PUFFIN BOOKS
Editor: Kaye Webb

THE SOUND OF COACHES

One stormy December night some time in the eighteenth century, a coach came thundering down the long hill outside of Dorking. It was *The Flying Cradle* making its usual journey between Chichester and London. But something rather unusual was to happen that night at the Red Lion Inn – for one of the passengers unexpectedly gave birth to a child.

That was how Sam Chichester came into the world, and how *The Flying Cradle* became a real one. Not till he was eight did Sam discover that the coachman and guard whom he called 'Pa' and 'Ma' weren't his real parents, that his mother had died when he was born, leaving him only a pistol and a cheap pewter ring as clues to his identity. His mysterious 'other pa', a figure sometimes ominous, sometimes magical, was to haunt the dreamy boy from then on – and it haunted coachman Chichester too. That sternly honest man, not given to showing his feelings but devoted to Sam, was terrified lest the boy had bad blood which must one day come out, and sometimes it looked as though his fears were well-founded. But Sam needed to grow up and leave home, to find love, some disillusionment and finally to uncover the truth about his parentage before he could come to appreciate the true worth of his adopted parents.

Leon Garfield has surpassed himself in this rollicking, racy tale, which tumbles along as swiftly as *The Flying Cradle* itslef, and as well as being an un-put-downable read shows a shrewd and deep understanding of human nature which makes it often very moving.

For older readers.

LEON GARFIELD

THE SOUND OF
COACHES

With engravings by
John Lawrence

PUFFIN BOOKS

Puffin Books, Penguin Books Ltd, Harmondsworth, Middlesex, England
Penguin Books, 625 Madison Avenue, New York, New York 10022, U.S.A.
Penguin Books Australia Ltd, Ringwood, Victoria, Australia
Penguin Books Canada Ltd, 2801 John Street, Markham, Ontario, Canada L3R 1B4
Penguin Books (N.Z.) Ltd, 182–190 Wairau Road, Auckland 10, New Zealand

—

First published by Kestrel Books 1974
Published in Puffin Books 1977

—

Copyright © Leon Garfield, 1974
Illustrations copyright © Penguin Books, 1974
All rights reserved

—

Made and printed in Great Britain
by Richard Clay (The Chaucer Press) Ltd,
Bungay, Suffolk
Set in Linotype Plantin

To John and to the memory of Vera

Let us take the road:
Hark! I hear the sound of coaches,
The hour of attack approaches,
To your arms, brave boys, and load.
See the ball I hold!
Let the chemists toil like asses,
Our fire their fire surpasses,
And turns all our lead to gold.

JOHN GAY: THE BEGGAR'S OPERA

Part One

Let us take the road:
Hark! I hear the sound of coaches,
The hour of attack approaches ...

I

ONCE upon a winter's night when the wind blew its guts out and a fishy piece of moon scuttled among the clouds, a coach came thundering down the long hill outside of Dorking. Its progress was wild, and the coachman and his guard rocked from side to side as if the maddened vehicle was struggling to rid itself of them before going on to hell without the benefit of further advice. Even the passing landscape conspired to increase the terror of the journey, and the fleeting sight of a gibbet – its iron cage swinging desolately against the sky – turned the five passengers' thoughts towards the next world ... of which destination there'd been no mention in Chichester where they'd booked their passage.

For some miles past a heavily built passenger in a corner seat had been eyeing every sharp fixture and fitting in the coach's interior and had at last succeeded in placing himself so that, in the event of disaster, he'd get off with no worse than a bruising. He frowned; he'd overlooked something.

'Young woman,' he began, moderately; but his voice was drowned by the uproar of the journey. 'Young woman!' he repeated, raising his voice to a shout and feeling, at the same time, an unreasonable conviction that he'd been ignored on purpose. 'That box. It would be safer in the straw on the floor!'

The female sitting opposite smiled feebly. She was clutching in her lap a long barber's box with brass corners as sharp as razors. Such a box, if the coach overturned, could become a terrible weapon. Not long since, a friend of his, in similar circumstances, had had his eye put out by an umbrella ...

'That box, I said. Put it on the floor.'

The young woman looked vaguely troubled and shook her

head; her hands tightened over her property. The heavy traveller shrugged his shoulders. Angrily he buttressed himself against the opposite seat, taking care to thrust his varnished boots into the folds of the young woman's voluminous black gown. She winced slightly, as if her flesh had been nipped; but she made no stronger protest than that.

She was a spiritless creature, with a pale, unhealthy face and sick eyes. There was the remains of prettiness about her which she'd struggled to preserve with vermilion and eye-black; but the effect was graveyard ...

Suddenly the tumult of hooves, wind and wheels took a turn for the worse. The coach shuddered violently as the horses struck an icy patch. Hooves skittered, the brake screeched on – off, on – off; and all the passengers were tumbled into a helpless confusion in which the heavy traveller, who prided himself on keeping his head, managed to seize hold of the young woman's box. He fully intended to hurl it away before it knocked his teeth down his throat. The young woman cried out in dismay, and, with surprising strength, held onto her property. For several moments there was a panting scuffle on the floor, then the vehicle righted itself and the danger was past. But the damage had already been done. The heavy traveller was bleeding profusely from a gash above his eye where the box had struck him.

'I warned her,' he said furiously to his companions, 'to put it down. She might have had my eye out!'

The other passengers nodded warmly. Their sympathies went out to the wounded one, regardless of the fact that he'd brought his injury on himself.

'If we live to see Dorking,' said one, 'I'll make it my business to see that box goes outside. And if she don't like it,' he added in an undertone that was meant more to exclude the young woman than to prevent her hearing, 'she can go with it. I have a little influence on this run.'

The young woman stared down at her box, then shrank

back in her corner with a helpless, pleading smile that endeared her to nobody. It was plain to all that there'd be no reasoning with her, and the four passengers felt exceedingly angry with her for forcing them to behave in an uncivil fashion. For some reason or other she and her box would not be parted, and by the time the coach swung into the yard of *The Red Lion* at Dorking she'd worked herself into a state of panic and dismay that seemed out of all proportion to the circumstances. She ate no supper and would take only a glass of gin and hot water before climbing heavily to her room at the top of the house, still clutching her box.

Idly the coachman and his guard watched her toil up into the shadows like a bulky moth with a camphor face. No one helped her; no one even wished her good night. There was something about her that repelled assistance or even common kindness. She had the air of an outcast.

Soon after, the remaining travellers went to their rooms, the local customers went out into the night and the landlord, the coachman and his guard were left in possession of the parlour. Cautiously the landlord examined the corners and shadows, then rose and fetched a bottle of brandy. The coachman held up his hand.

'Only a nip, Mr Roggs.'

Originally the landlord's name had been Poggs, but humorous clients had so made his life a misery by calling him 'Pox' and 'Old Poxy', that he'd renounced his birthright and changed to 'Roggs'.

He filled the glasses and offered the customary toast: 'To the horses'. As he drank he couldn't help smiling at how like horses the coachman and his guard had become. They had that same heavy, willing look . . .

Towards midnight the weather worsened; the wind rose to a tremendous pitch and every joist and plank in *The Red Lion* groaned with the effort of keeping it out. Outside the sign flew back and forth with a loud, monotonous banging, for all the world as if someone was pleading to be let in. Unconsciously the three in the parlour looked upward towards the stairs ...

'God have mercy on all at sea,' said Mr Roggs, passing the bottle again.

'God have mercy on all on the road,' said the coachman, glancing at his guard before dispensing a second nip.

'God have mercy on us all,' said the guard.

'Amen.'

They drank and the bottle passed again.

'Here's to *The Flying Cradle*,' said Mr Roggs, courteously. 'The steadiest coach on the road.'

'What was that?' said the guard sharply.

'To *The Flying Cradle*, I said.'

'No. That noise.'

'The wind.'

'Not the wind. It's more like the screech of a brake: on – off! On – off!'

They listened. The guard was right. On – off! On – off! It was coming from the top of the house – a harsh, regular screaming.

'It's her,' said the coachman, setting down his glass. 'That female passenger.'

The guard leaped up and made for the stairs. Already the other passengers had come from their rooms and were obstructing the stairway. The traveller with the wounded eye was looking extremely uncomfortable as if, in some obscure way, he was responsible for the young female's terrible distress. He wondered if he could have injured her ...

Roughly the guard pushed him aside. The screams were appallingly loud and reminded the coachman of the noise made by a hedgehog he'd once run over. The guard reached the little room at the top of the house and, without pausing, flung open the door.

The room was pitfully small ... scarcely larger than a coffin.

14

A candle guttered beside the narrow bed on which the young woman lay, like a coach overturned, with her thin, spoke-like knees twisting in the air. On the pillow beside her lay her precious box, which, from time to time, she attempted to bite as if to silence her own shrieks of bewilderment and fear.

'Quickly!' shouted the guard. 'Fetch the women! There's a baby being born!'

'A baby being born ... a baby ... a baby ...'

The words darted down the stairs like a ray of light dividing obstructions and finding face after face in the darkness, illuminating amazement, pleasure, concern, urgency ... Towels, sheets, bowls of steaming water like spirits ascending, passed up and down the stairs in the arms of a regiment of women; while the men gathered helplessly in the parlour, totally excluded from the proceedings.

The outcast, the sick-faced wanderer from the night, had suddenly become the centre of a mysterious world that had erupted in *The Red Lion* like a volcano; and the women ministered to it like priestesses ...

'It's always the same,' muttered Mr Roggs, who was the father of many children. 'They must always make a mystery of it.'

The shrieking had increased in violence and seemed to pierce every aperture in the night; two ostlers and a tousled potboy crept inquisitively into the parlour, blinking at the candles and the company in awe. Mrs Roggs, the landlord's wife, called reassuringly over the bannisters that it wouldn't be long now, but that the young woman was having a hard time of it. There was a shrugging of shoulders and the potboy, who was scarcely fourteen, nodded knowledgeably.

'Horrible,' said the traveller with the wounded head, 'to have a living creature wrenched from your insides.' He was still feeling that some blame attached itself to him and lost no opportunity of extending his sympathy.

'Pooh!' said Mr Roggs, with one eye on the stairs. 'They slip out as easily as ripe plums!'

'Many a mother dies of such plums.'

'There's danger in crossing a street, or eating mushrooms. When a man shaves of a morning he's kissing close to a cut throat,' said Mrs Roggs's husband contemptuously. 'Keep a sense of proportion, my friend.'

Even as he spoke, the screaming died away as if sensible of Mr Rogg's reproach. The company looked upward in expectation; then the racket started again and the landlord sighed. He clasped his hands behind his back, feeling that the extraordinary event which was taking place upstairs was somehow his property. He was keenly aware of his position as landlord and host; however babies might be born elsewhere, this one was by courtesy of *The Red Lion* and no philosophy or comment was called for other than the landlord's.

'It's all in the mind, you know,' he said firmly. 'I remember my first like it was yesterday. There was me outside of the room where the mystery was taking place. She – Mrs Roggs – howled and bellowed (this is nothing to it) till I was made to feel like a murderer for having brought it on her. Then I went in as sweaty as a piece of old cheese, and there was she with an object the size of a mutton chop and smiling all over her face. *I* was the one with labour pains of the spirit as if she'd passed an elephant instead of a red-faced mouse.'

A voice from the stairs interrupted with the news that 'she was squeezing regular but not quite hard enough. Nonetheless the babe was on its way and, God willing, would soon be in the land of the living ...'

'And may God have mercy on its soul,' said the coachman, rather sternly for so charitable a sentiment.

'And on hers – and on hers!' said the wounded traveller.

'Original sin,' frowned Mr Roggs, watching a bottle of his best brandy ascending with a barmaid who glanced down with an air of female reproach.

'It was Eve,' went on Mr Roggs grimly, 'what ate of the Tree of Knowledge first – and, as they say up north, copped a belly-ache. But Adam, being a higher animal, suffered in his head. One moment there he was, enjoying himself in a lawful, husbandly fashion, and the next – he was aware of consequence! Two words, my friends, were his downfall. *What if*. What if she dies in childbirth? What if the corn don't grow? What if the sun don't rise? What if I die in the night? What if my child goes to the bad? It was another world – a world of what *might* happen – a world with no bottom to it. Give me the bellyache every time to the torments of the mind.'

Once more the howling upstairs drained away – then a most terrific shriek split the night. It didn't seem possible that a human being had uttered it. Awestruck, the gentlemen in the parlour gazed to the stairs; then, in the hollow left by the enormous shriek, came the tiny crying of a baby.

The wounded traveller felt a ridiculous desire to get down on his knees; his mind was filled with childhood memories of Christmas plays – of babies born in inns ...

'It's a boy,' said the landlord's lady, coming down the stairs like a tragedy queen. Her eyes were full of tearful accusation, as if the tiny creature in the room upstairs already belonged among the careless sinners below.

'And – and the mother?' Unconsciously the wounded traveller touched the bloodstained bandage round his head.

'Gone. She lived just long enough to kiss her son and leave him her shabby old box. Then the blood came ... Oh, you men have it easy!'

2

W H O was she? Where had she come from – the dead young woman on the bed upstairs? Her waxen face, still pearled with sweat, smiled blandly up at all inquiry; and her hands, folded by someone across her breast, seemed to enjoin her body to secrecy.

Her baggage consisted of a bundle of underclothing and the brass-cornered barber's box; there was nothing in either by which she might have been traced. Her black gown, which had been laid neatly across the end of her bed, told no more. The women pronounced it to be of good quality, but pointed out several places where it was worn almost threadbare. Likewise her shoes, which had been placed carefully on a chair out of a sense of respect, had once been smart but were now battered and worn almost down to her often mended stockings.

In all likelihood she'd been a servant dressed in her mistress's cast-offs. Her whole fortune consisted of three guineas and a pretty green-handled fruit knife that had been found sewn into the hem of her dress. It was guessed that she'd stolen it from the house where she worked, perhaps out of spite for having been turned away when her misfortune showed.

Where had she been going so urgently that she'd taken a coach in her dangerous condition? God knew! She'd boarded at Arundel and paid her money for London and that was that. To her home, maybe? The coachman didn't think so. Her voice had been country; she'd never come from London. The more he thought of it, the more sure he was. He'd asked her if she wanted to be set down anywhere in particular, the town being such a great muddle of a place; but she'd shook her head and then asked if the coachman had heard of Covent Garden and where it might be. When he'd told her and promised to put

18

her off very near, she'd given such a sweet and thankful smile that he supposed she'd feared there never was such a place and accordingly was grateful to have had her fears put to flight.

'Then to find her lover, maybe?'

The coachman shrugged his shoulders; he was not a man given to conjectures.

'What's to be done?'

'The parish will bury her,' said the landlord.

'And her baby?'

'The parish will provide.'

A silence fell on the parlour, and the melancholy sound of the sign banging outside chilled all hearts. The very candles seemed to shrink and give a pinched and meagre light, lowering the shadows till eyes and mouths were bandaged up in gloom. The injured traveller lost his distinction; all seemed wounded . . .

The women were in the kitchen where the baby was asleep by the fire. No more had been seen of it as it had been carried down the stairs than a pathetic tuft of black hair poking out of a shawl. Tiny, nameless, helpless . . . yet most urgently alive. Mrs Roggs had held it – and the image of its swaddled form descending into the bannistered vale of shadows was imprinted on every mind.

Could it have dreams already? Disturbing thought. Were its mother's shrieks still echoing in its ears, even as they seemed to be echoing in the wind outside? Would the darkness last for ever, or would somebody make a sun and moon and stars and watch over him?

'The parish will provide . . .'

'I – I would like,' said the injured traveller awkwardly, 'to leave a little money with you, landlord, for the – the baby's future . . .'

Mr Roggs looked uncertain.

'I'll add to that!' came an abrupt voice from a corner of the room. The offer was so prompt that it seemed that all the speaker had been waiting for was someone to make a beginning.

'And I!'

'I will, too!'

'I'll spare a copper or so . . .'

'I got a bit here for the tiddly 'un . . .'

'I'm skinned,' said the potboy dolefully, 'but if you'll advance me a shillin' on me wages, Mr Roggs, I'll be 'appy to join in.'

The gloom vanished; the parlour was resurrected! Even the wizened fire in the hearth seemed to improve; *The Red Lion* was roaring again. Everyone was smiling and laughing and talking at once. What an original idea it all was! The injured traveller was congratulated on all sides. It just went to show how warm and straightforward life could be if one put one's mind to it! Think of it! There they all were – men of business, professional men, nobility (Were there any noblemen present? There weren't, but no matter.), and humble working men – all united in love and charity for – for a perfect stranger! Surely this is how the world was meant to be! Thank God they'd come to their senses in time . . .

A feeling of glorious happiness sprang up in every heart, where the images of the dead mother and the living child were radiantly enthroned.

'What day is today, landlord?'

'December eighteen.'

'His birthday! Let the four of us who knew his mother send a present every year.'

'To the tiddly 'un's birthday!' cried the potboy, who'd got hold of a glass with something left in it. He was quite overcome by the general sentiment and could only be calmed down by being sent to fetch pen, paper and ink for Mr Roggs to note down the names, addresses and donations for the benefit of the small posterity asleep in the kitchen.

'We'll send the gifts to you, landlord . . .'

'No call for that. Send 'em to me.'

It was the coachman who spoke. Until that moment he'd remained silent and, to all intents, disapproving.

'Why's that, coachman?'

He frowned and shook his head. More like a horse than ever, thought Mr Roggs, wonderingly; with something unnatural in his feedbag.

'His ma paid up her fare right through to London,' said the coachman, 'so the tiddly 'un is rightfully owed the rest of the journey.' His voice took on an aggressive edge. 'Stands to reason he can't take advantage of it now, so me and my good lady will shoulder him, as the saying goes, till he's able. It ain't charity, like yours; it's no more than lawful trading.'

He paused and stared round at the company. His long, bony face swayed from side to side. Any moment now, thought Mr Roggs, he's going to whinny.

'What say, Mrs C.? Do we shoulder the tiddly 'un? But only, of course, till he's growed enough to drive his own team.' The coachman rubbed his chin and looked inquiringly at the guard who'd come in from the kitchen. 'Is it a go, Mrs C.?'

The four travellers blinked; they were quite taken aback. For the first time they saw the coachman and his guard as something other than the furniture of the journey. And a very remarkable pair they were. Though weathered, stern and notoriously sharp with the gun, the guard of *The Flying Cradle* was indisputably female. She and her coachman were partners on more than the road; they were man and wife.

Who would have married her but him, thought Mr Roggs, unkindly; but the travellers, with more breeding, reflected that, with a dab of paint and powder, a week with a dressmaker and a month with a hairdresser, the needle-eyed guard of *The Flying Cradle* might have been almost handsome. But only if she wore gloves. Her hands were speckled and grained with sufficient gunpowder to have blown a man's head off if he spoke a word out of turn. All in all they admired the coachman's courage quite as much as his taste. Then they thought of the baby in the kitchen, and couldn't help wondering if the parish might not have been the kinder choice ...

However, no one was inclined to cross the formidable pair, even though, in their heart of hearts, they felt deprived of a little of their agreeable inner warmth. There was no doubt it would have been a far more romantic thing to be providing for an orphan thrown on the mercy of the parish than to be sending birthday presents to a coachman's child. But they were all worthy, honest people and had no intention of drawing back.

'What shall we call him?' asked one, determined to keep some sort of foothold in the child's life. Silence.

'Balcombe's a pretty place,' said the coachman carefully.

'You can't call him that! You can't give a human being the name of a place!'

'Why not? It's good enough for folk to live in ...'

'I wouldn't call a horse Balcombe!'

Ha – ha! thought Mr Roggs; but refrained from interfering. The coachman subsided, muttering something or other to his wife who shrugged her shoulders and went back to the kitchen with a faintly mysterious smile.

With the departure of the female, the parlour eased. Names began to be suggested, at first tentatively, and then in a real landslide so that a stranger, entering, would have supposed the place to be filled with invisible spirits being familiarly summoned: 'Ned! David! Walter! Harry! Richard! Hassocks! Sam! Christopher! Gideon! Moses!' And in every rest came the potboy's doleful voice: 'What's wrong with Joe?' Having mortgaged a shilling of his wages, he was eager to have his interest declared. His own name was Joe. At length Harry and Sam emerged as equal favourites, with Hassocks and Joe nowhere. Someone suggested tossing a coin to decide, but here Mr Roggs objected. Names, he said feelingly, were too dainty a matter to be left to chance. Folk grew into names, not names into folk; so 'Sam' was fixed on with the provision that, should the infant turn out to be more of a 'Harry', then Harry he'd be. But for the present he was known as 'the tiddly 'un'.

For the first time that Mr Roggs could recall, *The Flying Cradle* was late in leaving Dorking in the morning. With one accord the four travellers insisted on waiting until certain melancholy arrangements were complete. Partly out of sentiment and partly out of respect they stayed till the undertaker's men came with the coffin. Silently they gathered at the foot of the stairs while the dismal object was hoisted aloft. The coachman and his wife preceded it and entered the little room where Sam (or possibly, Harry) had been born.

'Look carefully, Mrs C.,' said the coachman quietly. 'Look at her face; look at her hands and fingernails. Look at the colour of her hair and, if you can stomach it, look in her eyes. Look at her lips and remember the smile on 'em. For what you see now is all the tiddly 'un will have. So make no mistakes. He'll ask, you may be sure. He'll want to know. And you must tell him, adding nothing and taking nothing away. Every detail, Mrs C. Whatever lies there of his ma is in your keeping . . .'

Patiently the undertaker's men waited on the landing. They were used to all sorts of oddities between the living and the dead.

'Finished now?'

'Finished.'

'What name on the box?'

'Call her "Arundel". That's where she got on.'

Accordingly, 'Arundel' was inscribed.

Downstairs the travellers watched, and, as the coffin made its swaying appearance, they lowered their heads.

'Watch it, there —'

The coffin jolted and cracked a bannister. The coachman stared at the damage as if that, too, was to be remembered. Then the little party followed the coffin outside into the cold grey morning and watched it being laid on the undertaker's cart. They frowned reproachfully as the undertaker's men came back to finish off their tankards of ale that they'd left on a window-sill. The coffin had contained something more than just a heavy weight ...

'May she rest in peace.'

'Amen ... amen ...'

The cart moved off and the party returned to the parlour where Mrs Roggs had laid out a funeral repast of cakes and wine. From the kitchen came the sound of the next of kin – crying.

'He knows,' said one of the travellers softly.

'He's hungry,' said Mrs Roggs, shaking her head with a melancholy smile. 'We'll have to get a nurse from the town. He must stay here till he's grown enough to take his nourishment on the road.'

Mr Roggs looked as though he was about to say something, but changed his mind.

'What about his inheritance?'

'Won't touch a penny of it,' said Mr Roggs sincerely; 'neither for his keep nor anything else. Forty-seven pound four shillings, including what was in the poor soul's purse. You were very generous, gentlemen. If his ma had lived, I doubt if the tiddly 'un had done half so well. It's an ill wind, as they say ...'

'And that box?' said the injured traveller, touching his bandage ruefully. Now he'd shown goodwill, he felt entitled to relax a little. 'I happen to know she set great store by it.'

'Oh, yes, the box. A very queer thing for a young woman to be travelling with.'

'Belonged to the baby's father,' said the coachman's wife abruptly. 'She told me, almost with her last breath. "His father's," she said. "Keep it for him, please." What sort of a man could he have been to leave such a keepsake? An old barber's box with nothing in it but a cheap pewter ring and a pistol ...'

3

'AND what's wrong with Balcombe or Hassocks?' mumbled the coachman, more to his pounding horses than to his companion, and pursuing a line of thought that had remained unbroken since the previous night. 'They're nearby, ain't they?'

His wife, long accustomed to reading his mind as well as his lips, patted his arm comfortingly, then resumed her careful scrutiny of the bushes and clumps of trees that flanked the road.

'Or we could call him "Red Lion",' she said dryly. 'Leastways, it was where he was born and he's surely got the voice and complexion for it.'

The coachman grunted. His wife's rare excursions into humour always succeeded in irritating him. He was still smarting under the thoughtless reproof that the name of a place wasn't even fit to bestow on a horse. As a case in point, his own name was Chichester – not because he'd been born Chichester, but because he worked the Chichester road. It was possible that, nowadays, he couldn't even lay his tongue to the name he'd been born with; he'd been Chichester when he married, and he'd be Chichester when he was buried.

The custom of calling a man after the road he worked was an ancient and honourable one, and certainly not to be mocked at. A man had only to go to one of Mrs Nelson's coachmen's gatherings at *The Bull and Mouth* in Aldersgate Street to understand the profound nature of names. Once a year she held them, lasting for three days over Christmas so that the most farflung coachmen might come together there: Exeter and Durham, Canterbury and Buckingham, Winchester and Warwick ...

There was a comfortableness about the meetings and a

sense of deep knowing; when a man spoke with Exeter, he spoke with a man as hard and grey as the ancient city itself, and as lanky as the road he worked. Then Buckingham, short and inclined to be crafty with a square mouth like the old town gaol. Sometimes it happened that a stranger appeared. 'Here's Weymouth!' someone would say; and the stranger was no longer a stranger. Straightaway everyone knew the road he worked, the inns he stopped at, and the proprietors who'd taken him on. They knew his life almost as well as he knew it himself.

'Bratsby, Bartholomew, Oxton and Skipping,' rumbled the coachman under his breath, contemptuously pronouncing the names of the four travellers. 'What manner of names are they? What's the meaning in 'em? Why, it would take a man a lifetime to get to know the streets you walk and the houses you visit! Strangers ... strangers ...'

In this frame of mind, which deepened rather than the reverse, the coachman felt quite embarrassed at the prospect of attending Mrs Nelson's distinguished gathering with the news that he and Mrs C. had acquired a tiddler by the name of Sam. He had really rather fancied a little Balcombe or a Hassocks ...

But the news had gone before them, and when the Chichesters entered Mrs Nelson's dining room which, as usual, was bright with candles and bunting – for Mrs Nelson was a proprietor's widow and did things in style – they were met by a silent crowd which suddenly parted to reveal a truly magnificent object on the long table. Overcome with confusion, the Chichesters stared at an enormous cake in the shape of a horseshoe across which was stretched a silken ribbon bearing the words: G O O D   L U C K   S A M.

Then the silence was broken by three rousing cheers accompanied by posthorns and they found themselves set upon with vigorous congratulations, thumpings on the back, terrific shakings of the hand (a coachman's grip is as fierce as new springs), while Mrs C., in particular, was terrified to find herself kissed times without number ... and a coachman's lips are as rough as frayed leather.

Inquiries and humorous reproaches were showered on them from all sides: Why hadn't they brought the tiddler? Weren't they good enough? Wasn't it Christmas?

'But – he's too little, truthfully ...'

'We wouldn't hurt him!'

'And – and there's his feeding ...'

'What's wrong with Mrs Nelson? D'you hear that, Mrs Nelson? Your food ain't good enough for Sam!'

'No – no! It ain't that, I swear!'

'It's all right. We know. We've all had 'em, Mrs C.'

Mrs Chichester smiled uneasily. She and her husband were not at all used to being joked with, and they had no real idea how to accept it. To be plain, they had never been a popular couple. Honesty had always been their drawback; the coachman himself was almost fanatical about it, consequently their presence tended to cast a blight on any company more easy-going than themselves. Generally it was held that the Chichesters were deficient in human nature.

But now all was changed; the Chichesters must turn human. The possession of a child, as every man knew, meant conniving, lying, shouldering the unlawful passenger for the wherewithal to buy a toy, and swearing that goblins dined on the road at night.

Though none of this was put directly into words, there was an undertow to the talk that seemed to be drawing the Chichesters helplessly into a huge conspiracy whose scope and aim was unknown. Feelings of apprehension and fear continually caught at them, and awe at the enormity of their action in shouldering the child.

Mrs Nelson, sensing rather than observing the Chichesters' distress – for she was well away, as the saying goes – took pity on them and, whenever she could, drew Mrs Chichester aside and offered her comforting advice.

'You don't want to worry too much about 'em, dear. Feed 'em and wash 'em and let nature do the rest. Ale doesn't come amiss when they're teething . . . or even a little brandy to flower the gruel. Sends 'em to sleep, you know. But never claret. colours their water, you know . . . Rum makes 'em sick . . . brandy, dear; nice and clean . . . wool next to the skin, of course . . . spots, you know. My youngest used to come out like a tabby cat. Wash him in his own water, I say. But not claret, dear . . .'

Bemused, yet oddly comforted, Mrs Chichester listened as Mrs Nelson rambled on.

'Here's a little something for him, dear,' murmured Mrs Nelson, somewhat later in the evening. She had vanished mysteriously from the gathering and now returned, fumbling in her gown. Presently she found what she was looking for.

'Been through the family,' she whispered, and pressed a battered silver teething ring secretively into Mrs Chichester's palm. 'Only see he don't swallow it, dear.'

Mrs Chichester was deeply moved. She would have thanked Mrs Nelson, but that lady had already gone off in a rattle of beads and only her high feathers could be glimpsed weaving among the sturdy coachmen like a portable bonfire.

Mrs Chichester stared down at the baby's ring. A great and unbelievable excitement filled her. The possession of this object somehow made her realize, to the depths of her soul, that she owned a child.

Thrice weekly *The Flying Cradle* called at *The Red Lion* in Dorking and the Chichesters solemnly inspected their property. Improvements were in hand and proceeding apace. The red, crumpled look had gone and the infant was beginning to resemble a human being. He was a windy child, which, Mrs Roggs declared, was only to be expected, considering the weather on the night he'd been born.

Bringing up the wind was an absorbing adventure and Sam's

triumphant grin when success was achieved remained long in Mrs C.'s heart so that her impatience to come into full possession of the infant grew out of all proportion to the size of its object. Weekends in either London or Chichester, which were part and parcel of the business of coaching, became times of terrible agitation. Motion was calming, but the helpless staying in one place away from the child was intolerable. In February when bad weather threatened to divert the coach through Reigate and leave out Dorking altogether, Mrs Chichester could scarcely hold back her tears.

'Don't go fastening too many hopes on him,' said the coachman, who was made of sterner stuff. 'There's many a slip, you know.'

'What do you mean by that?'

'For instance, what if the father should get wind of it? He'd have the right, over and above us, to take him. We'd have to give way to a blood relation . . .'

'A man what leaves a pewter ring with his sweetheart don't come back for his child.'

'He left a pistol, too, Mrs C. And that speaks of a violent, lawless nature. If he ain't hanged already, we must always be prepared.'

'Be honest with me, Chichester. It ain't likely, is it?'

The coachman looked momentarily serious, then he smiled. 'Nor's it likely that May won't come!'

If all went well, May was the month for Sam.

Without a doubt it was the longest winter in the world; and spring, when at last it came, moved like a cripple along the hedgerows and seemed scarcely able to reach the awkward bushes and left whole patches bare. Under such unfavourable circumstances, Mrs Chichester began to entertain serious doubts about the arrival of May: March seemed fixed for ever. And then, quite suddenly, it was May. The hedgerows were blazing all over and, on a Wednesday in the middle of the month, the coachman and guard of *The Flying Cradle* came into full possession of Sam.

They did not sleep a wink all night. When Sam cried, they rushed to see why; and when he didn't cry, they rushed to see why not. ('I think he's stopped breathing, Chichester.')

In the morning, much relieved to find him still alive, they took him out, fed him, covered him with shawls and blankets, and sat him in the neatly carpentered seat that Chichester had made, strapping him down as securely as a footpad off to gaol. The landlord and his wife, Joe the potboy, a barmaid and two ostlers came outside to see the brand-new family on its way. The men, including the interested passengers, drank toasts, while the women, for no good reason, felt it their duty to cry. Then the coach moved off to the accompaniment of fluttering handkerchiefs. The inside passengers – though it was no concern of theirs – waved back, while aloft, the proud coachman began gravely explaining the art of managing four horses to the astonished Sam.

Sam also was explaining something equally difficult to the Chichesters. He was explaining, at the top of his voice, that the cradle he was used to was not a flying one; that the ceiling he was used to was of a different colour and not so far away; and that the walls he'd always known did not rush by in such a dappled green confusion. He struggled to explain that, if it was at all possible, he would like things back as they were; but all that happened was that the coach halted and a spoonful of food was pushed into his open mouth.

At first he sought refuge in being sick, considering attack the best method of defence, then little by little, he resigned himself to a new world that thundered and moved and blew in his face, but at least had the good sense to stop when he howled. This was very interesting; and if only food hadn't been pushed into his mouth on each occasion he felt he might have benefited more.

However, Sam was of an amiable, endlessly inquiring disposition, capable of much sustained experiment. In no time at all he'd grown quite fond of the two large faces that had usurped his world. He could even tell them apart – though which of them would appear when he howled was still an impenetrable mystery. He knew there was a connection between his howling and their appearance, but as yet it was a very tenuous one. If only they'd stop poking food into him he felt he'd be better able to sort matters out.

Then, one night, as he lay in his cot listening to the Chichesters' musical snores, the truth flashed upon him. For some time past he'd observed that when they desired only to attract his attention, they called 'Sam!' There was no question of food at all. They simply called 'Sam!' and were not fed for it. Therefore: 'Sam!' he howled delightedly; or rather, '—am!' as he was still rather shaky on his S's. Almost directly the gentler of the two faces appeared. It looked intensely excited.

'Chichester!' she shouted. 'He can talk! He's hungry! He's calling for ham!'

There was no doubt that this was a set-back; the voyage into life was more perilous and intricate than he'd supposed. Many effects may proceed from one cause, and many means come to one end. Nevertheless he persisted with his experiments and by Christmas had uncovered the fact that his own name was 'Sam', and that his enormous companions were 'Mama' and 'Dada' respectively.

The thought of his earlier error caused him to chuckle mightily. His pa, attracted by the merry sound and thinking to prolong it, made a grotesque face. Sam frowned thoughtfully. What had happened? Which was the cause and which the effect? He chuckled again – rather hesitantly, this time; and the coachman, encouraged by such success, made another face. Sam stopped chuckling – and Chichester went away.

Sam brooded long, but finally gave up; he could make nothing of the problem. Whichever way he approached it, it was equally baffling; so for the time being he gave up intellectual pursuits and devoted himself to a certain mechanical problem that had long baffled him: namely, the secret of the buckles and straps that imprisoned him on the road.

'Chichester!' shrieked Mrs C. as *The Flying Cradle* approached the treacherous bend at the foot of Oakwood Hill. 'Sam's loose! The straps are undone!'

This adventure was related many times, in London, Dorking and Chichester, as an undeniable example of Sam's outstanding ability.

'He's unusual, all right,' was the general opinion. 'It's easy to see that the lad's come from remarkable stock.'

The Chichesters nodded, and not for the first time wondered uneasily what inheritance had been passed on to Sam along with the pistol ...

4

Dorking ... LONDON ... *Dorking* ... CHICHESTER ... *Dorking* ... Time was motion; and motion was a great turning wheel with Mrs Nelson's and the family room above the coaching office at Chichester at its outer rim, while Dorking was the hub, facing now towards Chichester, now towards London. Consequently Dorking sometimes wore a Chichesterish look, and sometimes a Londonish one; the very church and streets seeming to change as the whole town turned to face either north or south. It was always either Chichester–Dorking or London–Dorking for Sam; the town really appeared only as itself from Mrs Nelson's or from the coaching office in the south.

This sense of Dorking occupying a central situation in motion and time, though always present, was peculiarly strong during December and reached a climax in the days immediately preceding Sam's birthday. By skilful manipulation it was always contrived that this event was celebrated at *The Red Lion* – although the coachman himself would have had it otherwise.

There was no doubt that the Roggses meant well, but they took over the occasion to such an extent that the coachman couldn't help feeling ashamed at being unable to provide as lavishly himself. At times, even, he was made to feel more an acquaintance of Sam's than his parent. Though he and Mrs C. sat on either side of Sam, it was Mrs Roggs who provided the cake and Mr Roggs who bustled up to guide Sam's hand as he cut it. As it was Mr Roggs's brandy, it was he who proposed the toasts, beginning with: 'And now let's wet the little one's head, as they say up north.' He didn't come from the north himself, but liked to add the expression after anything that

33

struck an unusual note, considering it gave him a more cosmopolitan air.

Peevishly the coachman would withdraw into himself and put his hand over his glass at the third or fourth refilling. You can bring a horse to water, thought Mr Roggs, humorously regarding Chichester's long, dour face, but you can't make him drink. This quip occurred to him each year, but courteously he refrained from giving it tongue.

At last came the time of gifts; and even then the Chichesters' offerings tended to be overlooked in the greater variety of *The Red Lion*'s contributions ... the potboy, ostlers and kitchen-maids all adding their offerings to the pile before the bemused mite at the head of the table.

When this ceremony was over Mr Roggs would bring in the four mysteries. These were the parcels addressed to 'Sam of *The Flying Cradle*, care of *The Red Lion*'. The four travellers had kept their word.

Sam, three-quarters asleep by now, was permitted to unwrap his parcels – with the kindly assistance of Mr Roggs – and actually caught glimpses of various glittering articles of clothing such as would have graced an infant prince. Then Mr Roggs would pat him on the head and pass the presents round the table for all to admire and guess at the cost, ending up with the frowning coachman who laboriously noted them down in order to thank the senders.

Thereafter they were wrapped up again as it was universally considered that Sam had enough to be getting on with and was in desperate danger of being spoiled. At this point the Chichesters took charge and providently stored the costly gifts away in a high dark cupboard against the time when Sam should be old enough and wise enough to come into so valuable an estate.

Mournfully Sam watched, but bore no lasting grudge against the Chichesters for removing his property; rather it seemed to him that the best of earthly possessions were of a very transitory nature and doomed to cupboards soon after they were born. They were like butterflies, philosophized Sam; and one autumn, when the hedgerows were turning rusty, he ventured the observation that, 'butterflies put in cupboards now'.

Nevertheless the four travellers continued to send their gifts and the Chichesters continued to put them in the cupboard till that high, remote place became, in Sam's mind, something between heaven and a royal treasury. The only satisfaction he was given was being told that he had four mysterious benefactors called Bratsby, Bartholomew, Oxton and Skipping, who'd been on hand at his birth and whose generosity he'd one day go down on his knees and thank heaven for.

He was allowed no more information than that about his origins as the careful Chichesters believed in putting aside knowledge, too, against the time when Sam should be old enough and wise enough to make something of it. So Sam grew up in the reasonable belief that *The Flying Cradle* had been so named because he'd been born in it and that the hugely muffled figures who sat on either side of him through life were his natural ma and pa. Consequently his earliest ambition was to be a coachman like his pa and 'feel the mouths of four horses in the fingers of one hand', or, failing that, to be a guard and carry a shotgun like his ma.

'Thumb against the second weskit button,' explained Chichester to the attentive Sam, and laid the reins between his tiny fingers, thereby obliterating them entirely from view. 'Look, Mrs C. To the manner born!'

Sam frowned importantly, threw out his chest and in the innocent tones of a child of seven, bellowed a coachman's abuse at the horses. Mrs Chichester looked momentarily shocked, but the coachman laughed delightedly, feeling, perhaps for the first time, something of the pride and immortality of a father with a son to carry on. No matter where Sam had come from, he was now a Chichester through and through.

'As soon as his fingers has growed a bit, I'll let him take her out of the yard. That's a promise, Sam!'

Sam smiled dreamily, and thereafter, in addition to performing certain secret and painful exercises to increase the size of his fingers, he included in his nightly prayers an earnest request for their hasty growth.

These prayers, performed by his bed with all the solemnity of a cardinal, were very lengthy affairs and, at times, sorely taxed his memory. So many blessings had to be indented for. There was his ma and pa; there was *The Red Lion* and all souls in it; there was the safety of the coach and the health of the horses; there was Mrs Nelson and the turnpike keeper at Wickford Bridge who gave him an apple; there was Messrs Bratsby, Bartholomew, Oxton and Skipping and their respective families; and before he was able to finish up by reminding God to remove his soul in case he perished in the night, there was Arundel.

Why Arundel? Why should he ask for a place like Arundel to be blessed? He brooded on this question deeply, and whenever the coach halted in Arundel he looked out curiously and wondered if the whole town had once conferred a benefit on him, and whether that benefit, whatever it was, was hidden in the cupboard, too. He sensed there was something peculiarly mysterious and wonderful about it, because when he'd been first told to include 'Arundel' in his prayers, his ma and pa had exchanged odd looks; and then, at intervals had asked him almost secretively, 'Did you remember to pray for Arundel, Sam?'

His curiosity mounted to painful proportions; the possibility of his being the lost Earl of Arundel and that the entire family were travelling incognito had not escaped him. But there seemed no way of obtaining satisfaction – until he remembered Joe . . . Joe who lived in *The Red Lion*'s cellar and who doubtless knew many dark secrets.

'I prayed for Arundel, last night, Joe,' he said meaningfully to the cellarman who'd been *The Red Lion*'s potboy in days gone by.

'What the 'ell for?' said Joe. 'Is the old place fallin' down?'

Sam frowned; Joe was being evasive. It was going to be more difficult than he'd bargained for. 'I always pray for Arundel,' he said – a shade self-righteously, Joe thought.

Joe, now a rather thick young man in his twenties, privately considered that Sam was being brought up woefully. Not that he didn't respect the Chichesters, but he felt them to be too cautious by half over Sam. They treated him like he was the best glass. The lad needed a few corners knocked off; and Joe often thought he was the very one to do the knocking. He had a commendable desire to educate Sam in the ways of the world outside of coaching. After all, he had a stake in the tiddler. There was and always would be a shilling of his in Sam. Not a great sum, perhaps, but in his potboy days it had been as much to him as their guineas had been to the four travellers.

'I 'opes you pray for Joe, too,' said Joe suspiciously. 'Never forget *I* was a benefactor, eight years ago. Only a shillin', but it were a lot to me, and I joined in with the rest of 'em.'

Sam nodded and said he was much obliged. He was used to the notion of many benefactors; but still, what a whole town might have given him was a subject to be pursued.

'I pray for Arundel every night.'

'Do you, now. Lucky Arundel!'

'Why do I have to pray for Arundel, Joe?'

' 'Ow the 'ell should I –'

Joe stopped. His eyes lit up in a sudden remembrance; he expelled his breath in a low whistle of incredulity.

'Come along of me, tiddler,' he said softly, 'and I'll show you something.'

It was a fine September morning and the sun shone affably on the parish church, yellowing the grey stone and turning the weathervane to a private star. Although on that day he was indisputably in Dorking, the town, to Sam, seemed more Dorking than was natural, and to be pointing nowhere.

Uneasily Sam followed after the burly cellarman who himself was beginning to feel uneasy and wondering if, perhaps, he was taking a shade too much on himself in the cause of educating Sam.

They passed through the lych-gate and entered the churchyard. For a moment Joe paused, as if uncertain as to the propriety of his action; but the sight of Sam, struggling to look off-hand, reassured him. They began to thread their way among the tombs which seemed to Sam like a committee of milestones wondering where to go next. At length they came to the limits of the churchyard where the grass was ragged and tattered and wild flowers grew; here were laid the dead of the humbler sort. Joe halted.

'D'you know your letters, tiddler?'

'Names and numbers, Joe,' said Sam, who'd been taught to read from the road book as soon as he was able to hold it.

'Read what it says on that there stone.'

The stone in question was tilting forlornly in the shadow of the wall, as if the other graves had been giving it a hard time during the nights.

'Mary Arundel,' read Sam, still struggling ineffectually to appear off-hand, 'died December eighteen in the year of –'

'– That's enough,' interrupted Joe awkwardly. 'Rest in peace it ends up with. They all do . . .'

The name 'Mary' had been subscribed by the stonemason who'd not liked leaving plain 'Arundel'. Taking into account the romantic circumstances of that night at *The Red Lion*, he'd thought 'Mary' to be peculiarly suitable.

'Who – who is it?'

'It's your ma, tiddler. Your natural ma.'

'It's not. Mrs C.'s my ma.'

'No she ain't. Nor's Mr C. your pa, come to that.'

'It's not true.'

'True as your name's Sam. I was there, tiddler. I was in the parlour when you was being born upstairs and your ma died of it. I saw 'er brought down in the coffin what broke the bannisters; and you can see the place still. I even saw you asleep in the kitchen in Mrs Roggs's arms.'

'Was my pa – my other pa – there?' whispered Sam, quite overpowered by such a mass of circumstantial detail.

'In spirit, we 'ope. Judgin' by all anyone knew about 'im, 'e'd been 'anged, most likely.'

'Oh, I see,' said Sam, who didn't at all, but was unwilling to give Joe the advantage of knowing that he felt strange and bewildered. Suddenly he disliked Joe very much. He wanted to return to *The Flying Cradle* which, he recollected, was due to be off very soon. He wanted to be back in his old seat with his ma and pa close to him. He wanted to be far away from the churchyard that terrified the wits out of him . . .

He spoke to no one about his conversation with Joe. To all intents it had gone clean out of his mind. He seemed totally absorbed in some point on the road beyond the leading horses' heads and his unusual quietness during the journey to London was put down to his 'sickening for something'.

In a curious way, this surmise was not far from the truth; no matter how hard he tried – and his efforts were tremendous – he could not subdue a feverish panic that kept creeping round his heart. Desperately he cast about in his mind for some way of overwhelming Joe under a landslide of proof that the Chichesters were his true ma and pa; but he knew he would need things as real as a tombstone and a cracked bannister to demolish the cellarman satisfactorily. Worst of all was the fact that there was no one left he could ask. Joe had always been his customary mine of information, and though he loved and admired the Chichesters beyond anything, they themselves never invited confidences. They were practical folk, not much given to words.

That night at Mrs Nelson's, he said his prayers as usual; but then, when he was already in bed, he added in a whisper, 'And bless him who was hanged.'

Young as he was, Sam was not ignorant about hanging. Standing beside the road from London to Chichester were no less than three gibbets; and though they were mostly untenanted, he had seen, once or twice, a pitiful tarred object suspended inside the iron cage, and his pa had told him what it was.

It had meant very little to him at the time as the object had looked more like an ill-treated doll than a human being; but now, with Joe's words haunting his thoughts, the memory took on a horrible significance. What if one of them had been his other pa?

The night-candle guttered away and sent hasty shadows streaming up the walls. Hurriedly Sam retreated under the bedclothes, and presently fell asleep. But this proved to be a mistake. The dream room proved a good deal more alarming than the one he'd left behind; and it was no use longing to be back again.

The door opened and there on the floor outside was a small parcel addressed to 'Sam of *The Flying Cradle*'. Wonderingly he took it up; and, as no one was about to interfere, he began to unwrap it. Anxiously, and with mounting excitement he tore at the paper, but somehow the parcel seemed to grow bigger and bigger as he unwrapped. It grew to be bigger than Sam himself; and then, just as he was despairing of ever reaching the end of it, the parcel reared up and the last of the wrappings fell away to reveal his other pa, huge and shiny with tar, swinging gently in the air above him.

He attempted to cry out, but before he could do so Mrs Chichester appeared and said, 'What a beautiful deathday present. We must put it aside for him till he's old enough to make proper use of it.'

Then she took his other pa and put him away in a tall cupboard, locked the door and left the room. Quite distinctly Sam could hear his other pa's feet banging against the cupboard door: tap ... tap , ... tap ...

Tap ... tap ... tap ... Sam woke up. Where was he? London, Chichester or Dorking? The candle was very low. He stared at the table and saw one of Mrs Nelson's brown and white supper plates and bent fork. He was in London. Tap ... tap ... tap ... Was the sound inside or outside? A tall cupboard stood in the corner of the room. It bulged and wobbled in the flickering light. Tap ... tap ... tap ... The sound couldn't possibly be coming from inside the cupboard ...

The candle dipped and spluttered and the shadows on the walls climbed up to the ceiling as if desperate to escape from the room. The cupboard loomed and danced. Tap ... tap ... tap ...

Sam got out of bed. Half believing himself to be still dreaming, he crept towards the cupboard, taking up the fork on his way with some notion of defending himself.

He tried the cupboard door; it was locked. He listened; the tapping had stopped so he pressed his ear to the wooden panel. Was it his own breathing he could hear – or was it coming from inside?

He pushed the fork into the crack of the door and began to force it back and forth. He had to open the cupboard. Suddenly the frail lock splintered; the cupboard door swung open – and the child screamed.

A huge figure stood in the darkness, swinging ... swinging ... Then the candle went out.

5

THEY met him midway on the stairs, flying down in his night-shirt liked a doomed angel of the smaller kind. His eyes were starting, his hair standing up like a forest all in black.

'Sam!' cried Mrs Chichester, catching him in her gun-powdery hands and extinguishing him in her chest.

The child's screaming changed rapidly to a painful sobbing in which the words 'other pa' kept emerging with horrible clarity.

Panic-stricken, the Chichesters stared at Sam, not knowing what to say or do, so Mrs Nelson took charge and they all went upstairs to the room Sam had fled from.

Grimly Mrs Nelson surveyed the burgled cupboard in which the late Mr Nelson's topcoat (his very last purchase on this earth) hung from a hook in the wooden ceiling. Sam peered at his 'other pa'. His heart, already at a pretty low ebb, sank further. There was no doubt in his mind at that moment that the black spectre had treacherously changed itself into an item of clothing for the sole purpose of discrediting him. He prayed, as hard as he could, that this, too, was a dream from which he'd presently awaken.

'Sorry,' he mumbled, and retreated into tears. But the words 'other pa' had not been forgotten. Anxiously the coachman questioned him. What had he meant? What was all this about another pa? Sam affected not to hear; he continued to weep in the hope that they'd see he was fully occupied in lamentation and in no condition to answer questions.

Mrs Chichester asked him, and held him at arm's length so that he was unable to bury his face in her bosom. He obliged by shutting his eyes and shaking his head violently, possibly with the remote hope of its coming off.

'You'll get nothing out of him in this state, dear,' said Mrs Nelson shrewdly.

'I just want to know who's been talking to him,' muttered the coachman. 'Someone's gone an' told him something.'

'It isn't true!' cried Sam suddenly; then realizing he'd given himself away, retired hurriedly behind his moat of tears. He was terrified of betraying Joe and was resolved that, even if he was put to the rack, henceforth he'd not utter another word.

Miserably the Chichesters gazed at one another. Whether they liked it or not (and there was no doubt it was 'not'), the time had come to tell their child. They longed to lie to him, to keep up the pretence, but not knowing how much he'd been told or by whom, they dared not.

That the Chichesters should even have thought of lying was remarkable; affection for Sam had made sad inroads in their stern probity. Mrs Nelson, an almost unwilling bystander, felt a deep compassion for the couple whose voyage into humanity had suddenly struck so painful a patch.

'You had another ma, Sam,' said Chichester, striving to sound as easy as if he was telling a passenger the fare from Dorking to Aldersgate Street. 'And another pa, too. We – we just shouldered you, as it were ...'

'It wasn't that we meant to deceive, love ...'

'We was going to tell you when you was ready ... of an age, that is ...'

'We were – we were keeping it aside for you, Sam ...'

The child looked from one to the other. His expression was more bewildered than frightened; but thank God there was no resentment in it. Whatever were his thoughts at that moment, none present could surmise. Most likely he didn't know himself and felt only a vague sense of emptiness in which any straw was a world to clutch at.

'What – what was she like?'

Mrs Nelson heaved a sigh of relief; the worst was over. To her surprise she found herself to be crying; she smiled apologetically, as if suddenly conscious of having witnessed a deeply private scene. She offered the use of her own parlour, which the Chichesters gratefully accepted. They went downstairs, and in the small, brown-ceilinged room that Sam long recollected in its every brass and oaken detail, Mrs Chichester told him everything she'd so carefully remembered about his dead ma. At intervals during the recital, the coachman nodded his head and muttered, 'I told you that someday he'd want to know. That's how she was, Sam, exactly so.'

Dazedly Sam listened, feeling the whole circumstance to be weirdly festive. The lateness of the hour, himself being present in his nightshirt and Mrs Nelson's comforting good spirits all conspired to fill the room with an air of unforgettable kindliness. Ale and brandy were on the table and several pies that Mrs Nelson had sensibly provided, knowing that anything out of the way can make a child hungry. The last flies of the year woke up and buzzed unsteadily across the table, settling on food and fingers as confidently as if they'd come into money.

'She had fair hair, the colour of straw, I should say – nice fresh straw. All in all, you'd say she was rather pretty ... taking into account her condition, that is ...' Sam nodded, feeling it to be expected of him. ('He's all right now,' whispered Mrs Nelson to the coachman.)

'She had greyish blue eyes, like gunpowder in the sunlight, and an easy, soft mouth ...'

As Mrs Chichester went on with detail after detail, Sam dutifully tried to build a picture in his mind of the remote lady lying in the upstairs room of *The Red Lion* long ago. Nose, eyes and mouth jiggled in his imagination, but obstinately refused to come together in a face.

'Her voice,' said the coachman, taking up the story, 'weren't no hardship to listen to. Nothing rough or shrill about it. It were a good voice, Sammy, such as no one need be ashamed of. I noticed it particularly when she asked to be put off at Covent

44

Garden. That was the only place she ever mentioned. She sat, back to the horses, in the corner on the left, if you want to know. She never told her name so we called her "Arundel", after where she got on ...'

'I think he's asleep,' whispered Mrs Nelson. Sam's eyes had closed and his head had fallen against Mrs Chichester's chest.

But he was not asleep – or not in the generally accepted sense. Instead he'd drifted away into another world as he could make no sense of the one he'd found himself in. Why hadn't anyone mentioned his other pa ... the one who'd been most likely hanged? Why had Joe told him that? Joe couldn't be the only one who knew ...

'She kissed you before she died, Sam ...'

Words droned round him as meaningless as the flies.

He hated Joe with a deep, implacable hatred. It was all Joe's fault. He wanted to be revenged on Joe; he wanted with all his heart to be rid of him.

'Carry him back up to his bed,' advised Mrs Nelson.

'Come morning and you'll see he'll have forgotten everything. Children are like that.'

Next night at *The Red Lion* Joe was nowhere to be seen.

He secreted himself in various dark corners of the cellar, known only to himself, and whenever he was summoned, made brief, almost spectral appearances before vanishing with a rapidity that drew admiring comment from his employer.

The truth of the matter was that he felt he'd overreached himself in the educating of Sam and was anxious to keep out of everyone's way. The more he thought of it, the more he became convinced that the virtuous little tiddler would have betrayed him to the Chichesters. It stood to reason. In Joe's book, all unpleasant events stood to reason; agreeable matters seemed to happen of their own accord and for no reason at all. When he heard from the upstairs folk – grooms, ostlers and kitchen-maids – that Sam was looking for him, his worst fears were confirmed. He was for it. The Chichesters were out for blood. His panic increased and not for worlds would he have faced his 'little shilling's-worth', as he privately called Sam.

He succeeded entirely in remaining invisible till the morning – when he felt entitled to relax. Which was when Sam caught him.

The Flying Cradle was almost ready to leave when Joe poked his bristly face (he'd not yet had the leisure to shave it) into the yard. At once Sam flew out from nowhere, it seemed, and seized Joe's sleeve like a terrier.

''Ullo, tiddler,' said Joe, grinning furtively and looking round for the awful Chichesters. 'Where've you bin 'idin' yourself all this while?'

'Take it!' muttered the child, his eyes blazing with anger.

'Take what, tiddler?'

'Your stinking shilling!'

He struggled to push the coin into Joe's hand. Joe retreated blankly.

'Take it!' shouted Sam. 'I don't want no more to do with you!'

Helplessly Joe stared down at the tiddler, not knowing whether to laugh or cry. His mouth kept stretching in a foolish grin, but, at the same time, the realization of Sam's bitterness towards him was acutely painful. He'd never known such distress before.

'No,' he mumbled. 'No . . . I don't want it. No . . . no . . .'

He pushed Sam away and fled as if from the wrath of angels. Unluckily Joe never knew his own strength; it was always either too much or too little for the task in hand. This time it had certainly been too much, and Sam went flying against the coach wheel.

The Chichesters, hearing Sam's well-known howl, came hurriedly from the stables and found the child lying on the cobbles, weeping hysterically. Gently they lifted him to his feet and while they were inspecting him for injuries, the shilling fell from his hand and clinked on the ground.

46

'What's that, Sam?'

'Where?'

'What you just dropped.'

'Why it's a – shilling, pa.'

'I can see that. Where did you come by it?'

'Found it,' aswered Sam, in a sense, truthfully.

'Whereabouts?'

'Don't remember.'

'Do I have to shake it out of you?'

The coachman was agitated; the coach was due to leave and passengers were already staring impatiently out of the windows.

'Who give it to you?'

'Nobody.'

'Then you stole it!'

No answer; but more tears. Mrs Chichester attempted to interfere, but was brushed aside. She bit her lip; she knew perfectly well where the shilling had come from. Sam had thieved it from her pocket on the morning before, when they'd left Mrs Nelson's. She'd thought it best to hold her tongue as Sam had already had a great shock.

'I'll fetch the truth out of you,' muttered the coachman furiously. 'Tonight, my lad!'

Constant travelling meant that all crises in Sam's life had to be held in abeyance till the next full halt ... by which time they'd generally blown over. Sam nodded meekly and climbed up into his seat where he settled down, hunching his shoulders so that all but his eyes vanished into his coat collar.

Mrs Chichester watched him compassionately; and forlornly wished she'd had the presence of mind to have pretended she'd given Sam the shilling instead of helplessly watching him sink, axle deep, in a mire of evasion and deceit. From time to time she made efforts to soften the coachman, urging him to take into account the recent upheaval in Sam's life.

'Children forget things like that,' answered Chichester curtly.

'You heard Mrs Nelson – and she's got five on the road and ought to know.' Then his long, bony face set like granite and Mrs Chichester felt she was married to a stranger. She thought she knew all the depths in her husband's soul; now she was dismayed to come upon the unsuspected shallows. How could he be so hard about a shilling?

Furiously the coachman shouted at the horses – not that the animals were neglecting their duty, but he needed an outlet for his troubled heart. He knew that his wife thought him to be unreasonable, but she couldn't understand that his anger was for Sam's protection, even as he sometimes lashed at a leading horse to help it past a treacherous rut and save it from a broken leg.

The child's dishonesty, coming as soon after his nightmare about the 'other pa', disturbed Chichester profoundly. He was, and always had been, terrified of bad blood coming out in the child. Though he never spoke of it, and hoped with all his heart that Mrs C. had forgotten it, he himself could never forget Sam's equivocal inheritance – the pistol in the battered barber's box; and in his mind such weapons had always been associated with the pitiful tarred objects that had once been men, swinging against the sky. He would have given up his life to keep Sam from such an end. It was on that account that the stealing of a shilling worried him so horribly.

Sam was also horribly worried. Though he knew his ma was trying to do her best for him, he longed for her to keep quiet, or at least to stop talking about him. She wasn't giving things a chance to blow over. And, as it turned out, he was perfectly right: they didn't.

'Well, Sam,' said his pa in their room over the coaching office in Chichester that night, 'are you going to come out with the truth?'

'Borrowed it,' said Sam sullenly.

'I said the truth, the truth!'

His pa, who'd not yet taken off his coat, looked enormous

and terrifying. His ma had her back to him. There was nowhere to go; so Sam, as a last resort in a world he suddenly felt he had no business in, burst into tears and confessed. Chichester looked angrily at his wife who, he felt, had conspired against him. She turned to face him, but was unable, or unwilling to sustain his look. She put her arm round Sam's shoulders, and the coachman felt bleakly alone. For an unpleasant moment he hated the child who'd come between him and his wife.

Then he looked down at the small, tearful, windblown Sam, shifting from foot to foot and desperately trying to evade him. His hatred vanished and he felt suddenly frightened and ashamed to be the cause of such terror. Had he really become such a monster – he who had always been so careful of his courtesy and good name?

'What did you want the shilling for, lad?' he asked, meaning to change the course of the scene and turn it gentle.

'Don't know,' said Sam, unwilling to betray Joe.

The coachman repeated the question, and this time was not even honoured with an answer.

'For the last time, Sam, what did you thieve that shilling for?'

'Tell him, child,' murmured his ma, understanding that her husband needed some satisfaction for his dignity as a man.

'You got all my presents,' said Sam, quite at his wit's end, now that his ma had sided against him, 'so why can't I have a shilling?'

To Sam's amazement – for he never really expected to prevail – his pa looked utterly taken aback. He looked as if he'd been punctured and all the air gone out of him. 'So ... that's it!' said the coachman, with a world of startled bitterness. 'You think we've stolen from you! All this time you've been thinking that! Oh God, what goes on in a child's mind! Very well, Sam, if that's how it is, tomorrow, when we get to *The Red Lion*, you can have your property. Do what you want with it. I – I got an inventory, Sam. You can see it's all there. Neither your ma nor me's laid a finger on it. Tomorrow, Sam, you can have it all . . .'

'Tiddler!' cried Joe, the cellarman, who'd been lounging in *The Red Lion*'s stableyard and been caught unawares by the early arrival of *The Flying Cradle*, 'I 'ope I didn't 'urt you yesterday?'

Sam stared at him blankly; then he remembered and attempted to look offended; but it was impossible to keep it up. The events of yesterday were as a watch in the night and had passed . . . as even the blackest night must dissolve into the dawn, when giants turn into trees and coffins into cupboards . . .

'I'm coming into my property, Joe,' he said with dignity; and then grinned with delight. 'Right now!'

Before Joe could question him further, Sam had followed after his pa, keeping closer than a shadow. Joe couldn't help observing that the coachman's eyes were heavy from lack of sleep. He saw him glance down at the cracked bannister as he trudged up the stairs . . .

They reached their room and Sam apologized to his pa for pushing. They went inside and the coachman unlocked the high cupboard. Sam's heart thundered and he felt a strong inclination to dance.

'You'll find it's all here,' said Chichester coldly. 'Saving the money, of course. But we'll count that out for you later – in front of Mr Roggs,' he added with bitter irony. 'Till then, there's enough here to be getting on with. Take it, Sam. It's your own property. Do what you want with it; just so long as you never speak a word about it to me or your ma again.'

With that, he laid the boxes and parcels on Sam's bed, left the room and shut the door. He'd been scrupulous all his life, and he couldn't help hoping that Sam would one day realize how deeply he'd wounded him.

He paused, hoping perhaps that Sam would recall him to

put the parcels away so that everything should be back as it was, before the horrible night at Mrs Nelson's. He put his ear to the door. He fancied he heard a sound of sobbing. His hand was on the doorknob, when the sobbing stopped and he heard the unmistakable sound of paper being eagerly torn apart. Angrily he shrugged his shoulders and went downstairs.

The coachman and his wife waited in the parlour, watched inquisitively by the Roggses who, for once, refrained from interfering. Joe, too, was consumed with curiosity and kept emerging from the cellar like an enormous rat, to see if the tiddler had appeared again. On these occasions he was especially heavy on the potboy who had succeeded him – an ill-mannered little lout of twelve – whose place Joe had been saving up in his heart of hearts for Sam. The potboy who, among other things, was remarkably tired of being called 'Spare Joe', sighed and made up his mind for the hundredth time to seek his fortune elsewhere. Every time the Chichesters came, the cellarman turned nasty ...

Mrs C. smiled wistfully. 'I'd give anything to see his face when he undoes all his fine things.'

Absently the coachman nodded. The same thought had not been far from his own mind.

'Then what are we sitting here for, Chichester?'

'I was waiting on you, Mrs C.'

Mrs Chichester reached the door first, but as she was about to open it, her husband caught her hand and raised a finger to his lips. He knocked ... There was no answer.

'Sam,' called his ma. 'May we come in now?'

'Yes.'

They opened the door. At first sight the room looked to have suffered a comprehensive accident. The rich gifts of Bratsby, Bartholomew, Oxton and Skipping were tumbled over the beds and on the floor as if *The Red Lion* had overturned and flung them out. Tiny embroidered waistcoats, brocaded bonnets in the Elizabethan style, hats and velvet breeches for infant cavaliers and a satin coat with buttons as bright as guineas lay in a wilderness of brown paper for all the world as if some Herod of haberdashery had passed that way, slaughtering the garments of babes. Here and there great splits and rents, like swordthrusts, appeared in the material, dividing the seams; for Sam, ever-sprouting Sam, had grown out of his property before he'd had a chance to grow into it.

But the owner, sitting in the midst of his worthless fortune, was smiling nonetheless. There'd been one item in the cupboard treasury that still contrived to fufil his hopes.

'Stand and deliver!' said Sam sternly.

Obediently, the coachman's heart stood still. The child had found out the pistol – and was aiming it at his chest. He held it as if to the manner born. He was not yet eight years old.

6

So, the blow had fallen, darkness and a sickening dismay enveloped the coachman like a cloak of night.

'It's out – it's out!' he kept muttering to himself as if to a stranger. Then little by little his eyes seemed to grow accustomed to the inner dark ... and he began to distinguish between shape and shadow. In a few days he found himself to be curiously relieved that it had all happened. He was like a man who has suspected a venomous snake to be loose in his bedroom. Through the long night he lies, perfectly still, not daring to move and scarcely to breathe. Every scrape and rustle fills him with terror and disgust. Then comes the morning – and he sees the serpent coiled on his coverlet! His imagination has not played him false. He cries out with relief – and faces visible danger with almost a light heart.

'Leastways,' thought Chichester, 'there's nothing hid between us now. I can watch for him – and sooner or later he'll understand why.'

There was no doubt that the pistol was exceptionally handsome; Chichester had quite forgotten what a showy weapon it was. Its black butt was overlaid with a sinuous design of silver flowers and leaves, and its long steel barrel gleamed like a shaft of the moon.

This barrel unscrewed, and very early Sam discovered that he was able to insert his thumb into it, right up to the second joint. Getting it out was also interesting. Joe, the cellarman, ever practical, suggested firing it off with a small charge of powder; but Mrs C., knowing more about firearms, finally cleared Sam out with soap, water and a ramrod. Sam also discovered that it was possible to pinch his fingers in three distinct working parts; after which he and the pistol came to terms with each other and no further sudden treachery took place.

'I wonder where the other one is?' murmured Mrs C., coming downstairs one London night.

Chichester stared at her with quick hostility. It seemed to him that she admired the weapon instead of being disgusted by it.

'Gentlemen's pistols like that are always made up in pairs. Somewhere there'll be its twin . . .'

'Gentleman's pistol you call it? God save us from such a gentleman! I – I'd sooner it had been one of them footpad's guns, dirty and rusting! Some gentleman!'

Chichester's voice had risen in anger. There was an inhuman coldness and arrogance about the silver pistol that repelled and frightened him . . .

Mrs C. shrugged her shoulders. Her own feeling for firearms was on the practical side; had Sam's inheritance been rusty, she certainly would have cleaned it. Nonetheless, she too would rather it had been more commonplace. She had never forgotten her husband's half-joking warning during the months they'd waited to possess Sam. What if the father should come to claim his child? he'd said. Little had he known what misery that thoughtless remark had given her. Although no one might have recognized the boy, the pistol was unmistakable. Since the weapon had come into Sam's possession, her own fear had been even greater than the coachman's. Every journey, every new set of passengers made her sick with apprehension; and whenever a stranger happened to admire the pistol – for Sam couldn't be kept from flourishing it everywhere – her heart seemed to stop and she longed to fling the damning object far away, into the roadside bushes out of their sight and lives.

'We was just talking about Sam,' said Mrs C. awkwardly as Mrs Nelson came in. Obscurely she felt some explanation was called for to dispel the uncomfortable atmosphere in the parlour.

'You don't say,' said Mrs Nelson, sitting down. 'You surprise me. You really do. And there was me thinking you'd been chewing over the state of the nation – by them heavy frowns. So what's to be done? What horrible crime has that tiny little thing committed now? Burned the fleet, maybe?'

'We was talking about his pistol, ma'am,' said Chichester sullenly.

Mrs Nelson smiled but kindly. 'You poor souls. He'll grow tired of it. Children always do. And then you can put it aside again till he's older. Or throw it away, even ...'

But Mrs Nelson's words were confounded; Sam showed no signs of tiring of his property. Rather the reverse, his interest seemed to grow keener as time went on so that the pistol was rarely out of his hands. Even at mealtimes (till it was put a stop to), he laid it on the table beside his knife and fork, for all the world as if he expected to have to shoot his dinner on arrival.

To Sam, the silvery beautiful pistol was no ordinary toy (the looks his ma and pa gave it had long ago confirmed him in that); it was a rare weapon of defence against the loneliness of childhood and his lingering fear of cupboards and the dark. In the wintertime, when the nights were long and black, he was forever fingering the tracery of leaves on the butt and picking at the delicate tendrils; whenever he went upstairs to bed, the pistol always preceded him, peering round the door like a cold, stalking eye. Who could say what might be lying in wait, under the bed or against the wall?

Each scratch, each indentation in the weapon had been closely examined and its possible cause debated. Even the makers' names – *J. and W. Richards, London* engraved against a panoply of flags just above the trigger – had been scrutinized till that hard-working and doubtless respectable pair came to live in Sam's mind – for no particular reason – as a pair of dwarfs, hammering away and mostly drunk.

He imagined his other pa concluding some frightful pact

with them in exchange for the magical pistol ... for by now the weapon was certainly supernatural. When he held it in a certain way he felt strange powers coursing through him that enabled him to lead valiant patrols through the ravine between the beds, to fight desperate duels with tyrants, and to smile mockingly over his shoulders at pursuers as, one by one, he sent them to their doom.

'When are you goin' to get flint an' powder an' shot, Sammy?' asked Joe, half patronizingly, half enviously.

Sam frowned and coolly shrugged his shoulders. The question offended him. Curiously enough, he'd no wish to fire his pistol. The cruel savages and bloody tyrants who nightly melted away before the deadly barrel could only fall to bullets of the mind. Somehow it would have seemed clumsy and intrusive to have primed the pistol with common powder and lead.

'Milk fed, that's what 'e's been,' confided Joe disgustedly to the barmaid of his choice who served in the rival establishment of *The White Horse*.

'Oh, Joe!'

'I weren't like that when I were nudgin' on ten.'

'Oh, Joe.'

'I was goin' to give 'im some powder an' shot an' a flint for 'is birthday. But that milk-fed tiddler don't care for bangs.'

'Oh, Joe ...'

'A good kick up the arse, that's what 'e wants ... an' I've a good mind to give 'im one – for 'is birthday!'

'Joe!'

'Fer Gawd's sake, can't you say nothin' else?'

There was no doubt that the older Sam grew the more Joe felt that his shilling had been wasted. The boy never understood Joe's jokes, he never took Joe's advice, and he showed signs of becoming a dreamer – which human state Joe distrusted more than a leaking barrel. So for his birthday, instead of powder and shot, Joe bought him a pair of mittens, meaning the gift to be a sarcastic comment on Sam's fastidious nature.

However, to the cellarman's chagrin, the gift was taken in good part and he was warmly thanked for displaying so thoughtful a nature. Which was more than could be said for Messrs Bratsby, Oxton and Skipping. (Mr Bartholomew had passed away during the previous year so his parcels, like himself, had come to an end.) They remained true to their promise and scrupulously sent their yearly gifts; but in the matter of choosing them they consulted their hearts rather than their heads. Had they even consulted their wives, things might have been mended; but charity is a private satisfaction, and inclined to be selfish. So yearly, from the three warm hearts, came gifts for the baby who had kindled that warmth ... or at best, for an undersized toddler with illusions of grandeur ...

'No matter,' said Sam's ma, with her usual mixture of good sense and sympathy on these occasions, 'it's the thought that counts.'

Sam scowled in disgust and formed a low opinion of any thought that counted as hopelessly as this one: he was ten, not two!

He looked round the table. He had a distinct feeling there was something else to come. In fact, he had rather more than a feeling. He *knew* his pa had got something for him. Although he hadn't been able to discover what it was – not for want of searching! – there'd been such an air of secrecy and such an exchange of looks between his ma and pa whenever his birthday had been mentioned that Sam would have taken his Bible oath on there being another gift coming. For a time he'd feared it would turn out to be a book or something to wear; but he couldn't, in his heart of hearts, believe anything so monstrous of them.

'What are you waiting for, Sam?'

'Nothing, ma.'

'Not another present, surely!'

Everyone grinned and Sam blushed furiously.

'Why, what have we here?' said his pa as if surprised by a sudden apparition. He fidgeted and produced from nowhere a long, brown paper parcel. Elaborately he examined it, while Sam jumped up and down in his place.

'Why it says, "Sam Chichester"; and it's from –'

'Pa!' shouted Sam, almost falling into his cake in his efforts to reach his present.

'From his loving Pa!'

Sam had got hold of it and in no time had torn the wrapping to shreds. Somewhat wistfully the coachman watched his laborious writing vanish into unregarded fragments. But it was the gift that mattered.

'Pa!' shrieked Sam. 'It's what I always wanted! Look – look!'

It was a half-sized coaching whip with Sam's name engraved on a silver band round the handle. Next to a coach and four of his very own, it had been what the boy had wanted more than anything else in the world.

In high excitement he danced round the table showing his magnificent whip (which had cost more than Chichester cared to admit) to everyone. Mr Roggs opined that it was one of the finest of its kind and Joe declared it went handsomely with Sam's new mittens.

That night Sam went to bed and to sleep with the whip clutched firmly in his hand; and the coachman could have wept with triumph and relief. He felt that he had at last conquered the malignant pistol.

In the days that followed, the ordinarily stern Chichester forgave Sam a great deal; for most of his sins were connected with the whip. He flourished it; he cracked it; he swaggered through Dorking, Chichester and Aldersgate Street with it and found a thousand opportunities for displaying it to perfect strangers. Halfheartedly the coachman attempted to restrain him. It was meant for horses ... so! Never more than a touch; just so long as the horses feel it ... no need to make enemies of 'em ... Practise ...

Obediently Sam practised; and though it must be admitted that he never made enemies of the horses, he succeeded wholesale so far as everyone else was concerned. He nipped the tops off *The Red Lion*'s flowers, he caught Joe repeatedly behind the knees, and as an especial triumph, he took an apple off the head of a nervously obliging little girl of eight. Unluckily this child turned out to be the daughter of the Chichester coach proprietor whose mother, a fierce, unforgiving woman, bore down on Sam like a runaway coach as he was struggling to disengage his thong from the shrieking child's hair.

Grudgingly the coachman obeyed his wife and apologized to the mother and 'spoke sharpish to Sam'. He told him off roundly and packed him off to bed with a volley of threats and scowls. But afterwards he couldn't help chuckling and grinning into his supper no matter how sternly Mrs C. bade him be serious.

At last, wearied of carping and criticism, he got up to walk outside. As he did so he observed the offending whip lying on Sam's chair. With a faint, unreasonable pang of distress, he picked it up.

'I'll put it by him,' he muttered. 'He's sure to wake and miss it.'

He went upstairs and quietly entered the room. Sam was fast asleep. His features were composed most blissfully. The coachman began to smile ... then a sick dismay overcame him. He let the whip fall. He saw the cold, inhuman barrel of the pistol peering out from under the pillow.

The coachman stood perfectly still, gaunt as a spectre by the child's bed. He stared down as if striving to force his way into Sam's head and rage like a madman among his dreams, battering them into fragments.

There was a smile on the child's lips. What was he smiling

at? What instincts was the pistol awakening? Was he in touch with something sown long before he, Chichester, had known Sam? A secret meeting, perhaps, with the other pa ... ?

The coachman trembled as he watched the child's smooth face till it seemed to become alien and incomprehensible. They were strangers, he and the boy ... He turned away. Mrs Nelson had said that time would do for the charms of the pistol and, sooner or later, the murderous thing would go back into its battered box to be forgotten along with its tawdry companion, the unregarded pewter ring. This was commonsense. But commonsense, though it might drive horses and change a coachwheel, was no answer to the smile on Sam's lips nor the mystery of his dreams.

He bent down to pick up the whip. It had failed. In this, the last resort of sleep and dreams, he had been turned away by the too powerful rivalry of the mysterious other pa who dwelt in the pistol.

He laid the whip at the foot of Sam's bed and crept away.

7

THE *Flying Cradle* was an elderly vehicle, having been built in London some thirty years previously. Thirty years is a long, full life for a coach – even though it amounts to no more than wind, rain and fleeting sunshine passing in review across iron, wood and leather. Iron rusts, wood rots, and leather wears away. In lesser hands than Chichester's, *The Flying Cradle* would have been laid to rest long ago – maybe, even, with several of its passengers; but the scrupulous coachman so nursed its every rheumatic whine and grunt, seeming at times to commune with its very inanimate soul, that it outlived many a brasher equipage that spanked along only to fizzle out disgracefully in a ditch. Though here and there, in awkward places its decoration might have been a little tarnished, its reputation was not. Maybe it did take two days over a journey that others could have achieved in one, but it never failed to arrive nor had it ever been seen with its wheels in the air. Perhaps it no longer deserved to be called 'Flying', but surely it was still as safe as a 'Cradle'.

Twice a year, in July and September, it was taken off the road for renewal and repairs, first at the wheelwright's in Dorking and then at the coachmaker's in Town. On these occasions the Chichesters took another coach on the road and Sam was given a three-day holiday at *The Red Lion*.

Such prolonged halts in his endlessly travelling life seemed like halts in time itself. Motion, which was the very stuff of his real existence, was interrupted. The fields and hedgerows and even the passing season stopped, and all were petrified in a long, breathing moment. The very bedrooms in London and Chichester, that were at the rim of his wheel of time – each complete with its crackly ceiling, stained walls and particular dreams – dwindled away together with Chichester–Dorking and London–Dorking. He was at the hub and axle of existence, and *The Red Lion* stood firm for home.

Leisure spread in all directions and seemed like a microscope, magnifying the million details of a stationary life. Among these details, the least captivating was a well-meaning parson who nightly instructed Sam in the rudiments of theology and arithmetic. On the other hand, the occasional visit of a fair – on its way north to Smithfield, Tottenham or Southwark – more than made up for the solemn evening stint among crosses upright and askew.

Twice in his life before, Sam had been taken to the fair by Mrs Roggs, and the occasions remained like sunbursts in his memory; the prospect of a third visit filled him with an almost unbearable excitement. Not even the unexpected news that Joe, the cellarman, was to take him, reduced his exalted state by much ... though it certainly had a lowering effect on Joe. The cellarman had long been planning to take his barmaid from *The White Horse* when his employer's lady fell victim to what Mr Roggs called 'an inflammation of the spirits' and was confined to bed.

'It ain't often that we ask a favour of you, Joe,' said the landlord in a tone of voice that had alarmed him since his potboy days.

Joe nodded. He had to admit the justice of Mr Roggs's remark. He wasn't often asked to do something; he was generally told.

'You can take your Molly or Suzy or Bessy or whatever you call her just as well with Sam as without.'

At this, Joe offered his employer a bitterly incredulous smile.

'That's it, Joe! That's what I always like about you. You put a good face on things!'

Joe sighed. It always seemed his fate for his meanings to be missed. The real Joe – the bitter, sarcastic, biting, ironical Joe – remained totally unsuspected by the world at large, and was known only to Joe himself. 'Spare Joe' watched him uneasily from behind a chair, and then decided that for the next day or so, he'd turn into 'Scarce Joe'. After which he'd seek employment elsewhere.

The morning of the fair turned out gusty, with fitful sunshine and dark clouds lurking round its edges. The cellarman's mood matched it, being divided between pleasure at the prospect of his lady friend and gloom at being lumbered with the tiddler. He began by making his displeasure felt and forbidding Sam to take his whip to the fair. Then he found fault with Sam's hair, fingernails and neck, stressing the fact that he was going to meet a lady. When Sam retaliated by pointing out a road map of stains on Joe's best coat, the cellarman flew into a rage and warned Sam to mind his language.

'There's goin' to be a lady present, I told you; so watch them words. And manners, too.'

Sam's fingers closed menacingly round the butt of his pistol. His pace, as he followed Joe, took on a soft-footed, loping aspect, as might a hunter's on the trail of a wolf. Joe grew pointed ears and a long snout ... The market-day town shuddered into a forest, demanding sinuous stealth ...

'Can't you walk straight?' snapped the cellarman. 'Weavin' about like a boozy alderman!'

'Who's the lady what's coming with us?' asked Sam, giving up the forest and wondering how best he might demolish Joe.

'A certain Miss Amelia.'

'Ain't that Milly from *The White Horse*?'

Joe nodded curtly.

'But she's only a barmaid ...'

Joe stopped, regardless of the obstruction he caused in the busy street. A complication of emotions boiled up inside him. He glared at Sam.

'And who d'you think you are, eh? What sort of pa did you

'ave what gives you the right to abuse a lady? Answer me that!'

'Just as good as yours!' Sam had gone very red, and his voice had taken on a shrill, penetrating edge.

'Mine died in 'is bed,' muttered Joe, subsiding a little and beginning to walk on again, 'which is more'n can be said for yours. 'Anged, 'e was – and that's for certain sure.'

'You don't know that. You're just saying it.'

'Stands to reason . . .'

Silence for several moments while Sam scowled ferociously in an effort to uncover something that would undermine his enemy.

'What was your pa, Joe?' (Deceptively calm.)

'An ostler, if you must know.'

Triumph spread over Sam's face. 'Then he minded my other pa's horse! My other pa was a lord. And you can't say he wasn't because you don't know. You don't – you don't!'

This spectacular emerging of Sam's other pa from the awful blackness of cupboards into the aristocracy had taken much brooding and silent communion with the pistol to bring about. Consequently nowadays that shadowy personage whose total existence had once been confined in a barber's box blazed like a comet across Sam's secret sky, sometimes turning down on him the face of a prince, a general, or one of those legendary highwaymen whose gallantry elevated them to the stars. If he had been hanged at all, it had been for some truly spectacular offence; but more than likely he'd escaped at the last moment, cut the rope from his neck, and with a laugh and a shout, leaped to freedom on a miraculously convenient horse. Sam would have died in such a man's defence – and had done so several times already – so it wasn't to be wondered at that Joe lay bleeding like a punctured wineskin, begging Sam's forgiveness with his dying breath.

A shower of rain greeted their arrival at *The White Horse* where Milly was sheltering under the entrance to the yard.

'Why, it's little Sammy, ain't it?' she said, looking from Joe to Sam and then down to herself.

'No; it's the bleedin' Prince of Wales,' said the cellarman heavily.

'Oh, Joe!'

Joe shrugged his shoulders and sighed. The nearness of Milly with her glazed flesh and seasoned green satin always filled him with a strange excitement and awe. She was a mystery, like all women; one never knew what she was thinking . . .

Milly, on the other hand, being a woman, knew perfectly well what Joe was thinking: same as always – to get her on her own and make a beast of himself. But not this time.

'You come and hold my hand, Sammy love,' she said, extending her plump fingers invitingly. 'Don't want to lose you in the crowd, do we! Just you be my beau for today.'

Sam gave up his hand. There was a real splendour about Milly, and an intoxicating smell of flowers, port and femininity. In no time at all he was captivated by her; he grew a full twelve inches in as many seconds and when the rain stopped and they set off through the rinsed sunshine, he dropped a score of ruthless abductors in their tracks . . .

'Stop wavin' that pistol aboût!' snarled the neglected Joe. 'You'll 'ave someone's eye out!'

'Joe!' said Milly.

Sam frowned at the cellarman, bound him hand and foot and suspended him over a saucepan of boiling oil . . .

Stubs's Field – an unkempt patch of open ground to the south side of the town – was ablaze with a summer of flags and streamers. Booths and painted tents had sprung up everywhere and their loose battlements kept snapping and cracking in the stiff breeze like a festival of musketry; while shouts of laughter and excitement came from the escorts of young women whose skirts were billowing and rising and threatening to depart altogether. The narrow streets that had been created between the rows of bright pavilions were already deep in mud from countless surging feet; and at the backs of the premises, where battered vehicles and elderly horses were shambled up in a kind of clumsy twilight, roamed bands of lively and inquisitive youths like so many doubting Thomases, eager to poke their fingers through holes in the mystery. From time to time they were chased out by huge, ferocious women and fled among the crowds with shrieks of derision.

'You stay along of me, Sammy love,' said Milly, glancing suspiciously at these pockets of privacy in the fabric of the fair in which more might be lost than children. She hurried on, holding Sam with one hand and her windy gown with the other.

Her words were unnecessary; nothing was further from Sam's thoughts than letting go of Milly. His eyes were moist with admiration as he kept gazing up at her. He was head over ears in love; and when love comes to a lad of ten and three quarters, it comes like a landslide, sweeping all before it and changing the very contours of the visible world.

Milly was the most radiant, most beautiful being Sam had ever laid eyes on. She was an angel straight out of heaven, and the fact that she was forced to serve ale in the parlour of *The White Horse* lent her that crown of distress without which no beauty is complete.

Sam walked on air, stumbling occasionally over what could only have been the tops of very tall trees. He longed to show Milly his adoration, but at ten and three quarters there didn't seem much chance, so he contented himself with leaving piles of insolent dead to the right and left of her, shooting them down for no worse offence than an appraising look ...

They watched the conjurors, the rope dancers, the tumblers ... they ate toffee apples; they visited a fortune teller where Joe paid sixpence to the cruel-eyed prophetess who wore earrings like horse brasses and told Sam he'd live till he was ninety, never walk with a stick and die in his bed.

'Which is more'n can be said for 'is pa,' grunted Joe, who thereupon collapsed at the fortune teller's feet with a bullet through his chest.

Sam left him there; Milly squeezed his hand; he returned the pressure with interest.

'Ow!' said Milly. 'Sammy, love – you're *strong*!'

Sam felt like a king; he beamed.

''avin' quite a day, ain't you!' said Joe with biting irony. 'I 'ope you're enjoyin' every minute of it.'

'I am, Joe, I am, thank you,' said Sam, entirely missing Joe's meaning. He turned a gracious face on the cellarman and straightaway released him from the torture chamber in which he'd been screaming and allowed him out for an hour a day ...

Presently the morning went into one of its gloomy fits.

The air deepened ...

'Where's the sun gone?' wondered Milly ruefully.

'Don't you know?' said Joe.

'Behind them clouds, I suppose.'

'No it ain't. It's shinin' out of the tiddler's arse. Best get 'im ointment or 'e'll get blisters.'

Before Milly could reply, the rain set in again, this time in a pelting, gusty torrent. Shrieks went up from the crowd which began to surge and scuttle for shelter. Booths and tents of the more cultured sort, that had never attracted a soul till then, found themselves besieged; and a company of players who'd been performing the tragedy of *King Richard the Third* to an audience of about the same number, was overwhelmed by a sudden popularity. ('I never really reigned that day till it poured!' confided the King Richard, afterwards, when there were sufficient people about to appreciate the remark.)

Milly, Joe and Sam bought shelter in this latter tent, and it was here, with the rain coming down on the roof like gunfire, that Sam had his first view of the stage. Or, rather, a part of it, as he was small and those in front were large.

But he heard the great words thundered out and caught

glimpses of a wonderland that stretched his world beyond its natural limits. He saw King Richard, with withered arm and monstrous hump, wooing the lovely Lady Anne with a ring over her husband's corpse; he saw poor Clarence drowned in a butt of malmsey wine; and between sudden flashes of scarlet robes and silver braid, he saw a score of other murders plotted, executed and laughed away; he saw the gaudy ghosts haunting the king before his last battle; he heard the wicked king die ...

It was tremendous; it made an earthquake in his soul. Sam knew nothing of history. The world, so far as he was concerned, had always been constituted as it was. He knew there was a throne and a king upon it called George. Folk sometimes drank to him and that was proof enough. But the unexpected news that there'd been a King Richard (and plainly more than one) overturned his notions of a settled order.

But the real excitement lay elsewhere; it lay in the startled recognition of the world he knew translated into an astounded glory. There on the stage, larger than life, had been the representations of Richmond, Buckingham (deep, revolving Buckingham! how true!), York and Derby. It had been like the grandest of Christmases at Mrs Nelson's! In a flash, he saw the whole turbulent enterprise, with its sombre politics and murderous discord, as a mutiny of impossibly splendid coachmen against the crown. He was thrilled and enchanted. When the rain stopped and he came out of the tent, he was in a dazed state that remained with him for the rest of the day.

The cellars of *The Red Lion* were deep, mysterious and extensive. In a manner of speaking, they represented the darker portion of the mind of the premises above.

In this dark place, fancies, dreams, wild songs and poems were imprisoned in unseen vats and barrels where they fermented, muttering obscurely. As the eye grew accustomed to the gloom, several walls of bottles seemed to drift out of the shadows, like the high bulwarks of men-of-war, silently menacing each other with rank upon rank of small black cannons. From time to time, there would be a loud bang, terrifying to the unwary, as an unsound bottle exploded and discharged its contents on the floor. Then the air of the cellar would be pervaded by a sweet rottenness, such as one sometimes finds in an old garden . . .

Rumour had it that Prince Charles once took refuge there; but nowadays there was only Joe and *The Red Lion*'s motherly cat. Joe had an office in the depths – a kind of candlelit cave among the barrels, with a plank stretched across two of them upon which he kept his accounts.

'Who's there?'

Joe laid a large hand over a paper he'd been writing on; it was a letter to Milly and peculiarly private.

'Me.'

Sam came fumbling down the steps. The nightly parson had been and gone, the lesson administered and Sam was in search of company. The hostilities of the day were at an end; spirit came out to meet with spirit, bearing gifts . . .

'Do you think I could give Milly this?' asked Sam, humbly. He was holding out his pewter ring, the pistol's half-forgotten box-mate.

It was a cheap, clumsy affair, decorated with a piece of green bottle glass that pretended hopelessly to be an emerald worth a king's ransom. Yet in its way this ring was, perhaps, more mysterious than the pistol. Or, rather, it was the two of them together that made the mystery. The pistol might well have belonged to a gentleman, murderous though he might have been; the ring was from a different world altogether. The connection between them was so inscrutable that Sam never even attempted to fathom it.

'I know it's not real,' he said, 'but it's all I've got – at the moment, that is.'

Joe blinked, marvelling a little at Sam's growth from nothingness into the love-smitten lad who fidgeted at the edge of the candlelight. He was about to suggest, humorously, that Milly was a size too big for him, when an absurd feeling of awkwardness and delicacy overcame him. A furtive look came into his eyes; had the cellar been not so dark, it would have been seen that Joe was blushing.

The letter he'd been labouring over had been a proposal of marriage. He'd determined on this drastic course some months previously, but had been uncertain as to the best ways of persuading Milly to his way of thinking. She was so very particular ... and Joe, anxious to avoid humiliating mistakes in spelling, sometimes went a whole day in search of a desirable word, not liking to ask but furtively scrutinizing every scrap of print he could find. So far he'd been occupied in composing the letter for almost as many days as it had words. 'Dear Miss Amelia,' he'd begun, 'I am five and twenty as you well no and have good prospectuses' (he'd pilfered this word from an advertisement for a school that hung in *The Red Lion*'s parlour) 'and a little money put by. I have a loving nature as you well no and think I would suit even if you do better in time ...'

Joe's awkwardness increased under Sam's inquisitive eyes; he felt the words he'd written fairly tingling against his concealing palm. Like all people interrupted in some strong emotion, he endowed the interrupter with supernatural powers of penetration. He felt sure that Sam had guessed what he was up to, hence his delicacy in refraining from making fun of the lad. Sam might have thought he was jealous, and Joe was keenly aware of the wounding absurdity of such a state of affairs. The mysterious darkness of the cellar seemed to lend him unusual insight ...

'That was left to you by your poor ma,' he said reproachfully, indicating the ugly ring. 'You ought to keep it, Sammy. Your pa would tan your 'ide if 'e found out you'd given it away.'

'Which pa, Joe?'

Joe sighed. 'The only one what matters, Sammy. The one

what came into the parlour that night long ago and said, calm as kiss-your-hand, "We'll shoulder 'im." You could 'ave 'eard a bubble burst, tiddler. We all just stood an' stared.'

'And what happened then, Joe?'

Sam squatted contentedly on a barrel and turned his face towards Joe so that the candle burned double in his eyes. He never wearied of hearing about his origins; the details, as recollected by Joe, seemed to give him a real foothold in the world, and a strange sense of comfort. Many times he'd heard about Joe's shilling and the money laid out by the four travellers. (It seemed unreal that there were only three of them now; it was as if he'd been translated into history.) He liked to hear about Mr Roggs writing everything down, and most of all he was fascinated to hear of the glimpse Joe had had of his tiny self being carried down the stairs in Mrs Roggs's arms and thence to the kitchen ...

'And then, tiddler, we named you.'

Here was something new. On previous occasions the naming had slipped Joe's memory, but now it came back to him. Sam's eyes widened in disbelief. It had never occurred to him that his name had actually been chosen. If ever he'd thought about it at all, he'd supposed he'd come into the world complete, as Sam, and was well known as such directly. Most likely someone had called down the stairs: 'Sam's been born!' But now everything went back into the melting pot ...

'There was Hassocks and Ned, as I remember; but none of us went much on them.'

Sam nodded shrewdly. He didn't go much on them himself.

'Then someone thought of "Joe", which would have been suitable, but we couldn't 'ave two Joes, could we? So it came down to Sam – or 'arry. We took a vote on it and Sam won the day; so Sam you was, and Sam you are. But it were generally agreed amongst us that should you ever turn out to be a 'arry, then 'arry you'd be. But so far, you're still our Sam.'

Joe paused; Sam's expression had gone curiously remote. Joe wondered if he'd been offended.

'So I'm –' Sam began slowly, when a bottle exploded in the shadows with a tremendous bang. Sam started in alarm, then Joe reassured him and explained that bottles got excited no less than them that drank them.

'Here she comes,' he said cheerfully, as a ripe smell drifted through the cellar like a dream on its way to a party . . .

Joe looked inquiringly at Sam, waiting for him to finish what he'd begun to say; but the tiddler seemed to have forgotten. So Joe fidgeted with his papers, remarked, as if in surprise that he had work to do and that it was long past a tiddler's bed-time. He smiled expectantly, hoping Sam would take the hint and go as he was growing impatient to get on with his letter to Milly. But Sam seemed to have fallen asleep with his eyes open. He gazed into the dim caverns of the cellar with much the same dazed look he'd worn when he'd come out of the play earlier that day.

'What's malmsey, Joe?' he asked suddenly.

'Booze,' answered Jo. 'Sweet an' strong.' Then, remembering the only part of the play that had made an impression on him as it had touched on his profession, added humorously, 'Tastes a bit of dukes.'

Sam looked studious. 'Can I try some, Joe?'

'Too strong for tiddlers.'

'Just a sip?'

Firmly Joe shook his head; then he looked thoughtful . . . .

'It's by way of bein' a night-cap, Sammy. You'd 'ave to go straight up to bed.'

Sam hesitated, then he nodded in agreement. He'd seen enough of the weird power of drink to take Joe's word on it.

'Straight to bed it'll be, Joe. Promise.'

Joe shrugged his shoulders in a no-harm-seeing way. He rose to his feet and shuffled off into the dark. When he came back with a full ladle of wine, Sam had not stirred; he was still squatting on the barrel with his eyes full of dreams. But Joe could have sworn his letter had been shifted. He didn't want to accuse Sam of reading it, but it was impossible not to have his suspicions.

' 'Ere, tiddler; just a sip, then.'

Sam took the ladle. The heavy fruity vapour of the wine seemed to envelop him. He shut his eyes, wrinkled his nose and drank . . .

'Just a sip, I said.' Joe's attention had momentarily wandered to his letter. Had it or hadn't it been shifted? 'Gawd! You've sunk the lot! You boozy little soak, you! You'll 'ave an 'ead on you tomorrow, my lad! Up to bed with you! And look sharp before that drink really 'its you!'

Sam stared at Joe, as if amazed by his vehemence. He stood up. What nonsense Joe was talking. As if sweet wine could hit one like a fist! One wasn't swaying about, as some folks did . . . the stairs were as steady as a rock; one went up like a feather. One wasn't likely to fall down them so there was no call for Joe to stand behind one with that silly look on his face and his arms spread out. Feathers don't fall . . .

Ah! that was better! Fresh night air. Lucky one had one's pistol with one; the night looked dangerous. All them stars and shadows . . . One couldn't quite recall how one had got out into the night – there must have been doors somewhere; but after all, one couldn't be expected to remember *everything*. One wasn't an effelunt . . . elemunt . . . E L E P H A N T. One was Sam, who might have been Harry. And why wasn't one Harry? Hadn't one turned out well enough for a Harry? One was insulted and nobody really understood why. Of course one was Harry and always had been. Sam was just a disguise . . .

One should have drowned Joe in that butt of malmsey – and pushed his letter in after him. Harry would stop him wedding Milly. Now one was Harry one could afford to be brilliant and dashing . . .

Oh lovely Milly . . . Milly . . . Milly . . . I want my Milly . . .

73

'And who do we say's asking for her?'

An enormous face, full of whiskers and stinking disagreeably of liquor, grinned suddenly into his own. Several other faces, dizzily similar, crowded behind.

One was in the parlour of *The White Horse*. How had one got there? Don't ask silly questions!

'Shog off,' said Sam curtly. 'I want Milly.'

'Give us your name then ...'

'Harry.'

'Why it's that tiddler Sam,' said the landlord, easing slantways through the crowd. 'Sam from *The Flying Cradle*.'

The landlord looked extraordinarily villainous and threatening; Sam took aim ...

'I hope that thing's not loaded –'

'Sammy, love!'

'Milly! I've come ... to give you – that is, to give you ... this ring ...'

'He's boozed to the eyeballs!'

'Shockin'!'

'Shog off, the lot of you. I – I – oh!'

'Stand back, there! He's goin' to be sick!'

'Oh, Sammy, *love* ...'

8

JOE was the villain of the piece; there could be no doubt of that. Mr Roggs was disgusted with him, and would deal with him severely whenever he could be found. There was no sense it trying to blame Sam; the tiddler wasn't at all well. Besides, when all was said and done, he was only a child.

Patiently Mr Roggs explained matters to the Chichesters on the following day when they came to collect *The Flying Cradle* and Sam – only to find the coach a good deal more road-worthy than the child.

'Some child!' shouted Chichester, beside himself with indignation. 'A child what goes whoring after a barmaid and threatens a landlord with a pistol! Some child, I say!'

Mr Roggs sighed and rolled his eyes upwards in an expression that might have been pious had it not been joined with a tightening of the lips. The coachman's scrupulousness and probity were sometimes hard to bear. He himself was as honest as the next man – always allowing for the next man having a fair share of human nature – but Chichester's honesty would have driven a saint to drink. Once, long ago, Chichester had happened to find out that Mr Roggs sometimes hired out the coach horses for private riding. He'd never forgotten the coachman's attitude on that occasion. One would have thought he'd done a murder.

But Mr Roggs, by and large, was a forgiving man.

'You wouldn't carry on like that, Mr Chichester, if you'd seen the lad carried back in Milly's arms, half crying, half sleeping and then never settling because of his fear and shame of what you'd say.'

'Much he cares!'

'Ah! there you do him an injustice, sir. That tiddler dotes

on the pair of you. Why, sir, the sun and moon are nothing beside his love for you.'

This was no exaggeration; at the moment, the sun and moon came pretty low down on Sam's list of affections. If pushed, he'd have parted with them for a good deal less than the Chichesters.

The coachman was partly mollified; and Mr Roggs promptly pressed home the advantage by listing Sam's good points. The tiddler was healthy and quick at learning; he had an affectionate heart, and, though his countenance wasn't exactly 'Greeshun', it was a countenance that he, Mr Roggs, was never sorry to behold.

'He's handsome enough,' admitted Chichester grudgingly. 'He'll turn a few heads when he's grown.'

'He's made a good start,' chuckled Mr Roggs, who, in spite of efforts to the contrary, couldn't help regarding Sam's escapade as being in the way of a manly adventure. There was no doubt, in Mr Roggs's book, that the lad who sometimes didn't take a drop too much and chase a barmaid round the house, was a poor fish indeed. No better than a woman. Mr Roggs held all women in contempt, but was courteous enough never to come out with it where it might give offence.

The coachman went off into one of his long, silent ruminations and Mr Roggs's roving eye fell on 'Spare Joe', lurking round a table and collecting glasses as if he was pilfering them. He jumped a foot in the air when Mr Roggs addressed him and asked him if he'd seen Joe yet. 'Spare Joe' hadn't. Then would he have the goodness to go and find him as Mr Chichester wanted a word. 'Spare Joe' nodded and, with surprising willingness, departed; a singularly vindictive smile was playing round his lips as he took a candle to seek out the cellarman in his lair. Divide and rule, thought Mr Roggs with satisfaction.

'Of course you'll leave the lad here?' said Mr Roggs affably to the coachman. 'He'll need a day taking it easy. A coach ride would finish him off right now. I know; I've seen it happen.'

Chichester hesitated, frowning. Like all men of scrupulous habit, he hated any alteration in the regular run of his life. He had an almost superstitious dread of change, however temporary, and felt it an omen of disaster. But this was hard to explain to a man like Mr Roggs.

'It weren't my fault, sir.'

Joe had emerged from the cellar; there was no sign of 'Spare Joe', and Mr Roggs wondered fleetingly if the cellarman had done him in. Thoughts of explaining the calamity away occupied his mind.

'It was the play what put malmsey wine in 'is 'ead, sir . . .'

Ah! but who put it in his belly? thought Mr Roggs wittily, but refrained from coming out with it. 'Load of rubbish, them players,' he said aloud, seizing the opportunity of shifting any blame from his premises. 'But they're away tomorrow, Mr Chichester, so there'll be no more trouble of that kind.'

The coachman grunted. Plays and players revolted him. Theirs was a world of fraudulent dreams and pretence, the ever-willing bedfellows of lying, thieving and the crooked way. What was an actor but a wretch living by deceit? How could such a fellow, filling his days with pretence, ever know the difference between the truth and a lie? Habit must have corrupted him rotten.

Upstairs Sam lay in bed. His face was turned from the light and was very white and deathly looking. From time to time he attempted to shrivel into the bed-clothes and vanish without a trace. This was when he thought of Milly and the shame of the previous night.

He was ruined. Henceforth, if he survived, he could never leave his bed; he would become the upstairs invalid of *The Red Lion* of whom no one spoke.

'Best take a little broth, Sam,' shouted his ma, thundering over the boards.

He closed his eyes. Joe had poisoned him out of jealousy; if it was malmsey wine he'd had, it wasn't to be wondered at that it had finished off a duke.

'It weren't my fault, Mrs C.'

Joe had come in, sorry as a crocodile.

'How much did you give him?'

'Only a ladle, Mrs C. And I warned 'im ...'

'How big was the ladle, for God's sake?'

'Shade under a pint, ma'am ...'

'*Full?*'

'That's 'ow it comes up from the barrel ...'

'Couldn't you have tipped some back?'

'Too dark to see properly down there. Might 'ave spilled it ...'

Mrs Chichester stared at Joe in amazement, then called him an offensive name; the cellarman abjectly departed. Outside the door he scratched his unshaven cheek, then went slowly down the stairs, contorting his arm above his head in various positions as if manipulating a ladle.

'Just show me 'ow to tip it back without spilling an' I'll do it ...' he muttered contemptuously.

Sam stirred. 'Don't go, ma,' he whispered piteously. At that moment his ma was the only living soul he wanted by him.

Mrs Chichester compressed her lips. She'd recovered from her first anger and was now genuinely alarmed about Sam. There was no telling what a pint of strong wine might have done to a young stomach.

'I'll be back,' she said; and Sam watched her mournfully, wondering if he'd last out till she returned.

Mrs C. hurried downstairs, passing Joe on the landing where he was doing something odd with his arm. She found Chichester and Mr Roggs in the parlour.

'If you don't mind, I'd best stay with him, Chichester,' she said quietly. 'That is, always supposing you can find someone to ride guard in my place.'

'No trouble at all, ma'am,' said Mr Roggs courteously.

'One of them ostlers can go. Glad of the ride . . .'

The coachman said nothing; he stared at his wife in angry disbelief. Had it come to this? Had the child come so much between them? A feeling of helpless rage filled him, and a creeping bitterness . . . What if he had an accident on the way, he brooded? She'd be sorry then. Thus his thoughts ran, perhaps not so grandly as Sam's might have done, but much in the same spirit.

Mrs C. had gone; Mr Roggs rose to go to the stables to 'sort out one of them dozy layabouts', as he put it. Chichester followed.

'Women!' said Mr Roggs, after he'd instructed an elderly employee to make himself ready.

Gloomily Chichester looked up at *The Flying Cradle* which had been greased and polished till it shone like a new coach. She ought to be on it with him. After all, it was their life . . .

'Women!' repeated Mr Roggs, suspecting that the coachman's thoughts lay in that direction. Impulsively he patted him on the arm and wished him a safe journey. Then he retired to his kingdom of the parlour.

Unlike Mr Roggs, the coachman held no personal view of women. He divided all humankind into passengers and otherwise; he entertained no other distinction. Mrs Chichester, being the only woman he'd ever really known, he considered his equal in some respects and his superior in others. She was a better shot than he, and, though he was stronger, she was better able to endure the weather. She was more naturally learned than he and was able to converse with Sam in a manner altogether beyond the coachman's capacity. He'd always admired her for this, even though it had been with a tinge of regret. In the past, before the time of Sam, he and Mrs C. had always been a silent couple, content to exchange nods rather than words and spend the travelling days watching the fields go by and the changing weather. It was only after one of them had been absent on some necessary errand that they blossomed into chatter – as if they were unconsciously afraid that any gap, however small, in each other's lives might widen and never be bridged unless filled in directly with every detail ... But Mrs C. had turned out to be a wonder; she and Sam always found so much to talk about, even, Chichester reflected sadly, at the expense of the road itself.

'Look!' the coachman would cry.

'What, pa? What was it?'

'It's gone now,' Chichester would grunt, being quite unable to explain why, maybe two soldiers taking their ease at the edge of a harvest field, or a bramble hedge caught by the sun, had been worth looking at. He'd frown and feel momentarily like some clumsy vehicle, severed from its gossiping horses, and trundling slowly backwards into the night.

'Ready, Mr C.'

The ostler had appeared, accoutred like a general, carrying an enormous shotgun with a muzzle that could have accommodated a plate. Chichester frowned at him, and the ostler shifted uncomfortably.

'I don't like no talking on the road.'

'Agreed, Mr C. I'm inclined to be silent myself.'

'Horses changed round in twenty minutes.'

'To the tick, Mr C. I ain't one for loitering.'

'No shouldering of passengers. No more on the top than is lawful.'

'Honesty is the best policy, I always say, Mr C.'

'Use the brake when I say. Don't take it on yourself.'

'Won't lay a finger on it. Till you say, that is ...' He patted his weapon and prepared to mount.

'And another thing,' said Chichester fiercely. 'You'd best take Mrs Chichester's shotgun. Leastways it's clean.' And hers, he added inside his head.

'What's that?' moaned Sam as a crashing thunder filled his ears and rocked his poor brain.

'*The Flying Cradle* off to Chichester,' said his ma coldly. Now it was done, she couldn't help feeling angry with herself, with Sam and with the world at large that the coach had gone without her.

Sam shrank further under the sheets; Milly and the horror of *The White Horse* had risen in his mind again. He recalled he'd given his name as 'Harry'. Ah! if only he'd been called Harry, then Sam wouldn't be in this pitiable mess.

He dropped into a half sleep and dreamed of Harry fighting hump-backed King Richard for the favours of Milly-Anne; but it was to no avail. The wicked king proved unkillable; he kept appearing round corners, wiping the blood from bullet holes and chuckling. 'Drown him in malmsey,' said the king to the landlord of *The White Horse*. Joe and 'Spare Joe' advanced towards him with a barrel. 'He's only a tiddler,' said Mr Roggs, 'so use the ladle.'

'No!' shrieked Sam, desperately. 'You're my other pa!'

'My son's called Harry,' smiled King Richard, clapping his hands. 'You're Sam. You'll never make a Harry so you're better off drowned ...'

By that night, Sam had recovered sufficiently to take nourishment; and by the next day his illness was no more than a memory.

'Let's hope,' said his ma, 'that your pa had a good journey.' Mrs C. was anxious to heal the rift that she sensed had opened up in the family, so she and Sam waited on the road itself to greet *The Flying Cradle*.

At last the coach came – an hour late. It seemed to be driven by a madman – a stranger with white face and staring eyes. There had been an accident. At the bottom of Oakwood Hill, where three roads met, Chichester had been shot.

9

THE guard was almost speechless with dismay; he was terrified of facing Mrs Chichester. He had to be half dragged into the parlour and strongly dosed with brandy before he was capable of uttering a sensible word.

They'd seen the man waiting by the side of the road. He looked ordinary enough ... a traveller carrying a bag ... looked as though he had walked a long way. Waved his arms at the coach ... shouted. But the coach was full. 'You know Mr Chichester – never an extra on the top to save his life. That is, you know what I mean ... "Don't touch that brake," he said to me. But we had to slow down else we'd have run the fellow down. "Get out of the road!" shouts Mr Chichester. The fellow didn't seem to know whether he was coming or going. Then he pulls the pistol. "Stop!" he yells. Mr Chichester takes one look at the pistol and goes mad with anger. He lashes out with his whip and catches the fellow round the wrist with it ... then there's a God-almighty bang – and Mr Chichester gives a grunt and goes over sideways with the blood pouring out of him like a tap ...'

The parson from Stone Street had heard the explosion and come running out. He'd been with the troops as a young man and mercifully knew enough to stop the flow of blood. He'd wanted to take the coachman back to his house, but Chichester had mumbled and mumbled about Dorking that it seemed best to take him on and pray that he lasted out the journey. It had been that same parson who'd driven the coach, being glad to exercise a skill he'd picked up in his youth. The man who'd shot the coachman had got away – running like a hare, the guard said.

The huge, inert figure of Chichester had been carried into

the kitchen and laid on the table there; and a surgeon from the town was with him. It seemed that the pistol had been discharged when the front of the coach was already gone by as the ball had struck the coachman in the small of the back. The surgeon had succeeded in removing the ball and declared that it was a miracle Chichester had survived long enough to be brought back to his family. He must have had the strength of a giant. Taking this into account, it was possible that the coachman would recover consciousness before he died; but it was by no means certain . . .

Mrs Chichester and Sam sat by his head, not daring to move away in case they missed the last of life. Mrs C., unable to weep, stared and stared at her husband's long still face. A thousand thoughts and memories passed through her mind. She traced each bony feature over and over again . . . and as she did so, the coachman's words came back to her: 'It's all in your keeping now.' She remembered how he and she had stood over the bed of Sam's dead mother, and he'd told her to store up the image for the child. Who was she storing up Chichester for?

Sam's feelings were of terror and loneliness. His real pa was leaving him; and he knew he had no other. Neither he nor his ma had any thoughts to spare for the murderer.

The parson-coachdriver – a powerful looking man getting on in years – was examining the ball that had been carefully washed and laid on a shelf by the fire.

'Given another chain of circumstances,' he mused, half to the surgeon and half to himself, 'and this lead might have been part of a church roof . . .'

The surgeon smiled faintly. 'Are you saying that this unhappy affair is Fate?' (There was no mistaking the capital letter.)

'A man of God cannot accept a heathen notion like Fate. What I meant was that if only we could trace the various lives and tiny incidents that have nudged, so to speak, this tragedy on its way, we might find some quite different meaning in it. This battered piece of lead is, after all, only the last thing ... the end of the road. In itself, it is quite blameless.'

'But what of the finger that sent it on its way?'

'What of the finger, you say. I say, what of the reasons that drove the wretch to be where he was. What of the causes of his desperation? And why was it this coachman and not another? Why was he not a half an hour later? What forces pushed him on towards this moment?'

The surgeon shook his head in amusement. 'By your argument, sir, there's no responsibility anywhere for anything. I'd have thought a man of God would at least have brought in the devil to take the blame.'

The parson frowned as if trying to re-organize his thoughts. An inclination to philosophy had always been his downfall, bringing him invariably face to face with unanswerable untruths.

'He's awake! Quickly!'

Somehow Mr Roggs had managed to be first with the news. The surgeon hurried to the coachman's side. Chichester's eyes were open; he was staring dazedly at the ceiling. The surgeon felt his pulse.

'The fellow has the strength of the devil,' he muttered. Now it was the parson's turn to smile. 'How can I blame the devil when you give him all the credit?'

Mr Roggs asked urgently, 'Is he going to make old bones, then?'

For answer, the surgeon spread out his hands which were still filthy from Chichester's blood. 'I doubt it ... I strongly doubt it.'

'Then let's pray that his strength doesn't truly come from the devil,' murmured the parson.

Chichester's eyes flickered from side to side, as if he was struggling to determine where he was. He saw Mr Roggs, the surgeon, Parson Talbot – all mightily concerned for him. Perhaps he was wondering with surprise how come that he, Chichester, the unregarded fixture of *The Flying Cradle*, should suddenly be an object of universal anxiety?

'I'll clear out my office,' said Mr Roggs impulsively. 'He can stay there as long as – as he's able . . .'

To do the landlord justice, the thought wasn't uppermost in his mind that his charity was unlikely to be exercised for long. There's a property in tragic events that seems to give off a warm vapour, so that all present are infected by it and impelled to act for the admiration of others rather than the benefit of themselves.

The coachman's eyes turned to Mrs Chichester, and lingered there. There had been a lifetime of speaking silences between them; surely they had no need of words now? Her face was infinitely striving – and infinitely dismayed; there was silence even behind her husband's eyes.

Then he looked at Sam. The child felt an inexplicable embarrassment; the feeble look seemed almost to knock him down. Though he'd followed little of the talk between the parson and the surgeon, he'd understood enough to sense his own guilt in the horrible happening. Was his pa of that mind now? Was this the last he'd see of him? With all his heart he prayed for his pa to go on living. He offered up sacrifices: his whip, his dreams, his beloved pistol and childhood itself . . . if only the figure on the table would come warm again, speak angrily to him, cuff him, even . . .

'All I say is, that if he survives the next three days,' said the surgeon, preparing to leave, 'then he has a chance. Not much . . . but a chance.'

Whether through force of prayer, the surgeon's skill or his own granite strength, the coachman did survive . . . though had he known the outcome, he might well have wished it otherwise. As, day by day, he gained ground and the abyss retreated, it became apparent that certain disabilities remained and that Mr Roggs's charity would need to be exercised to a wholly unlooked-for-extent.

'Madam,' said the surgeon gently to Mrs Chichester, 'we must all thank heaven that he's alive. As for the other ... D'you see, the ball has broken his spine ...'

For the rest of his life, the coachman of *The Flying Cradle* would be condemned to watch the road and the changing seasons he knew so well from a cripple's chair. His legs were paralysed beyond all hope of a cure.

Part Two

To your arms, brave boys, and load.
See the ball I hold!

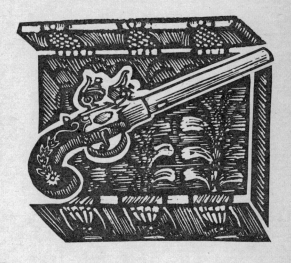

IO

WHEN a man takes it into his head to go into the business of coach-proprietoring, he embarks on a perilous enterprise in which there seem to be more hands than there are pockets to put them in – and more scoundrels than any man is entitled to expect.

To begin with, he grasps his money firmly in both hands, and looks about him for a road. He may be guided in his choice by affection, pleasant memories – a childhood journey to the sea, maybe, when the road was magical and the inns enchanted – but most likely he falls in with two partners who already have a road between them and are finding the business too heavy to manage on their own. It seems there was to have been a third, but that partner-to-be died unexpectedly – thus leaving a golden opportunity lying in the *open* road; just waiting to be picked up.

Without more ado, he closes with them. He never asks anyone's advice; he's sensibly afraid of losing a bargain by delaying; and besides, he feels that he is the best judge of his own affairs.

Forthwith the road is parcelled up and he finds himself the proprietor of some thirty miles in the middle, for which he undertakes to provide the horses. To be a 'middle road man', he is assured, is a terrific advantage as he will bear no responsibility for the turn-about at either end. All that's required of him is to 'horse the coach through', for which he will receive, each month, a third share of the profits. There's no doubt that he's bought a piece of road with a great future.

This mention of a road with a future is his first intimation that the road's present circumstances leave room for improvement. Nevertheless he has great faith in his own judgement and sets about buying horses. The necessary number to keep a public coach on the road turns out to be one horse per highway mile; but as he is a 'middle road man' and therefore relieved of the turn-about responsibility, he agrees to provide forty horses – ten more than his due.

He answers advertisements: 'Strawberry gentleman's mount – owner deceased', 'Brown nobleman's hunter', 'Good goer in harness', 'One lady owner'; he visits sundry secret mewses, has shrewd conversations with knowing stableboys and genuine-looking grooms ... and lays out money for some ten horses whose combined ages would have seen them back to Julius Caesar. Already he has discovered that more lies are told in the field of human transport than in all other mortal undertakings put together. It would seem that the concepts of shifting and shiftiness are indissolubly united in the human soul. He leaves the purchase of the remaining horses to the coachman who has his own personal safety to consider and so he buys the best stock at the highest prices. Now the proprietor is ready to go into business. His stock is stationed at staging inns in the charge of reputable persons. The coach begins – and he settles back, a proprietor with a future. A month elapses, and he meets his partners for the share-out. He rubs his hands – only to discover that there have been additional expenses that none could have foreseen. Repair to a lamp, a new hat for a traveller who lost his on a sharp turn ('Good God! Was it made of gold?'); and four fresh horses as the coachman had rejected four of the existing stock as being unsound in wind and limb.

Very well; he awaits for the second month. Alas! the road seems to have been totally unpopulated; four journeys with no more than ten passengers all told. But these things happen, he is advised; passenger traffic is seasonal and, anyway, it is a road with a great future.

Next month turns out to be the time for paying the Government duty, which, in addition to tolls, turnpikes, wages and hiring of the vehicle, scarcely leaves enough to pay a surgeon seventeen pounds for attending a lady with a bruised hip, occasioned, unfortunately, over the middle road.

And so it goes on; a new coachman proves hopelessly dishonest and must be pocketing many a fare for himself. Horsekeepers neglect their duties, giving the animals short measure and pilfering the difference. Consequently horses rarely last to work out their cost and have to be sold off as 'Fast lady's hunter', or 'The property of a gentleman who is giving up hunting'. Drearily he receives back a fraction of the money he's laid out ... and knows by now that it is useless to accuse knowledgeable horseboys and genuine-looking grooms of robbing him at every turn. And worst of all, everything that happens, happens on his stretch of road: injuries, loss of clothing, scrapings of paintwork ... the list never ends. 'Ah!' say his sympathetic partners, 'but then you don't have the responsibility of the turnabout. Middle road men can't have it all ways.'

He sighs and submits, feeling at the same time that he's not getting it any way at all. Yet folk make money out of coaching. Maybe he hasn't given it long enough? Somehow he must manage to hold on till things improve and some intrepid explorer discovers the road he's invested in and spreads the good news far and wide.

So, being by now well soaked in the morality of transport, he turns to a little fraud on the side; a touch of false pretences, maybe, and then a stealing by finding ... in an acquaintance's house.

Unluckily, though he's pretty well versed in shiftiness, he's not quite so deft at shifting yet. He gets caught, tried and convicted. He is sentenced to transportation and notices appear in *The London Daily Advertiser*, *The Bull and Mouth* in Aldersgate Street and at the *The Red Lion* in Dorking to the following effect: 'For disposal by private treaty. Thirty miles of prosperous, well-run road. Proprietor forced to sell. Going abroad.'

Patiently Mrs Nelson of *The Bull and Mouth* in Aldersgate Street and Mr Stacey of the coaching office in Chichester waited for a middle road man to turn up. At last, to their embarrassment and surprise, a person in holy orders appeared, and, after much discussion and hard bargaining, Parson Talbot joined with them in the proprietorship of the London–Chichester road.

This extraordinary man, who'd tried his hand at many things, had suddenly taken a fancy to coaching. Perhaps the furious, life-saving drive from Oakwood Hill to Dorking had inspired him? But that, after all, was only one thing. No action is the result of a single impulse. Many forces must come to bear before a man acts ... the last being but the tip of the arrow, so to speak. What of the bowstring, the hand that draws it, and the thousand and one chances that have brought the archer to that very spot at that very time and at no other?

Infinite chains of circumstance. Parson Talbot was obsessed by them. Deeply moved as he'd been by the tragic plight of the Chichester family, he could not fail to wonder at the chain of circumstances that had brought him to cross their path at the very moment of disaster. Half humorously, he mused that, if he hadn't spilled wine on his summer waistcoat while dining at Warneham Place, he would not have worn winter clothing on the following day and consequently kept his windows open and so heard the shot from nearby Oakwood Hill. The coachman would have died, his family gone to ruin ... and he himself would have failed destiny.

Once having taken this larger view, it was impossible for him to return to his own concerns unscathed; and Mrs Nelson and Mr Stacey detected an underlying seriousness in their new partner's attitude to his investment.

Not that this was undesirable; Mr Stacy in particular had

been feeling the strain of trying to make both ends meet with no man in the middle, so to speak. Although he and Mrs Nelson had agreed to pay a small pension to the paralysed Chichester, the demands of a costly wife and an extravagant daughter made him ponder more and more the truth of charity beginning at home.

Parson Talbot, learning of this state of affairs from sundry inadvertent remarks passed by Mr Stacey, promptly offered to take Mr Stacey's obligation on his own broad shoulders – and Mr Stacey was sufficiently grateful to yield certain turnabout privileges to make the middle road a little smoother.

'As I see it,' said the parson, still taking the larger view, 'the pension must be continued for at least five years, or until the boy Sam is old enough to take on the coach. Then, as is proper, he will become the support of the family.'

'I don't want to shock you, Mrs Nelson,' said Mr Stacey quietly, when the profound and powerful parson had left them, 'and I wouldn't have you think me inhuman.'

He paused, and Mrs Nelson said encouragingly, 'I wouldn't do that, Mr Stacey. I would call no man inhuman till he was dead, God rest his soul.'

'Exactly so, ma'am. Dead. I wouldn't have thought it right to speak if I'd still been committed. But now that our clerical friend has – you know what I mean – and, having no axe to grind on my own account, as they say – I think I can come out with it and say that, from *all* points of view wouldn't it have been better for the old fellow to have died on Oakwood Hill? It would have been a mercy, ma'am, as much for himself as for *everyone* else. From all one hears, he's no better than a shell – a great heavy shell of flesh with neither motion nor sense . . .'

This was not wholly true; with the help of crutches and his immensely strong coachman's arms, Chichester was able to drag himself about the ground floor of *The Red Lion*. Stairs,

93

of course, were beyond him, and the outside he avoided like the plague. Mostly he sat in the little room that had once been Mr Roggs's private office and stared out of the window onto the kitchen garden. Cabbages outside, and a great hulking cabbage within, thought Mr Roggs, but as usual, did not come out with it. He had grown quite bitter about the loss of his room. Having made what he'd been led to believe at the time was a deathbed promise, he now felt deceived and betrayed, and lost no opportunity of taking silent digs at the grim, granite-like inhabitant of his personal retreat, furnished as it was with his most intimate thoughts.

There's no doubt that, when the blaze of tragedy is over, so also is the warmth it has engendered; it leaves behind only burnt-out feelings, grey as ash. Sam and Mrs Chichester travelled the road together with a series of temporary coachmen; and for a long time persuaded themselves that they looked forward to the nights at Dorking. But in their heart of hearts they found these nights hard to bear, and had it not been for Parson Talbot, they would have been harder still.

At first Sam, with childish invulnerability, regaled his pa with news of the road – of the state of the fields and the hedgerows, of the seasons and of a small company of troops bound for the north, resting by the wayside and playing at dice on a drum . . . The helpless man would seem to listen, then his eyes would go bleak and he'd heave himself out of range with a muttered exclamation of impatience.

Sam, mildly offended, would make as if to follow, but Parson Talbot, who was always on hand when *The Flying Cradle* came in (protecting his investment, he called it), would restrain the boy with a gentle shake of his head.

'It'll come,' he'd say. 'In time – in time. When I was a boy, we'd play rather cruelly with snails. Have you never done the same, Sam? We'd put them on a wall and wait for their heads to come out to see where they were. Then we'd prick at their

94

horns with a holly leaf. Back they'd go and we'd wait, making wagers on whose snail would venture out again first. We'd crouch there, quiet as mice, watching the motionless shells knowing all the time that something living was dwelling inside, wrapped up in itself – perhaps, for all we knew, even thinking in its own darkness. But sooner or later, being alive, they would have to come out ... Your father, Sam, has been pricked by more than a holly leaf; but sooner or later, he will emerge from the darkness ...'

Whenever he could, Parson Talbot unfolded matters to Sam in terms of forest, field and ditch, believing that this would encourage the boy towards that larger view of affairs that he himself so ardently cultivated. Certainly there were times when it did so; but as often as not the boy got hold of the wrong end of the stick and was persuaded into taking a very bizarre view of human nature indeed. He took to watching his pa intently for that longed-for peeping forth of his spirit – for all the world as if the coachman had somehow gone inside a real shell from which he could no longer see Sam's urgent eyes fixed upon him.

The learned cleric who, in days gone by, had instructed Sam in the rudiments of arithmetic and theology, now found himself unnecessary; he transferred his custom to *The White Horse* where he would wryly comment on the fickleness of the young and the conceit of the elderly. But Parson Talbot, unaware of having put anyone out, was delighted to have a free hand with the forming of Sam's mind. He transported quantities of books from his house in Stone Street to *The Red Lion* and loaded them on a shelf that Joe had hammered up by Sam's bed. These books seemed to embrace the whole of mortal knowledge, and Sam felt that when he had read them he would be a human being of inconceivable value; even turning the pages and looking at the pictures improved him.

Nowadays his bed was in the little room his pa inhabited, and he often wondered if, when he was away, his pa ever read the books ... and if Parson Talbot had had it in his mind that one day the grim, silent man might do so. But so far as Sam could tell, the books were never disturbed from one visit to the next. The only thing that seemed to fascinate the coachman, and about which he was prepared to talk, was a complicated system of ropes and pulleys that Joe had fixed to the ceiling so that the cripple could raise himself without assistance. This ingenious device had been adapted from an old hoist in the cellar and Joe was inordinately proud of it.

Once Milly came to see Joe's handiwork – and cried her eyes out afterwards over the coachman's terrible plight.

'An' I'm fixin' one in the privy, too!' said Joe, quite carried away by his own engineering genius.

'Oh, Joe!'

'And I never even had to tell him to do it,' said Mr Roggs wonderingly – as if he'd had the idea in his own mind and had Joe not spent hours of his own time on Chichester's behalf, he, Mr Roggs, would very soon have told him to do so.

The creak and squeal of the pulleys would waken Sam in the early morning. He'd lie quietly and watch the huge figure rise upwards like a clot of black smoke, then the dim morning light would catch his pa's eyes and he'd hurriedly shut his own, peeping out from time to time to see what would happen. For hours, it seemed, in that dead while, the coachman would just sit on the side of his bed while the silent boy would watch and wonder what thoughts were inhabiting him. Was he thinking of the man who'd shot him?

Although Sam had kept the promise he'd made to God if his pa should be spared and had returned the precious pistol to its battered box never to bring it out again, he had not been able to sacrifice his dreams as well. But now it was the monster who'd wrecked his pa that haunted his thoughts – and nightly he hunted the murderer down and slew him.

But it was always a monster without a face. Unluckily there had never been any clear description of him. The frightened passengers remembered him in bewilderingly different ways so that it seemed that the man was a ghost or a spirit, capable of an infinite number of faces. Each passenger, striving to recollect, was reminded of someone or other he knew – and each inevitably described a different acquaintance. In seeking to fix the unfamiliar by means of some common factor, they had lost the reality in the image.

Perhaps the only true description would have been the coachman's; but to all inquiry he grimly shook his head and muttered, 'I don't want to recall such trash!'

It was this strange attitude that provoked Mrs Chichester to one of her rare outbursts against him. One evening when she came in from the coach and Chichester was in the parlour, explaining something about his crutches to Joe, she laid her shotgun on the table and brushed her lips against her husband's stony head. He nodded and smiled remotely.

'A good run, Chichester.'

He nodded again.

'There was a man standing where them three roads meet – at the bottom of Oakwood Hill.'

The coachman frowned and turned to Joe who fidgeted awkwardly.

'He was tallish – about your height – and with a bent nose. He had thin lips and a pointed chin. His hair – if it were his own – was sandy-coloured.'

As he listened, Sam marvelled at the precision of his ma's observation from a moving coach.

'Were it – him, Chichester?'

The coachman stared at his wife.

'How should I know? I told you, I don't choose to recall trash like that!'

'For God's sake, man, tell me! Don't you know that every day, every yard of the road I'm looking – looking for him? Don't you know it's all I live for now – to shoot that murdering bastard down? What was he like? Tell me – tell me!'

'Them crutches,' said Chichester to Joe, 'need to be a good half inch shorter.'

'Jesus Christ!' cried Mrs Chichester, turning to Sam. 'What's become of us?'

'Tell her, Sam. You should know from all them books the parson's lent you, and from all the watching you do of a morning when I'm sitting on me bed not wanting to get me crutches for fear of waking you. Tell her to let well alone. I don't want for no more blood than me own. I don't want *nothing* but what's me own.'

Sam stared from his ma to his pa in fear and misery . . . then Parson Talbot came in and somehow the very presence of this man with his gentle obsessions calmed Sam and awoke in him an ambition that was to burn, sometimes in anger, sometimes in pain and despair, until it should be fulfilled.

Luckily this ambition was not put into words, else even Sam might have been abashed by its childish innocence. More than anything else in the world, he wanted to make the Chichesters happy.

II

S A M ' S thirteenth birthday marked a giant step forward for the imaginations of Messrs Bratsby, Oxton and Skipping. It was as if time, that spoiler of mirrors and steepener of hills, had woken them one morning so that they exclaimed:

'Is it really so long ago – that famous night of ours at *The Red Lion*? Why, he must be almost a man by now!' Consequently there arrived at *The Red Lion*, for 'Mr Sam, care of *The Flying Cradle*', a gold-topped cane, the Complete Plays of William Shakespeare, and a set of razors in a leather case.

It would seem he'd jumped straight from infancy to manhood, without the bother of having been a boy. But for once, time had been slow off the mark – the travellers' imaginations had quite outstripped it; Sam's cheek was still as smooth as worn harness and the most careful scrutiny revealed no more than a down that would have mortified a day old chick.

Nevertheless, there were the razors, like seven gleaming tongues of steel, and Sam had found a bristle somewhere on his chin. Everyone looked – and took his word for it; so Parson Talbot gave him a brush, a glazed jug and a cake of Newcastle soap, Joe fetched him hot water and Mr Roggs instructed him in the art of forming a lather. The operation was performed in the kitchen.

'You want a good boss of lather,' urged Mr Roggs as Sam brushed away, scattering suds like a snow-storm.

'One would have thought,' said Mrs Roggs admiringly, 'that he'd been at it all his life! And it only seems yesterday that I carried him down the stairs ...'

Sam glowed, and blew soap out of his nose and mouth. The coachman grunted impatiently and Mrs C. bit her lip to hold back a smile.

'That's what I call well bossed up now,' said Mr Roggs. Sam laid down the brush and peered in the mirror. He was greeted by a wild landscape under a heavy drift of snow with toppling peaks of lather reaching almost to his eyes. Familiar landmarks had vanished; he stared past himself to the faces beyond: Joe, Mr Roggs, his ma ... They seemed far, far away, as if bidding him good-bye ...

'Tools of the trade, tiddler. In the right hand.'

Sam reached for the razor – and 'Spare Joe' reflected bitterly that *he'd* been shaving regular for two year now, and no one cared.

'Left-hand side of the neck and upward with a gentle sweep – like you was stroking the cat,' said Mr Roggs.

'*I* always start at the top an' work me way down,' said Joe.

And it always looks it, too, thought Mr Roggs, contemptuously.

'Hold the razor like you would a whip,' said Chichester sharply. 'You ain't writing a letter with it, Sammy.'

Mrs C. dabbed her eyes and smiled ... and Sam boldly approached his face to the steel. A moment of real panic seized him. How was he to know for sure how thick the soap lay on him? Razors were that sharp he might cut his throat before he knew he'd got to it!

Slowly and with many an uneasy pause the steel sank into the suds – until at last it came to Sam. The small shaver sighed with relief, and cautiously set to work. Broad pink highways appeared like magic among the white, with, here and there, a tiny trickle of the brightest red. At last all the soap had been swept away and Sam turned a shining countenance – liberally decorated with brown paper to stem the bleeding – to the kitchen company. He felt his chin; the bristle had gone – shaved or frightened away.

'Now you're a man, tiddler,' said Mr Roggs affectionately. 'Come next birthday and you'll be wanting a shave again.'

Sam frowned at Mr Roggs whom he did not like. Thirteen is

a dangerous age; the business of becoming a man is a slithery, uncertain enterprise; neither steps forward nor slippings back are occasions for humour. He detested being called 'tiddler'.

Nonetheless he was sensible of the landlord's generosity to his pa, so he endured him and put the razors away with his most important possessions.

The old barber's box was still there; he hadn't opened it since the time of the shooting. He stared at it with almost a sense of shock – and a host of memories rose up in his mind. Uneasily he reached out to touch the box, then drew his hand away as if he'd been burned. So strong was his superstition that he felt that, if he broke his promise and took out the pistol, God would kill his pa. He knew he ought to throw the box and its contents away ... but what then of his other pa? Surely that sardonic being who had both plagued and inspired him would also be entitled to revenge?

Suddenly it occurred to him that the box was not exactly as he'd left it. He pulled it out, meaning only to shake it and make sure its contents were still there. So intent was he on this that he never heard the scrape of crutches and the creak of the door. The door swung on its hinges – and Sam turned.

The crippled coachman was hanging there, like a bird on immense wooden legs, and staring down at him and the accursed box. His eyes, ordinarily so dull and dead-looking, were screwed up in an almost insane rage.

'I – I –' he began, then cursed violently (a thing Sam rarely heard from him), heaved about and dragged himself away.

Sam dreaded the coming night; he had been severely frightened; but to his relief the cripple said nothing about his outburst; he seemed to have shrunk more firmly than ever into his usual gloomy silence. The boy lay awake a long time, thinking of Parson Talbot and his snails; he wondered how long must go by before he knew for certain that his snail was dead in its shell?

Next morning, as a mark of his premature accession to manhood, he was allowed to take the coach out of the yard. He felt, rather than knew, that his pa was watching him; so he mounted in style, reins in the left hand with a foot of slack for the off-side, then up, change hands, separate the leathers, hands again – and then the whip.

'Re-markable,' said Mr Roggs, surveying the young coachman high on his seat. 'It's re-markable, I say.' He nodded and looked round at *The Red Lion* that had nurtured the prodigy in front of him, as if the whole miracle of birth and growing up had been a strikingly original notion of his own.

During the following March there was a heavy fall of snow that laid up *The Flying Cradle* in Aldersgate Street for three days. It turned out to be at a time when Parson Talbot was there on business with Mrs Nelson.

This admirable, deviously kind man, who lost no opportunity of fulfilling destiny, was pleased to have the unexpected company and couldn't help reflecting that it must certainly be for a purpose. With some amusement he observed that Sam was beginning to eye Mrs Nelson's prettier barmaids with a thoughtful eye. The boy was truly growing up. The parson shook his head. He knew that Sam was unlikely to receive much help in the way of natural knowledge from his obstinately reticent mother and father – they would rather have died than reveal the secrets of birth – so at the first opportunity the parson drew Sam aside. It was in the stable yard where Sam was industriously constructing a snowman.

For a few minutes the parson assisted him, but only in order to allay suspicions of any ulterior motive. Then, when he judged the mood between them was level and easy enough, he asked: 'Do you happen to know how you came into the world, Sam?'

'Yes,' answered Sam shortly. 'It was upstairs in *The Red Lion* and Arundel – she was my natural ma – died of it. You can still see the cracked bannister where they fetched her down. Joe told me. Can you keep on making up the back, sir, while I do the face? It'll fall over, else.'

Obediently the parson laboured in the snow, enjoying it in a freezing sort of way; then he tried again.

'You're nearly a man, now. I think it's high time you were told what we call "the facts of life", Sam.'

'You mean about earning me own living?' said Sam. 'I know all about that. I'll be coachman on *The Cradle*.'

'I mean how babies come into the world, my lad.'

'Oh, yes,' said Sam, privately thinking it rather an unsuitable conversation for the snow and the parson.

'In your travels, Sam, have you ever seen a cow being served by a bull?'

'Once or twice,' said Sam, vaguely relieved that the parson was going to confine himself to the farmyard. 'Only it's usually too far off to get a good look. Can you get on with the shoulders, now, sir?'

'Did you know, Sam,' went on the parson firmly, 'that it's the same with men and women?'

'Yes,' said Sam. ' "Spare Joe" told me.'

'Oh. And what else did he tell you?' asked the parson, feeling suddenly unnecessary.

'That you can try it out for a shilling in Saffron Hill, sir.'

Parson Talbot struck the snowman a great thump and all but dislodged its head.

'And did he tell you nothing about love, Sam – your worldly "Spare Joe"?'

Sam shook his head: plainly love had been outside 'Spare Joe's' range. Awkwardly Parson Talbot reflected that he'd be better advised to attend to Sam's inner advancement and leave the rest to nature and the two Joes.

He toiled away in silence while Sam reproachfully repaired the snowman's neck.

'How about a clay pipe for him, Sam?' The parson was anxious to make amends. 'Shall I fetch you one?'

'I've waited, Parson Talbot,' muttered Sam, scraping out the hollows of the snowman's eyes. 'I've waited, like you said. But my snail won't come out of his shell. How much longer will it take?'

'And a hat, Sam. Would you like me to get one of my hats?'

'Will he ever come out, sir?'

Deeply moved, Parson Talbot put his arm round Sam's shoulders.

'I think it's like this, Sam,' he said quietly. 'Your father has known the road so long and loved it so well that he's planted it all with his own thoughts...thoughts that have grown like trees and hedgerows all along its length. So – so when you come in from the coach and tell him of all the wonders you've seen, he thinks to himself that there was another coachman on the seat, driving his road. He feels robbed and trespassed against. But when the time comes for *you* to take the coach, Sam – when you take it on your own, *then* I think he'll come out to meet you. So I beg you, Sam, have patience till that day ...'

The skill and knowledge of a craft may be acquired very early; but the shading can only come with time. Nothing can replace this, neither the most exact measurement nor the most scrupulous care. Even an apothecary, hamstrung by science as he may be, knows that all must give way to that curious instinct that warns: 'This is not right.'

When Sam was no more than fourteen, he was as accomplished a coachman as could be found on all the roads of the kingdom; he was accurate with the whip, he was as familiar with the harness as with the veins of his left hand, and he knew the width of his vehicle down to the last coat of whitewash on the archways of the stableyards. But the shading was wanting. He still lacked that instinct that warns of ... *something round the bend*, or of a rut that is deeper than it seems.

'No one can tell you how, lad,' the coachmen would tell him. 'You just come to *knowing*.'

He began to take over the reins for short distances, at first along the better-mended London–Dorking road, and then the more difficult Dorking–Chichester run. Little by little these distances would be extended; the supervising coachman would nod approvingly to Mrs C. The shading was coming; did Mrs C. notice how the lad judged the last bend?

'Brake, ma!' Sam would cry – at the very point on a hill where Chichester himself would have shouted. 'Just a touch, ma!'

The brake would screech, on – off! on – off! and *The Flying Cradle* would steady, then really seem to fly under the skilful hands of the grown child it had carried and rocked for so long.

By the time he was sixteen he was taking the coach over the whole distance; his ma was constantly amazed by his skill, and could never get over how readily she took his orders and how natural it all seemed. Nevertheless, for a multitude of reasons she kept putting off the day that she knew, sooner or later, must come. The boy was not quite ready – the road was in a bad state – the horses were playing up . . . in short, anything rather than give up her place and set Sam free to take the coach on his own. Long since her desire for vengeance on the man who'd shot Chichester had dwindled to a dullish ache; but now even that old passion and fear was dragged up to support her efforts to delay the freeing of Sam. What if the guard who rode in her place failed to protect his coachman?

At last, in the May following Sam's sixteenth birthday, when the road was at its sunny best, her excuses ran out and she gave in to Sam's constant pleading. He was to take the coach without her from Dorking to Chichester and then back to Dorking again.

'He'll be all right, ma'am,' said the retiring coachman.

'I'll watch after him,' said the incoming guard.

Mrs C. nodded, but could not subdue a panicky sense of loss.

'Well, tiddler,' said Mr Roggs, 'I should have a good shave before you set off. We don't want no close ones on the way, do we?'

Sam laughed. Not even Mr Roggs could subdue his soaring spirits. His simple ambition of days gone by had grown and become complicated by many feelings and desires. His need to make the old coachman happy was no less – the stern, granite-like figure still haunted and moved him inexpressibly. He longed for the power to melt the granite, to change it back to flesh and blood. Was it then just power he wanted? No; there was a deeper feeling ... the feeling of a freedom almost within his grasp; a remarkable feeling the like of which there was no words for ...

His pa was restless. The old man kept scraping and heaving himself from place to place. He went out into the yard and peered at the coach's wheels; he examined the sky ... and whenever he thought he wasn't observed, he watched Sam's hands intently. He was even heard to remark to the passengers, in an off-hand fashion, that they were likely to have a good, smooth run; perhaps the best they'd ever had.

Tears of pleasure came into Sam's eyes. Parson Talbot came up and shook him warmly by the hand.

'I think – I'm sure it will be all right, son,' he murmured.

Sam nodded. He was extraordinarily confident that the day he'd waited so long for had come.

'But remember, lad, don't take it into your head to go hunting for murderers on Oakwood Hill. Vengeance is mine, saith the Lord, *I* will repay.'

Sam nodded again, but this time more slowly. The parson had touched on a tender spot. Sam was beginning to mount when Parson Talbot, seized with a desire to return to the larger view, added:

'You're not a child any more, Sam, playing games with snails on a garden wall. No holly leaves – if you know what I mean?'

12

A DREAM coach sped through the countryside; a coach that was at once old and new. So smooth was its passage that it seemed that fields, villages, trees and smiling mansions were but embossed garnitures fixed to the rim of the road which turned and turned under the hovering coach. The wind, the world and the hours rushed by to the splendid drumming of sixteen hooves; although whether or not these hooves ever touched the highway was a matter for doubt. The four brown rumps, berried on the bars, flashed and danced with such consummate ease that it seemed as unnecessary to change horses as to interrupt the ticking of a clock. But changed they were, in the twinkling of an eye . . .

'As neat and quick as in the days of old Chichester . . .'

Sam sang as they went, snatches of coachmen's ballads, half remembered, half made up; and the guard, a real virtuoso, harmonized on the high horn. Billingshurst – Amberly – Houghton – Arundel. They passed like the chimes of hours, leaving only an echo behind . . .

'Not since the days of old Chichester . . .'

The guard smiled as the young coachman, his eyes bright and his lips parted, exercised the skill of his craft and plainly felt himself to be flying. The sensation was intoxicating; the joining of hand, eye and spirit in one harmonious whole. The horses were but an extension of his thought and the coach itself was a little gilded kingdom, set in a sea of speeding air.

'You're a born coachman, my lad!' said the guard admiringly that night in the parlour of *The Old Cross Inn* in Chichester.

Sam's brow momentarily darkened as he recalled his equivocal inheritance, buried years deep in the barber's box; then he laughed aloud.

'The Lord knows *what* I was born – but I'm a Chichester now! Did you never feel the mouths of four horses in the fingers of one hand? Wonderful – wonderful!'

At last Sam believed he knew what must have been passing in his pa's mind for all of his paralysed years; and his heart ached for him. But henceforth, everything would be changed; he felt he had the strength to lift the cripple right off his crutches and set him alongside on the bounding seat of *The Flying Cradle*. He truly believed he had got to the heart of the matter.

Next morning the coach was full; six passengers inside and five on top with the baggage.

'To the Chichesters of *The Flying Cradle*!' toasted Mr Stacey, the gentleman proprietor. He'd taken time off from his costly wife and extravagant daughter to see his investment on its way, and he was honestly delighted to find Sam in sole command. He'd long felt that Mrs C. had stood between the lad and his full excellence; apron strings and reins should never be tangled together. As the town clock struck ten the coach pulled out with the customary wavings and shoutings and running alongside with last minute provisions for late travellers Mr Stacy stood, watching its squat, old-fashioned back swaying and jerking over the cobbles and had sundry vague, philosophical thoughts on the passage of generations and whether inanimate objects retain some imprint of human presences so that the old *Flying Cradle* would always go as Chichester used to drive it no matter how hard young Sam tried to make it his own. The old Chichester had given way to the new; but they were really one and the same. For a moment Mr Stacey really fancied he saw two coachmen on the seat, the one young and eager, the other hunched and grim. 'It's my coach,' this second one seemed to be saying. 'Change my ways at your peril, son ...'

The proprietor's thoughts were the thoughts of any father with a child eager to surpass and supplant.

On the outskirts of the town lay a road that forked to the right where there is a windmill and a fingerpost to Goodwood House. In olden times a gallows stood on this spot, but now only a single post of it remained ... although, according to some, its moon-shadow was still as it used to be, even with a figure swinging from the bar. But there are always those who see what used to be – as if the sun and moon had nothing better to do than to remember to skirt the outlines of dreams.

Straight into the rising sun went *The Flying Cradle* as the great fiery light toppled the gallows' post and made clear seeing impossible. Sam scowled and squinted as he glimpsed something vaguely wasplike leaning against the post. He drew near and saw that it was a young woman in a yellow and black striped gown. She waved a parasol at him imperiously; he reined in the horses sufficiently to shout that the coach was full.

'Sam Chichester!' she cried. 'Stop the coach directly!' Surprised that she should know his name, Sam slowed to a walking pace while the young woman – she was scarcely more than a girl, really – hobbled along angrily beside him; the passengers looked on with some amusement.

'I want to go to Arundel.'

'Then you'll have to walk,' said Sam with all the haughtiness his high perch gave him.

'Sam Chichester – do you know who I am?'

Sam peered down inquiringly at her upturned face that was framed by a wide, many ribboned hat. It was a reddened face; it was an indignant face; and it was certainly familiar.

'The Princess of Wales?' offered Sam humorously. The guard smirked and several of the passengers laughed aloud.

'You're a rude bumpkin!' cried the young woman furiously. 'I'm your employer's daughter! And well you should know it!'

Sam stared, and all but let the reins go slack. Suddenly he remembered his childhood days ... a little girl of eight, shrieking with alarm as he untangled his birthday whip from her hair ...

'It's Caroline Stacey!' he said with a pleased smile of remembrance. 'And I see you've still got apples on your head – or are they plums?'

Miss Stacey's hat, of which she was inordinately proud, did indeed resemble a basket dangerously full of fruit. She tightened her lips, but was unable to remain angry in the presence of her own memories and Sam's infectious smile.

'You villain!' she said good-humouredly. 'And are you still as dangerous with the whip?'

'Shall I show you, Miss Stacey?'

'No! How dare you!' cried Miss Stacey, clutching her bonnet in mock alarm. '*Please*, Sam Chichester, for old time's sake, take me to Arundel. I must go shopping before my father comes back.'

'It's against the law, Miss Stacey. The coach is full.'

'I'm not that heavy, Sam Chichester.'

'Oh, I don't know about that,' said he, eyeing her rounded figure with an exaggeratedly doubtful air.

'For pity's sake, Sam Chichester, take me to Arundel!'

'Tell you what,' said Sam helpfully. 'I'll keep going like this, and in no time at all you'll find you'll have walked to Arundel. It's only eight miles.'

'I'll –' began Miss Stacey, then changed her mind. 'You can shoulder me, Sam Chichester – and keep my fare for yourself.'

Sam laughed and shook his head. He was thoroughly enjoying himself. The day was fine, the girl was pretty and the audience were grinning their heads off.

'Step it out, Miss Stacey. We'll be there in less than three hours.'

At this point one of the passengers took a hand. The sight

of the girl, hobbling along on unsuitable shoes, touched him. He was one of those gentlemen who affect great gallantry to all the fair sex except their wives. Also he didn't much care for the notion of keeping up the present snail's pace all the way to Arundel.

'Come along, coachman. Enough's enough. You've had your little joke; now we'll all make room for the young lady.'

There was a murmur of general agreement; Sam looked to the guard. He shrugged his shoulders.

'It's only eight mile, after all,' he said. Sam halted the coach and Miss Stacey climbed aboard.

'You can sit next to me, if you like,' said Sam with a rush of gallantry.

'I'm not sure that I want to, Sam Chichester.'

'It's considered a great honour, Miss Stacey.'

'Who for, Mr Chichester?'

Thus they bantered and bickered as they sat side by side on the broad seat, their feelings wearing words like armour against sudden looks, flushes and arrow-sharp silences.

'How is your father these days, Mr Chichester?'

'Well enough,' answered Sam, cooling slightly, as if a shadow had come between him and the sun.

'I suppose you're wondering how I'll get back from Arundel?'

Sam said the thought had never crossed his mind.

'Well, there's a young gentleman who'll drive me in his own chaise,' said Miss Stacey with satisfaction. Though Sam could have been little more than a footman to her, she was unable to keep from flirting with him and inviting his jealousy.

Sam grunted and exerted himself at the practice of his craft; although jealousy was ordinarily foreign to Sam's nature, they did, on occasion, talk the same language.

'I hear Arundel is something rather special for you, Mr Chichester.'

Sam's heart faltered uncannily. How did she know about

Arundel-rest-in-peace? An uncomfortable sensation of bewilderment gripped him as he understood he'd been talked about, pondered over and generally made the subject of thoughts and conversations out of his hearing and knowing. What image of himself had been presented – and what had been done with it? He felt incomplete, and acutely vulnerable.

He leaned forward, flicked at the leading horses and executed several dazzling manoeuvres that had little effect but presented an extremely dashing appearance. He longed to recapture that sense of flying that had so enthralled and inspired him on the previous day.

Miss Stacey watched him dreamily; she was thinking of the milliner in Arundel and of how soon she'd be there; but Sam, vain Sam (how he wished he was Harry!) fancied she was remembering old times and thinking how splendidly he'd grown and how dexterous he was in his craft.

Beyond Crocker Hill, for a mile or more, the highway ran straight as a stretched ribbon; 'a fine fall of road', Chichester used to call it, and often hummed as he bowled along, though none heard him as his voice was always pitched in the middle of the harmony of wheels and hooves.

'Now!' shouted Sam as he came to it, and flicked at the leaders' rumps with his whip. The coach seemed to lift and take wing; the air rushed by; Miss Stacey cried out and clutched at her bonnet.

'Now!' shouted Sam again – and again his long whip flashed and cracked. He glanced sideways; the girl's face was transfigured with excitement. She turned towards him and the wide brim of her hat clapped her cheek windily while her hair streamed away, dark as a chasing night.

Never a king sat on his throne more exultantly than Sam Chichester on the seat of *The Flying Cradle* as it careered into the eye of the rising sun. The road ahead seemed a wilderness of fire through which he was driving unscathed;

he felt a hand reach out to grip his arm. He turned again to the girl; he couldn't keep his eyes away from her.

'For God's sake! For God's sake!'

The guard and the passengers were shrieking. What was wrong? On the road, directly in his path a vehicle had appeared from nowhere. It was rushing straight at him!

He dragged at the reins; the leaders screamed and panicked; the wheelers ran on. The bars perked and cracked – the horses furiously mounted the bank. The whole coach swung horribly, reared up, then crashed on its side, breaking open like an old, dusty box.

Sam received a distinct impression of the world suddenly coming loose and letting its parts fly off at an abnormal speed. Legs and faces belonging indiscriminately to men and horses tumbled upwards; there were wheels rolling everywhere ... fifteen or sixteen of them – twisting and toppling and gyrating absurdly ... and a storm of belongings on the bank and in the ditch. But most striking of all was the bursting and splitting of wood and leather and a terrible cry that, even as he heard it, Sam knew was inside his head. It was the anguished voice of Chichester. *The Flying Cradle*, fragile and elderly, had been utterly destroyed.

Just before passing into a brief unconsciousness from a glancing blow on the head, the guard heard him cry out something about a holly leaf ... but could make nothing of it at all.

13

'HE came at me like a madman!' declared the driver of the colliding vehicle – a careful sober gentleman with a gig – attempting to account for the accident and remove any lingering doubts as to where the blame lay. 'I couldn't believe my eyes! The horses were going like steam and he was whipping at them as if all the devils in hell were after him. I tell you, he never looked to see what was coming. I've never seen a coach driven like it. He's a danger to all on the road!'

By the greatest good fortune there'd been no worse personal injury than the guard's breaking his wrist; the passengers and coachman alike escaping with a bruising and a general wrecking of clothes. Miss Stacey's smart gown had been almost ripped off her and she'd been in a pitiful state, divided between womanly modesty and childish panic at what her father would say if he found out she'd been on the coach.

'You don't have to tell him, do you?' she kept sobbing, believing in her frightened mind that everything would be all right if only it could be kept from her father.

Sam stared at her, his eyes filled with tears of disbelief. What did her pa matter compared with his? They were both, in those moments following the disaster, most miserably, most selfishly young – with not even each other to cling to.

The door panel of the coach that bore its name in red and gold letters, was taken back to Dorking; and Chichester was told.

Sam waited in the yard; he hadn't the courage to go inside. He talked to Joe and 'Spare Joe', but it was all dreamlike. Presently Mr Roggs came out.

'Is it – is it all right?'

'Take a look through the window, Sam,' said the landlord

shakily. 'But don't let him see you. Then come into the kitchen, lad.'

Sam went round to the front of *The Red Lion*; he reached the parlour windows, crawling on all fours. Even to raise his head and peer through the glass cost him all the strength he had.

The panel with the words, *The Flying Cradle*, lay propped against the fireplace wall. His ma, Parson Talbot and the guard were standing with their backs to him. Chichester himself was half turned, gazing at the panel. The coachman's face seemed like that of a drowned man. Tears were running helplessly down his stony old cheeks as if to wear fresh furrows in them. His shoulders were heaving and shaking so that the single crutch he was grasping kept banging on the floor. He caught sight of Sam.

'Get out – get out – get out!'

His voice cracked, so that it was more of a howl than a shout. He half rose and, with an enormous effort, supported himself on one hand; with the other he lifted the crutch and hurled it at the face in the window! Sam moaned and fled; it was only when he reached the kitchen that he discovered his face to be all cut and bloody from the smashed window glass.

'I don't believe it's happened,' said Mr Roggs in the kitchen. 'I just don't believe it's happened.'

Sam sat at the kitchen table, trembling as in a fever.

'There's forty-seven pound due to you, lad,' said Mr Roggs, coming back from the door where he'd been muttering with his wife who'd gone off with a look like death. 'It's your birthright, you know. It's what was collected on that night. Mrs Roggs is just gone to pack your things. P'raps you'll come back in a little while? The old fellow will miss you ...

'Here's an address, Sam. You might be able to make use of it. It's that Mr Bratsby's. Go and see him ... or them other two. But don't go hungry, Sam – or do anything foolish. It ain't the end of the world. Keep in touch lad. I should go to Aldersgate Street and see Mrs Nelson, if I was you. After a day or two, that is. Give it time, Sam. The great healer, you know; better than all the doctors.' Mr Roggs paused on this last piece of wisdom, then added, shaking his head very solemnly; 'Sam ... I'm sorry. I truly am.'

'Didn't he say – nothing else, Mr Roggs?'

'Not really, lad.'

'What was it, then?'

'I'm sure he didn't mean it, Sam ...'

'Mean what, Mr Roggs?'

'You'll come across it in the purse, lad. There's an extra two pound.'

'He gave it to me?'

Mr Roggs nodded unhappily.

'It's your fare, tiddler. He said you was owed it. Your ma, you know – the one who died, that is – well, she'd paid right through ... to Covent Garden. He said you wasn't to think it was kindness or charity. It's lawful trading. He said he wanted to be clear of all debts.'

The box containing his possessions was heavy; 'Spare Joe' gave him a hand with it down to the town.

'Parson Talbot presents his compliments,' said 'Spare Joe', as if he'd just remembered it. 'He says to come and see him at Mrs Nelson's.'

Sam nodded. 'Spare Joe' watched him shrewdly. He'd used up his small stock of sympathy and his thoughts had turned, as always, in a favoured direction.

'I hear,' he said, 'that you got an introduction to the gentry. Mr Bratsby, ain't it? I'd be much obliged if you'd mention me name. I'm on the look-out for an opening elsewhere, you understand ...'

There was a farm cart going to Croydon where he stayed the

night, and from there he took a coach to London. He thought several times of going to Aldersgate Street directly, but decided to take Mr Roggs's advice and give it time; instead he found lodgings in a small public house in one of the narrow streets between Fleet Street and the river. The premises were called *The Bunch of Grapes*, which cheerful fruit was represented on a sign outside in a singularly ghastly fashion; and this turned out to be prophetic of the state within.

Drearily Sam unpacked his possessions and disposed them about the wretched room he'd been given as best he could. He came across the whip Chichester had given him on his tenth birthday – and wept till there were no more tears left in him. He searched further, hoping against hope that his ma would have put in something for him. But there was nothing.

He stood up and began to walk about, attempting to fix his thoughts on some sort of future. But always there came into his mind the terrible sight of the coachman's crutch flying at his face. He wished it had killed him. Presently there came a knock on the door.

'Come in!' he cried, with the totally unreasonable hope that it should be someone from *The Red Lion* come to take him home. But it turned out to be a maidservant with a candle.

'The guv'nor says you'll be needing this.'

With quite a shock Sam realized it was dark already. He took the candle and sat on his bed. The girl smiled inquisitively at him, then went away. He heard her loitering down the stairs, one at a time, as if she expected to be called back; then she finished up with a sharp and irritable clatter.

Sam took hold of his old barber's box and held it close to his lips.

'Where are you now?' he whispered. 'Are you with me in this room somewhere? Have you come back for me after all this while? From the churchyard and the gibbet, perhaps – or wherever else you may be? I'm alone, now, don't you know.

Me, Sam, who came out of your love. Ghosts – ghosts, come and keep me company!'

He opened the box and stared down at the ring and the pistol that had once belonged to his other pa. What blood was it that really ran in his veins? A murderer's, a soldier's, a cut-throat gambler's? A ring – and a pistol. A madman's, perhaps? He took out the pistol, and the sudden chill of the metal made him shiver. He remembered his promise to God. Had he just killed Chichester, then? Vengeance is mine, saith the Lord. I will repay. Could even God care what Sam did any more?

There was a small knot of linen tucked in a corner of the box. He picked it up and undid it. Sixteen golden guineas were inside – one for each year of his life. There was also a scrap of paper. 'God bless you and keep you, Sam,' was written on it in his ma's small uneducated hand.

He knelt on the floor in silence; then he stood up, replaced the pistol in its box and left the room. He could no longer bear his own company.

He walked down the steep hill towards the river, imagining lapping solitude and heaven knows what else besides. He crossed between trees and gardens, striving to lose himself in the shadows as if to avoid the eyes of the night. He came to the embankment ...

The night was full of stars; and at first he thought they were reflected in the wide black water. But they turned out to be the lanterns of watermen's boats, waddling sturdily up and down stream. Here and there, larger vessels glinted, fidgeting slowly on their fevered reflections ... and beyond, to the west, stretched Westminster Bridge, lanterned from bank to bank. Lights moved and twinkled everywhere, and on the opposing side, where dark spires rose, dividing the constellations into bright columns and wedges, a thousand flickerings weaved in and out of the darkness as link-boys, cabs and coaches threaded the unseen streets.

Spellbound, he stood and watched the night-time town, while passers-by pushed and jostled till he turned round and round to stare after them. A multitude of faces filled his brain: eyes narrow and keen, eyes wide and silver as shillings; crinkled eyes full of knowingness; eyes with lids like funeral hatchments; women's eyes that seemed to scrape him to the bone, and an old, old man whose lids and pouches cuddled his eyes as if in a tumbled bed. The old man stumbled; involuntarily Sam put out his hand, but the old man pushed him aside and hiccuped on his way till he was lost in the huge dark family of the night.

Long, long Sam stared after him, recalling every detail of his battered, time-insulted face; then he returned to his lodgings, dazed by various incomprehensible sensations that not even Parson Talbot could have put into words. Little by little, as he lay in bed, his mood turned calmer until at last he was able to close his eyes and face the darkness in his head.

On the following morning he rose early, put on his best clothes, took his gold-topped cane and set off for Panton Street to wait on his benefactor, Mr Bratsby.

Before he left *The Bunch of Grapes*, he took it into his head to ask if Covent Garden was nearby; he was told it was scarcely fifteen minutes' walk away. At once he felt a strange excitement – even though his connection with that place derived from no more than a fragile mention some hours before he was born. It was impossible for him not to wonder what would have been the course of his life – if the young woman of long ago had reached Covent Garden instead of stopping short at *The Red Lion*. What or who was it she'd hoped to find there – and could it still be there after sixteen years? He felt quite strange when he thought that it might have been he himself, growing and pressing inside her, that had forced her to make her terrific, ill-fated journey! Now at last he was within fifteen minutes' walk of the very place for which he'd been destined. But it was no use; the vital reason for it lay under the stone in Dorking churchyard.

'God bless Arundel and him who was hanged,' he murmured from force of habit.

Mr Bratby's house in Panton Street stood next door to Mr Sidall's, the chemist. It was a plain, modest house that had recently been improved by a Grecian portico and a large new door. Brimming full of destiny, Sam knocked.

'Doctor Bratsby is not at home,' said the footman who answered. He seemed to lay emphasis on the '*Doctor*'.

'Will he be back soon?' asked Sam, feeling his destiny slipping away into commonplace circumstance.

'Tonight. Will you leave your card?'

'No, no,' said Sam, drawing a pattern on the pavement with his cane. 'Just tell him Sam Chichester called. Sam Chichester of – of *The Flying Cradle* ...'

'Why that's –' began the footman, startled into curiosity. 'Just wait a moment Sa – Mr Chichester. Don't go away, now!'

Excited and flustered, the footman vanished into the house. Sam waited with revived hope. Presently the footman returned.

'Mrs Bratsby's compliments, but you're on the early side for a call in London, you know. Or most likely you didn't. Things is very fussy in town, sir. Mrs Bratsby says to tell you to come back at half after eight o'clock. The doctor will be home by then.'

Sam backed politely away as the footman kept staring at him. Then at last that splendid personage could bear it no longer. He beamed.

'So you're the one, are you? Well, well – who'd have thought it?'

14

'SAM – Sam Chichester! My dear Sam Chichester – what can I say? How good – how very good it is to see you! Grown up – marvellous, marvellous! Really, Sam – if I may – I'm lost for words! Absolutely lost!'

Dr Bratsby, always a heavily built man, was now quite massive. Patients beholding him drew great comfort from his size, feeling that he would be unlikely to counsel abstinence. And they turned out to be right. He was a believer in good eating and advised a liberal diet so expansively that one might have supposed he was paying for it. He made as if to shake Sam by the hand, then, changing his mind, clasped him by the shoulders, giving off a powerful smell of sickroom and herbs.

'My dear boy – my dear boy! Let me look at you!' He released Sam, stepped back and gazed at him from head to foot, shaking his head all the while in wonderment.

'But why are we standing out here in the hall? Come in – come in! I have a surprise for you. Mr Oxton and Mr Skipping are with us tonight! I told them as soon as I heard. Not a word more now, Sam (how extraordinary it is to be actually talking to you!), save it all for the three of us. Come inside. Sam Chichester ... *Sam Chichester*!'

Relieved of his hat and cane, Sam was drawn into a dining-room that seemed all light and smiles and overflowing kindness.

'Here he is – here he is!' cried Dr Bratsby joyfully. 'The boy himself! Our little one, eh? Oxton, Skipping – what d'you think now? Has a good job been made of him? Mrs Bratsby, Mrs Skipping ... this is him – Sam Chichester. *The* Sam Chichester! Isn't it amazing?'

While the ladies were agreeing that it was amazing, Sam

was seated at the foot of the table. Much moved and not a little bewildered, he gazed at his three benefactors, trying to determine which was Oxton and which was Skipping. He felt a great inner warmth, a desire to cry, and a strong sense of being a prodigal coming home.

The joy and kindness on every face overwhelmed him; he sat nodding and beaming under Dr Bratsby's torrent of reminiscenses and ceaseless urgings to eat to his heart's content. Sometimes, even, the hospitable doctor heaped his plate for him, declaring professionally that young bones needed all the nourishment they could get to grow.

Little by little, Sam's high mood sank under the weight of the dinner; he felt his eyes becoming glazed from inward pressure. He longed to undo the top of his breeches, but the superiority of the company and the grandeur of the room stifled him and he suffered in silence. At last the ladies left and port and brandy filled their places.

'Drink up – drink up!' insisted Dr Bratsby, floating down the length of the table, his cream and silver waistcoat billowing out before him like a cloud. Like many a large man, the doctor was remarkably light on his feet, though tremendously heavy on everything else. His chair creaked ominously as he returned to it. He gazed moistly and sentimentally around him.

'Do you remember?' he began, and touched his forehead above his left eye. A tiny scar was still visible. He smiled and shook his head.

'It was before you – you came among us, Sam,' he said, dropping further into his misty mood. 'She was – was very lovely, Sam ... your mother, you know.'

'And very lady-like,' said Mr Skipping. 'I remember thinking it at the time. What a lady-like young person, I said to myself. Good heavens! it seems like it was yesterday!'

'What a shame Bartholomew never lived to be here this night,' murmured Mr Oxton to his glass.

'Drifted away,' said Dr Bratsby. 'Just drifted away. I saw it coming, of course. Drink up there, Sam!'

'What a shame, though. Bartholomew would have been so happy.'

'Perhaps he is?' said Mr Skipping, glancing piously upward to the swaying chandelier.

'Do you remember how we all waited in the parlour? And that potboy with his shilling?'

'And the landlord!'

'And that moment when the coachman came in!'

'How is he, Sam? How is dear old Chichester? Still as gruff and good-hearted as ever? And his lady wife? Still the great markswoman?'

One would have thought from the familiarity and warmth of their recollections that the three gentlemen had known the Chichesters all their lives, instead of being the chance acquaintances of a single night. With a start, Sam recollected himself. Somberly he told of Chichester's accident and his present tragic condition. Dr Bratsby was shocked; Mr Oxton was shocked – and so was Mr Skipping. Why hadn't they been told? They were sure they could have done something. People are so selfish about tragedies ...

'If only Bartholomew had lived,' said Mr Oxton, confiding in his glass again.

'He had a good life,' said Dr Bratsby, as if he'd arranged it; and Chichester was quietly laid aside.

'Do you – do you remember that moment when we all knew it was a boy that had been born?' asked Mr Skipping, determined to wring a few more drops of pleasure from his memories.

'That was you, Sam,' explained Dr Bratsby. 'Drink up – drink up!'

Sam smiled weakly – and tried with all his might to enter into the cheerfulness that flickered all round him like candles he couldn't quite see.

'Do you remember ... do you remember ...' His bene-factors trundled off again, shedding years like clothes in summer; while Sam, lost, neglected Sam, sat at the foot of the table, deeply mined with food and drink and feeling that he'd missed out on a great occasion by being too young to appreciate it.

'I – I –' he began several times; but what could he say?

They looked at him sympathetically, smiled and reminded him of how he'd been held in Mrs Roggs's arms and how his hair had tufted over the blanket. Then Mr Skipping gazed at him almost reproachfully and said it didn't seem possible, and Mr Oxton shook his head and regretted that Bartholomew hadn't lived to see it, and Dr Bratsby diagnosed that time flies by ...

'If only *she*'d lived,' sighed Sam. He meant nothing in particular and was only expressing a deep feeling to be part of *something*.

'I know what you're thinking,' said Dr Bratsby. 'And I can assure you that everything humanly possible was done for her.'

'It was God's will,' said Mr Skipping, looking up at the chandelier again.

'I would have attended her myself, Sam ... but it was plain, from the very beginning, that nothing could be done. Take my word for it, young man ...'

Dr Bratsby had really come to believe this and had entirely forgotten a certain nervousness and guilt he'd felt at the time that had led him to conceal his profession.

'Under the circumstances, my boy, it was as well she – she passed away. Although, I've no doubt, she was a fine woman, Sam, there was no father. You were very fortunate, Sam; very fortunate indeed. The Chichesters are fine folk, and – and –' he trailed off, feeling perhaps he'd been guilty of an unnecessary sharpness. 'Drink up – drink up, Sam! This is a happy occasion ...'

Sam looked at Dr Bratsby uncomprehendingly. The change

in the doctor's tone had been disturbing, even frightening to Sam in his present rootless state. Oxton and Skipping were glancing at him uncomfortably, and then looking away. Mr Oxton even shrugged his shoulders at the confidant that resided in his glass.

Of a sudden, Sam felt that his benefactors were perhaps not altogether pleased to see him. They wanted the baby back. He, grown hopelessly out of reckoning, was a trespasser ... a wrecker of dreams even as he'd been a wrecker of coaches. He was a destroyer; his very growth was destruction. For a moment he saw Chichester's anguished face howling at him across the table; then it dissolved and he saw his benefactors seeming to say, 'We've dined you, we've wined you; we've faithfully remembered your birthdays. What more can you want of us? Don't press us, lad. Don't force us to turn our backs on you. We *have* been charitable ...'

'I – I must go now,' said Sam, abruptly rising to his feet.

'So soon? But we've hardly talked yet ...'

'Coach time-table, eh? Well, well, we mustn't keep you, dear Sam.' There was a hint of eagerness in the voice.

Sam nodded. He had said nothing of his reason for calling nor of his disastrous break with the Chichesters. It had seemed quite pointless to mention it.

'Come and see us again, Sam Chichester. Don't forget us now!'

'Our kindest regards to your mother and father.'

'A pity you didn't come sooner. Poor Bartholomew would have been so happy!'

'You know where we live ... always a welcome ... always ... always ...'

The affectionate sentences echoed in Sam's ears as he left Dr Bratsby's house for the shadows of Panton Street

'If only Bartholomew had lived,' he muttered to himself. If Bartholomew had wanted to see him he could have visited *The Red Lion* at any time and enjoyed himself to his heart's content. Perhaps Mr Bartholomew had been the most sensible one of all by dying with his dream intact.

The object of charity ought never to show itself after the first warmth. Bitterly Sam wondered which was the worse fate for good intentions: to be worn away to the irritable bone – as they'd been at *The Red Lion* – or to be carried along like painted masks at a funeral – as they were in Panton Street?

'Damn you, damn you, damn you all!' whispered Sam, tears running down his face; then, in the next moment he despised himself for his own ingratitude.

'Mr Chichester – Mr Sam Chichester!'

Dr Bratsby's footman was running after him. Sam's heart leaped with hope. Had his benefactors awoken to the living Sam?

'You left your cane, sir.'

Sam thanked him ruefully and, on an impulse, asked the way to Covent Garden. The footman told him, then, seeing his tear-stained face, murmured, 'A moving occasion, weren't it? May I, Sam Chichester?'

May he what? Sam saw the man was holding out his hand to be shaken. Sam obliged and clasped it.

'I was there, you know,' said the footman, working Sam's hand energetically. 'I was there that day when the doctor came home. He told us ... and we all drank your health, Sam Chichester. It seems like yesterday ...'

Covent Garden: huge, dark and lurid with torches and lamps that seemed to spread the teeming blackness rather than dispel it. The reek of the morning's market clung everywhere, and cabbages lay on the cobbles like traitors' heads.

Sam crept down the arched Piazza, staring, staring for something that might awaken a chord deeper than any memory in Panton Street. He wrestled with the very air to reach back before the grave. *He was here*; he was at the end of the journey. Surely there would be something ...?

Every house, every tavern, every stall drew him. He peered up at them despairingly, as if the ghost of 'Arundel' was watching for him from a window. Faces there were in plenty that looked out ... and faces that passed him languorously by. Faces painted as if over the bare bone so that the lascivious smiles seemed skull-like.

'Dear boy – handsome boy, where are you going?'

'Lovely boy, won't you come inside?'

'Two shillin's lover. Only two shillin's.'

He hastened on, past shops with dingy tallows flickering in their windows. Hot baths for ladies and gentlemen ... and other services on request.

'Would you care to step inside, young gentleman?' A face full of beauty spots, with graveyard dust between ... and a mouth like the entrance to hell.

A shop with two old women sitting at a table, chewing, chewing and taking what looked like fat grey tongues out of their mouths and putting them in a bucket and covering them with a wet cloth. Best papier-mâché chewed here for the trade. Munch, munch, munch ... huge jaws good for nothing but chewing paper ... Had they ever been young?

'Buy me a drink, dearie? My hair's real ginger in the day; and I'm real ginger at night! Hot spice ginger – smoking, smoking hot!'

A sweet voice; and the ginger hair hung down over an old child's eyes.

And still Sam walked and walked, with the horrible fear growing round his heart that 'Arundel', had she lived, would have come to this. Why else Covent Garden?

He went inside a huge, noisy tavern called *The Shakespeare's Head*, where he found a corner to lose himself in. At last he believed he knew the significance of the pistol. Destruction; destruction of memories, hopes and dreams. But what of the ring?

15

THE days that followed were desolate ones for Sam. When he saw vehicles, even humble carts, swaying and bumping along the streets, he was seized with an actual pain in his chest; he would stand and stare after them, convinced they were all bound for Dorking.

Night after night he would dream he'd been left in some gigantic inn-yard. He would run from group to group of travellers, falling over mountains of baggage, plucking at coats and begging to be told when the coach was coming.

'Coach?' they'd answer. 'There *are* no coaches coming. This is the end of all journeys.'

He'd run to another group – only to hear the clatter of hooves on the cobbles behind him. He'd stumble and turn ... too late. The travellers would have vanished and the air would be full of the roar of wheels.

Sometimes this dream would take a more sinister turn. The travellers' baggage would be replaced by stacked coffins, all marked 'Arundel, with care'; and this time when he plucked at coats, they'd fall away in dusty heaps till all the inn-yard was empty. A horrible dread would grip him and he'd try to escape before the coach came. He'd hear a sound of crutches, and then a clatter of hooves; and he would wake up, trying to scream ...

More and more frequently he resorted to Covent Garden, trudging through the market, visiting the coffee houses and ending up by finding a corner for himself in *The Shakespeare's Head* ... At first he took the pistol with him in the fantastic hope someone would recognize it; but finding that pickpockets swarmed everywhere like maggots, he left it behind at *The Bunch of Grapes*.

He felt deeply drawn to Covent Garden – and had no trouble in deceiving himself that this feeling was somehow constituent to his blood . . . as if his mother's acute longing had flowed out of her and into him at the moment of death and birth.

At the beginning, he went alone, but sooner or later the ceaseless badgering of pimps and prostitutes and easy-money-men so frightened and repelled him that he was glad enough to take Jenny.

Jenny was the maidservant who brought him his candle and tidied his room. Otherwise she helped in the bar, helped in the parlour, helped in the kitchen, helped in the cellar and some-times in the stable down the road. She'd got it into her head that Sam was a young country squire of means – and deter-mined it was high time she helped herself.

Although she was no beauty, she possessed lively grey eyes, a wide, dreamy mouth and the beginning of a barmaid's figure. In addition to these advantages, she 'kept herself clean,' as she put it, and would never be ashamed 'to meet with a lord or an accident'.

On the debit side, it couldn't be denied that Jenny was not particularly honest. She lied as effortlessly and as soothingly as oil. Pilferings, breakages and lost messages were denied almost before she'd been accused, and with such a torrent of circumstantial detail that the point at issue had vanished long before she'd done.

Sam, gloomy, lonely and, as Jenny put it to herself, 'as smelling of hay as they come', was no match for this slippery scrap of female London, and became helplessly attached to her.

It often happens that strong friendships are formed in adversity – though whether they ever survive prosperity is another matter. However, Sam's prospects were in no danger of improvement; the only thing that was able to prosper was his fondness; which it did.

He confided his history to Jenny; but her belief in his independent means remained obstinately unshaken. It's only natural he should be cautious, she reasoned. She had already discovered and counted his stock of money, and that in itself was a tidy sum to go travelling with. His gold-topped cane, his silver-work pistol and his leather-bound *Plays of Shakespeare* were further evidences of his superior situation; and as for the ring with the great green stone – well, it was the smartest thing Jenny had ever seen.

Though Jenny's life was spent in clutching at straws, she possessed the golden gift of being able to convert them into state barges, capable of supporting her admirably. She was entirely convinced that Sam was hiding something rather grand from her. Nevertheless she was no fool; she knew well enough to pretend to believe every word he said and to offer him suitable advice and encouragement. When he talked of his mysterious birth, his coaching life, his benefactors and his crippled pa, Jenny would tighten her grip on his arm and wink inwardly. Sooner or later he'd come out with it; it stood to reason he'd want to be sure she wasn't just after his money.

The Shakespeare's Head, where they spent most of their time, was abnormally full of actors. The Covent Garden Theatre had suffered a recent blow; one Dr Croza, following a benefit performance, had absconded with the proceeds and there were notices posted everywhere offering thirty pounds to secure his person. It had not been secured and opera, which had always been the chief support of the house, had come to a standstill. However, it turned out to be not so ill a wind after all, and all the penniless dregs of the theatrical kingdom had come valiantly to fill the breach. In times of disaster, each player is loyal to the stage. Little men with enormous booming voices strutted in the tavern, exchanging confidences and experiences as if none but they were present; and all the while their threadbare eyes would roam the smoky room for some shrinking manager they could seize on and bear away as a rich prize to be plundered in private.

Sometimes it happened that an actor from the theatre itself – a man actually in present employment – would slip in between the acts. He'd drift through the door like some fantastic dream of ancient Rome, toga'd and painted to the eyeballs and grinning like the emperor of the world. At once he'd be the centre of attention. Friends – for want of a better word – would crowd round him, congratulate him on his performance (which they'd not seen), and take some pains to remember him in his lesser days. When he'd gone, they'd speak of him awhile with affection ... then one would stab, then another and another till Julius Caesar fell again, drowned in an envious sea of blood.

Sam and Jenny sat in their corner entranced; and lately Sam had taken to bringing his 'Complete Plays' so that he could look them up and tell Jenny who'd come stalking in. There was no thought of ever going to the play itself; the gallery was always full of footmen and the rest of the house taken up from early afternoon. But the tavern, with its loud voices, grand gestures and its sense of a world removed, exercised a tremendous fascination. Soon Sam and Jenny became familiars, and the booming atoms, sensing admiration as keenly as a dog sniffs out a bitch on heat, warmed towards them and offered indulgent smiles.

'I'm sure I've seen him before,' whispered Jenny discreetly jerking her thumb at a gentleman who sat nearby.

The gentleman sat by himself. He was shortish, with bushy grey hair and a somewhat mottled complexion. His face, in repose, was ordinary enough; but when anything animated it, such as port wine, it became immensely lively and charming. His eyes, in particular, had a trick of attracting the light.

'He's here every day,' muttered Sam.

Jenny shook her head and kept insisting that she knew the stranger's face as well as she knew her own and Sam's. Sam, knowing Jenny's nature and freedom with the truth, guessed that she'd been fascinated by the stranger and was trying to scrape an acquaintance. Sam shrugged his shoulders, and, to oblige her, kept glancing politely across at the stranger. He was more than old enough to be Jenny's father, so Sam did not consider him to be a rival.

Presently the gentleman decided to admit that he had noticed the attention; he inclined his head with a sudden smile.

'Yes,' he said quite loudly. 'You are quite right. I *am* Daniel Coventry.'

'So you're on the coaches!' cried Sam with involuntary pleasure. To a familiar of Mrs Nelson's, the name Coventry could only have meant a worker on the road to that place.

The gentleman looked mortified. 'I am an actor,' he said coldly; and turned his back.

Afterwards they discovered that Daniel Coventry was a player of some fame, though now a little past his prime. His memory was apt to play him tricks, and it was said that sometimes he tended to forget what play he was appearing in. There was a tale told of him – and vouched for – that he had been performing in *The Suspicious Husband* at Richmond when he'd got it into his head that he was in *Othello* and to everyone's consternation had proceeded accordingly. So powerful a performance did he give that player after player was overwhelmed as they came on until *Othello* won the day. Sam longed to apologize to Mr Coventry for his unlucky mistake; but whenever the actor saw him he scowled and turned away. It was plain that Sam had unwittingly dealt him a severe wound. Practical, commonplace Jenny suggested making it up by buying him a glass of port wine; but a natural delicacy prevented Sam bribing the offended player into setting aside his pride. He felt he would rather have him as an enemy than as a bought friend ...

'Believe you me,' said Jenny shrewdly as they left *The*

Shakespeare's Head and walked arm in arm towards Russell Street, 'I know his sort. He'd take the coat off your back before he'd take offence.'

Sam shook his head. He could never keep pace with Jenny's worldliness.

'How old are you, Jenny?'

'Seventeen.'

'I'm only sixteen and a half . . .'

'In two years, that is,' said Jenny easily. 'I thought you meant how old was me ma when she had me. Honest I did. I'm fifteen, actually. Cross me heart and hope to die. Just right for you. A gentleman should always be a bit older. Am I your first – lady friend?'

Sam thought. He stretched a point.

'Not quite.'

'How old was you when you had your first?'

'Eleven,' said Sam, remembering Milly and exaggerating her.

'Lor'! The things you get up to in the country! Still I suppose being a squire makes it different?'

'How old were you, Jenny?'

'Fifteen, of course! Give us a kiss, Sam. I just fancy one.'

'Here? In the street?'

'No. Here – on me lips!'

Sam laughed and put his arm about her. Momentarily he caught a glimpse of a pair of ancient prostitutes watching them with frozen grins. He shut his eyes. After a moment he felt Jenny begin to fidget. She drew away.

'What's that old scarecrow watching us for? Ain't she never seen a kiss before?'

'She's jealous of us, Jenny,' said Sam, opening his eyes and looking irritably around. 'She's – oh, God!'

Standing not two yards away was a tall, gaunt figure, looking indeed like a scarecrow. But a scarecrow with terrible eyes and a trembling mouth and a weathered face suddenly drained

133

of blood. It was Mrs Chichester! Even as he stared, unable to move, she turned on her heel and hastened away into the bustling night.

'She must have been looking for me ... tramping the streets ... everywhere ... all this time ... and then ...'

Jenny, desperately worried, took Sam back to *The Shakespeare's Head*. She sat him down and let him go on and on. She'd never seen him look so ill and frightened and wretched.

'She – she –' mumbled Sam, and buried his face in his hands. He felt Jenny's fingers endeavouring to pull his own away, when an extraordinary gentle voice broke in:

'Let him pass! He hates him
That would upon the rack of this tough world
Stretch him out longer.'

Sam looked up. Mr Coventry was gazing down on him. The actor's face was full of compassion.

Jenny sighed gratefully.

'Might I make so bold as to buy you a nip of port wine, Mr Coventry?' she inquired nervously. 'Meaning no offence, of course ...'

The actor looked momentarily nonplussed, then gave a sudden dazzling smile.

'Good faith, little one; not past a pint, as I am a soldier.'

16

ALAS, poor Jenny! the sight of Sam's Ma, bony with anguish and all too plainly pinched by circumstance, quite demolished her dream of a squire with an estate. At first she was exceedingly angry with Sam for having deceived her by not deceiving her, so to speak. How was she to have bloody well known that he'd been telling the truth? Never in all her life had the truth done her any good, and now it turned out that she'd really thrown herself at the head of a bumpkin coachman. She was fully persuaded that she'd passed up many a better opportunity for the sake of humdrum Sam.

Then, after a little while, being Jenny and as bright and current as a worn shilling, she found that there was still hope. After all, the old scarecrow wasn't his natural ma; there might still be an estate coming to him from somewhere. Besides, there was always that tidy little sum in his room and all his handsome possessions; and he wasn't bad looking ... So she kept up with Sam, telling herself that one didn't throw out the dirty water till one had one's hands on fresh.

Taking all this into account, Jenny considered it her duty to prod Sam about his future. After all, she might have to share it. To her constant irritation, Sam responded by sliding away from any mention of it; if ever he thought of a future at all it was as something so vague and unlikely that he was ashamed to talk about it. 'Money don't grow on trees,' said Jenny persistently. 'Even in the country they must have taught you that.'

'What's the matter now?' said Sam irritably. 'We don't go short of food or drink, do we? I've got enough to carry on with. I'll start worrying when it's gone.'

'Hark at my gentleman!' said Jenny witheringly, to *The*

Shakespeare's Head at large. 'Fifty-five pound and he thinks it'll last a lifetime!'

Several faces turned in amused interest; Sam blushed but Jenny stared them out.

'Fifty-five pounds? Did I hear fifty-five pounds? A young man of property, eh?'

Sam and Jenny started. Mr Coventry stood over them. The mottle-faced little man was swaying slightly. He tapped the side of his rich nose and repeated: 'Property.'

'Boozed,' diagnosed Jenny, 'right out of his mind.'

Without waiting to be asked, Mr Coventry sat down, at first almost missing the chair and then deftly righting himself. Sam stared at him. The actor had not approached them since that terrible evening when Sam had seen his ma. He'd usually been engaged with a friend – a tall, melancholy looking gentleman – and had favoured Sam and Jenny with no more than a casual nod. But now, for some reason or another, he'd chosen to cross their paths for a second time . . . Idly, Sam wondered why.

'I was only joking,' Jenny was saying. 'He's not got a brass farden, really. We was making it up . . . so you just put it out of your mind, Mr Coventry. Meaning no offence, of course . . .'

Jenny was in an agony of remorse for having mentioned the money. She was convinced that all the world was after Sam's property and prospects (to say nothing of his person) and she was prepared to defend them against all comers. She'd found him first; Mr Coventry could take himself off and find his own bumpkin.

But Jenny's fears proved unfounded, or, at least, premature. The actor's melancholy-looking friend had appeared; he beckoned and Mr Coventry, swaying to his feet, bowed to 'the young man of fortune', and departed. Jenny heaved a sigh of relief. She didn't know who Shakespeare was, but she'd felt that his Head had suddenly been a place of great danger.

On the next night Mr Coventry was sober. He approached Sam and Jenny rapidly; it was almost as if he'd been lying in wait for them, and before Jenny could push Sam to safety, the actor had made a low engulfing bow.

'*Why here comes in the sweet o' the year!*' he declared loudly, and to Jenny's undying embarrassment, offered her a large red rose.

She took it, not knowing what else to do; and to her further mortification there was a distinct ripple of applause for Mr Coventry's gallantry.

It turned out he'd saved places for them and Jenny, blushing to shame her rose, sat in a corner and poked the flower cautiously down her bodice. No one had ever given her a flower before; and in spite of herself she was immensely proud of it. She kept glancing down and sniffing it; and when the occasional thorn pricked and stung, she bore with the pain, regarding it as a small price to pay for the distinction.

Mr Coventry, his gallantry undiminished, ordered refreshments for the three of them – but was unluckily called away by his melancholy friend whose name was Robinson before the glasses arrived and had to be paid for. He returned, full of apologies and straightway offered to re-imburse Sam.

But by the time Sam had worked out how much he was owed, Mr Coventry had changed the subject and was paying court to Jenny and her flower, comparing her to a summer's day and a great many other beautiful things. Sam listened and marvelled that Jenny took it all in. He began to fidget slightly when Mr Coventry, perhaps sensing 'the young man of fortune's' mild annoyance, turned to him and said, with a sudden, rueful smile:

'Though I'm old enough to be her father, I'm still young enough to wish I wasn't.'

All in all it was a mixed evening; but on the way home through the stirring market, Sam was suddenly moved to buy the radiant Jenny a bunch of flowers the size of cabbages.

'That's right,' said Jenny. 'Throw your bleeding money away! I don't know. I really don't know!'

There was no flower for Jenny on the night that followed; but there was a bow and Mr Coventry kissed her hand. Jenny wished to God she'd scrubbed it better, but the actor didn't seem to notice. Sam watched him enviously; he seemed to do everything so effortlessly, and he caught so many admiring eyes.

This time he absolutely insisted on buying the wine; he really didn't want to be seen preying on 'a young man of fortune'. No one stopped him and he looked a little crest-fallen. Nonetheless he paid up good-humouredly. Indeed, he was in a peculiarly good humour and presently confided that he was soon to join Mr Robinson's company and tour the Provinces.

Although he'd appeared many times in the chief London theatres, he loved touring best. It was like setting out in a grand coach of adventure, he said, with a rare and intrepid crew. (At the word 'coach', Sam leaned forward in an access of almost painful interest.)

Kingdoms were built in a night, went on Mr Coventry enthusiastically; in York, Bristol and even remote Penzance ... and applause from country hands was always as sweet as nuts. Sometimes, when the sun shone, they rehearsed on the road itself, making some woodland place their theatre and fairly charming the foxes from their holes. Sometimes they played in inns, before roaring fires where oxen roasted whole; thus their supper enjoyed them before they enjoyed it. Or eastward into Kent, between Canterbury and the sea, where some great noble might bespeak a night. Then to the mansion – huge rooms and chequered floors – maybe to play a royal tragedy beneath the very rafters that saw it first, and feel or even see the bloody ghost of a murdered king creep among the players for a better view of his own unhappy fate ...

Bewitched, Sam listened to the actor's lilting voice that seemed addressed almost secretly to him, and Jenny had some difficulty in rousing him when it was time to go home.

Even on the way back, as they crossed the Strand, she found

it necessary to push and pull him out of the way of dangerous carriages and lurching shadows: he was walking so peculiarly ...

This was because he was King Richard, the Duke of Clarence, 'deep, revolving Buckingham', and occasionally Julius Caesar ... But Jenny, who wasn't educated enough to know it, saw only her Sam, swooping about the street like a drunken sparrow. Suddenly it dawned on her.

'You don't fancy yourself an *actor*?' she said incredulously. Sam flushed angrily. 'Maybe.'

'Christ,' said Jenny.

They reached *The Bunch of Grapes* without mishap and Jenny, anxious to make amends, said with amorous affability,

'See you later, love? Upstairs?'

'I don't know,' said Sam ungraciously. 'I might be going out again.'

'Not back to Covent Garden?' A sudden fear seized Jenny. She saw Sam, complete with his property and prospects, washed away in a tidal wave of port wine.

'Perhaps,' said Sam, unwilling to expose himself to reproach and argument.

'Then I'll come with you!' offered Jenny eagerly.

Sam shook his head. 'I'll see you later,' he said. He smiled. 'Upstairs.'

Thereupon he disengaged her arm and stalked off into the night, Covent Gardenwards. His brow was furrowed, his expression was serious as if he was attempting to suppress whatever hopes were stirring within him for fear they might be dashed.

'Guess what,' said Sam, sitting up in bed as Jenny came creeping into the room in a nightgown tied with a pink ribbon so that she looked like an Act of Parliament. 'I'm a genius.'

'Oh yes?' said Jenny, seating herself on Sam's bed so that the candle lit her best side.

Sam's eyes were shining like stars and his face was flushed. Jenny studied him uneasily.

'Daniel Coventry said so.'

'What have you gone and done, Sam?'

'Daniel Coventry said he'd make me the greatest Hamlet of the age. His very words. On my honour.'

'In a pig's eye,' said Jenny, terror mounting within her.

'I read to him, Jenny,' went on Sam, in a voice trembling with excitement, 'and he was honestly amazed. He said he'd never known anything like it. He said I had the finest talent he'd ever come across. I swear it! He's promised to teach me everything he knows. *Daniel Coventry!* Think of it! Oh Jenny, Jenny! I'm going on the stage! I'm going with the company to the Provinces. York – Bristol – Penzance ... Dublin even!' he went on with prodigal geography. 'I'm apprenticed! And it's only costing thirty pounds! Thirty pounds!'

'Thirty pounds?'

'Mr Coventry's arranged it. It's half the usual articles, but he's promised to persuade Mr Robinson. Now what do you think, Jenny? What do you think of my future now?'

'I think,' said Jenny, trying to control the furious tears of dismay that threatened to engulf her, 'that Mr Coventry's hit on an easy way of parting a country fool from his money. That's what I think.'

Sam turned on his side and scowled savagely. Although he might have expected such a response, it was bitterly hurtful when it came. He'd been so sure he'd found his home in life; all had seemed so bright and clear, all questions had been resolved, all doubts set at rest. He had been happy. Already in his private mind he'd been the foremost actor of the age; he'd been sweeping up and down his room with intolerable grandeur, pausing only to acknowledge applause that exploded like broadsides from cupboard, table and chair. In fact he'd only just hopped into bed when he'd heard Jenny coming. And now she'd called his prophet, Daniel Coventry, a liar and a thief. It was more than he could bear. Savagely, and with his voice muffled by his pillow, he accused her of judging everyone by her shifty self.

Jenny shrugged her shoulders.

'You asked me,' she said. 'So I told you.'

'I pity you,' said Sam, with quiet dignity; and then, seeing Jenny begin to shudder into tears, his mood softened. Her anger and contempt were only expressions of how much she'd miss him.

'You'll not come and watch me, then?'

'If my next gentleman cares to take me. I'm not paying out good money of me own.'

Sam sighed wearily and called her a sixpenny bitch. Jenny, on familiar ground, lost her temper and asked him who'd made her a sixpenny bitch but the penny-pinching young gentleman upstairs? She had always kept herself clean, and in spite of countless high-class offers, had lived like a nun, wanting only the veil to render her an object of reverence and pity in Fleet Street and the Strand. She was thankful her mother had not lived to see her ruined and abandoned by an unfeeling brute of a coachman's assistant and would most certainly have disposed of herself in the adjacent river if it wasn't highly probable that something better would turn up as soon as Sam went out of the door. Not that he was to lose any sleep over her — as if his sort ever did! He might go his way rejoicing on how he'd taken her in with all his fine talk and possessions which now turned out to be all he had. She had always been warned never to trust gentlemen up from the country; now she had learned her lesson.

'But,' began Sam, somewhat confused.

And well might he go red in the face! Thirty pounds to an — an actor! What had he ever given *her* save a mouldy handkerchief and four and a half yards of muslin that she'd had to bargain for herself as he hadn't been man enough to open his mouth. And anyway it tore as soon as you put a needle near it. And now along comes Mr kiss-my-arse Coventry and walks off with thirty pound and enough port wine to wash St Paul's in.

'But I –'

Not, as it happened, that Mr Coventry was all that disagreeable. It was possible that he rather fancied her. (He *had* compared her to a summer's day; and at *his* age, too.) It all went to show that she wasn't hard up for admirers. Did Mr Coventry really say Sam was talented – or had he made that up like his country estates?

'I swear it –'

Well then, certainly it was something to think about. It would be wrong to ignore the opinion of a famous person like Mr Coventry. Personally she'd often suspected something of the kind herself and felt that there had been more to Sam than met the eye; but being a lady she hadn't liked to say so. Would he forget her when he was a famous actor with all London at his feet? Would he fall ears over his bumpkin head in love with some actress or other? Actresses never kept themselves clean and there was no telling where they'd been. What parts would he be playing, and would he always remember to wave to her when he came on?

So it was a sort of genius who was sitting there, fixing his burning eyes on her! Would he, in view of their special friendship, give her a small sample of his skill?

Sam, more bewildered than ever by the weird convolutions of Jenny's mind, beamed uncertainly and reached for his book. He found a place:

> It gives me wonder great as my content
> To see you here before me. O my soul's joy!
> If after every tempest come such calms,
> May the winds blow till they have wakened death –

'What does it say down there?' asked Jenny, pointing to a place lower down the page.

'It's a stage direction,' said Sam. 'It says they kiss.'

'Ah!' said Jenny. 'That's where I can help. Mr Coventry may learn you all the rest, but this part's mine.'

'God bless Ma and Pa Chichester, Joe and Milly and all in *The Red Lion*; God bless Mrs Nelson, Parson Talbot and all my benefactors; God bless Arundel and him who might have been hanged. God bless Jenny and please, not to forget my soul to take if I should die before I wake ...'

Thus Sam in the strange darkness after Jenny had left him. He smiled sadly as the old words – neglected for so long – came flooding unaccountably back. His face was soaked with tears.

He had a curious sense of saying good-bye almost to himself. Maybe this was because he'd given Jenny the ring she so coveted. He'd regretted the offer as soon as he'd made it; but he knew she'd think he never intended to come back to her if he refused. Now all that was left of his beginnings was the pistol. He held it in his hands, tracing the silver design on the butt as he'd so often done in childhood; he waited breathlessly for his wild dreams to return; but the magic that had resided in the pistol seemed to have been used up. He was unable, even, to conjure up the old, sardonic image of his other pa; the enormous excitement of his future kept intruding and pushing aside everything but the prospect of overwhelming success.

'*There is a tide in the affairs of men*,' Mr Coventry had said, when faint doubts had assailed him, '*Which taken at the flood, leads on to fortune.*'

'God bless William Shakespeare and Mr Coventry,' murmured Sam, and fell asleep.

Part Three

Our fire their fire surpasses,
And turns all our lead to gold.

17

To be an actor a man needs more talents than ever God intended to be contained in a single mortal frame. He needs a powerful mind, a pleasing manner, a superhuman memory, a deft body, a fine voice; he should know enough of kings to be one, and enough of beggars to crawl for a penny; he should be a dancer, a fencer, a singer and a dier for love at the drop of a hat. And over and above all, there should be grappled to his soul, with hoops of steel, the three prime qualities: Imagination, Idealism and Sincerity – and the greatest of these is Sincerity.

Mr Daniel Coventry had Imagination, Imagination and Imagination; and the greatest of these was Imagination. For example, the thirty pound premium asked for and obtained of Sam Chichester had been a very small figment of Mr Coventry's imagination. As Jenny had rightly surmised, Mr Coventry had hit on an easy way of parting a country fool from his money and Mr Robinson was entirely unaware of it; but she thought that the actor would at least keep his word and teach Sam to make the best use of his undoubted talent.

There was nothing to be gained from further criticism of Mr Coventry. Jenny could see that Sam was as drunk with the man as if Mr Coventry had been solid port wine ... which he very nearly was.

'Sometimes I wonder if it's all real,' Sam confided to Jenny. He looked at her as if he was uttering the greatest profundity; and, so far as he was concerned, he was.

Problems of reality had been weighing pretty heavily with Sam. Try as he might, he couldn't help being troubled by the ease with which he'd sloughed off his despair. It suggested too shallow a nature for his own comfort and self esteem. He kept trying to find some sort of *real* self in his own heart; but however deeply he probed, there always seemed something else, stirring beneath. It was like trying to part water with spread fingers.

'Even Daniel Coventry himself seems like a dream at times . . .'

Jenny smiled faintly but sadly. She said nothing. It didn't seem worth risking her gentleman for the sake of thirty pounds.

With this in mind, she said good-bye to him two days later at the costume warehouse in Monmouth Street with a minimum of tears, a maximum of advice (he was to keep himself clean, etc.), and a tender storm of kisses administered quite regardless of the company bustling back and forth from Mr Robinson's vehicle to the warehouse, mountained high with clothes. He was to write – he was to give a close account of every penny he earned or spent – he was to inform her in detail of every scrap of success. In return for all this, she would wait and keep herself clean, etc.

The company's vehicle was a huge, battered conveyance that looked grandfather to *The Flying Cradle*. Two horses, that must have been condemned to it for some equine offence, pulled it and were roughly of the same vintage; they resembled animated lessons in anatomy such as not even the hardest-headed trader would have the courage to look in the mouth. Nevertheless, when Sam climbed aboard, a multitude of aching memories beset him . . . as if the vehicle itself was acquainted with his history and was reproaching him with it.

Northward lay their direction, and Jenny ran alongside till the end of Monmouth Street when her shoe came off and Sam saw the last of her hopping into the road to recover it. Then he abandoned himself to all the old sensations of motion, losing himself in a thousand unprofitable recollections while he was pushed, trodden on and generally taken in as a full-blown member of 'Mr Robinson's'.

At the outset, Mr Robinson's company consisted of ten

souls and almost as many bodies – Mr Minchin, the comedian, having a wooden leg. They were extraordinarily noisy, cheerful and wonderfully full of hope. They waved and shouted to passers-by pelting them with any removable portion of the coach – and kept bowing grandiloquently till the jerking of the vehicle sent them headlong into each other's laps. There was a fiddle player among them who scraped up a number of tunes till the whole rocking, ancient affair burst into song on the outskirts of Islington.

There was something grand and unearthly about it all – a sense of a journey begun at the very opening of time; fragments of scenery flapped as they went along, someone put on a crown, an old sword flashed in the diminishing sun. A piecemeal universe was moving through a fixed world – a loose universe, crammed into the head of an invisible god, complete with painted skies, suns, storms, forests and boiling rivers ...

My darling Jenny: we stayed the night in Barnet. I spent a shilling and the bed was tolerably clean. We are bound for Norwich, but I doubt if I'll be fit to make an appearance so soon – even though Mr Coventry says I improve hourly. I miss you tremendously and have neither eyes nor thoughts for our actresses, you'll be pleased to learn. Your ever-loving Sam.

There were two such professional ladies in the company – a Mrs Jamieson and a Mrs Clarke; but as they were both not so much past their prime as having missed it altogether, Jenny had been able to regard them with unusual calmness of mind and to believe that Sam did likewise. They had that bony, scorched look frequently met with among ageing actresses and known in the profession as 'having good bones'. (Curiously enough, no one said the same about the horses.) They disliked and despised each other, would have stabbed each other with a pair of scissors rather than yield an inch of stage ... and yet would readily have parted with their last shilling if the other had been in need.

So it was with all of them; in that lower, drearier world, where the wind blows meanly, where men catch cold and underwear goes into chilly holes, they could be moved by pity to an openness of heart marvellous to behold. And yet – and yet it was rumoured that Mr Minchin had lost his leg in a dispute over a part, and no one thought it unreasonable that he should have done so, or even unlikely.

In the world of spirit, they were savages; but in the world of savages (for such seemed everyday), they were spirits of the finest temper, closing their ranks against misery, despair and oppression with humour, good fellowship and inexhaustible kindness of heart.

My dearest, loveliest Jenny: happy to report am still clean and hope you are the same. Mrs J. says she would be happy to play Juliet to my Romeo – but Mr Coventry is against this as he says I still walk like a coachman! As if a coachman can't be in love! Would you like to be an actress, darling Jenny? You and me could play them quite a love scene! Yesterday we performed in Bishop's Stortford and made ten pounds of which my share was four shillings. Mr Robinson takes five shares to everybody else's one on account of expenses. Perhaps I ought to think of becoming a manager? But the company are very grand to be with and I think you would love them as I am beginning to do. In a few days we will be in Norwich, and if Mrs J. has her way, I will appear!! But don't count on it as I don't; Mr Coventry is far from satisfied with me. Everyone hopes for great things from Norwich, particularly Mrs J. who is going to have a benefit there. She is a real lady and must have been exceedingly beautiful when she was young. You should see her as Queen Katherine, surrounded by enemies and oppressors. It makes your heart bleed. I dream of you every night. Your ever-loving Sam.

If ever a soul was oppressed, it was Mrs Jamieson's. She was surrounded by oppressors: landlords, tailors, butchers, candle-makers, lace-makers, wine-merchants – and any one else who was coarse enough to press for the payment of debts. But she was a player – and never gave in.

Mrs Jamieson (haughtily, yet with a touch of distress): 'Mr Robinson; when are we to leave this horrid town?'

Mr Robinson (wearily): 'What's wrong now, ma'am? Didn't you get fourteen pound ten for your benefit?'

Mrs Jamieson (indignantly): 'That's the bloody trouble, sir. I can't get out in the street without being plagued by every coarse ruffian from here to Covent Garden for money!'

Sam: 'Why don't you apply to the justice, Mrs J.?'

Mrs Jamieson (savagely): 'You shut your mouth!' (continuing in former indignation as if there had been no interruptions) 'So how am I to play Desdemona when –'

Mrs Clarke (ironically): 'The lady wants to know. Tell her.' (laughs bitterly).

Mrs Jamieson (deeply offended): 'I'd be obliged if you'd shut your bleeding mouth, ma'am, before I knock your last tooth down your throat. So help me I will. Seriously, though, how can I give of my best when there's twenty wretches in the audience holding up bills like banners and an ill-natured lout bawling out in the middle of me death scene, "Don't finish her off, blackie, till she's paid me!" What's to be done?'

Mr Minchin (gravely): 'Settle with 'em, ma'am?'

Mrs J. stares at him like he was Judas. For a moment Mr Minchin sustains the look, then he smiles, then he bursts into laughter. Then all follow suit and Mrs Jamieson laughs loudest of all, relieved that no one expects her to settle her debts.

Sam is laughing away with the best of them, but when he is alone it passes to an uncomfortable wonderment and then to a burning shame at the company he is keeping. Pa Chichester had called them 'trash'; and certainly to the grim old coachman, with his fanatical sense of honesty, Mr Robinson's company would have seemed contemptible indeed. Childish in their vanity and in their evasion of responsibility, often reeking from week-old make-up, they would have appeared to him no better than refuse, blown along the roads of the kingdom to stink and fester wherever they rested.

Yet these same blow-flies, once upon a stage, became heroes and heroines of the loftiest nobility. Mrs Jamieson, who would sooner have gone naked through the streets of Norwich than pay a poor man what she owed, turned into an Imogen capable of raising every slut in the audience – for the space of the play – to something like beauty of mind. Her raddled face would become lovely, her movements youthful and her whole dissolute being a paragon of excellence that stayed in the heart and ennobled it.

'To be an actor,' said Mr Coventry, perhaps divining Sam's inward confusion, 'is the highest art of all; and most likely the Almighty's will.'

Maybe one day, thought Sam wistfully, Pa Chichester will come round to that way of thinking . . .

'Every man's an actor,' went on Mr Coventry, 'engaged for three score years and ten to play a single part. But look about you and see how slovenly he plays it! All the world's a stage, my boy . . . but we are the blessed ones who are properly trained for it!'

My soul's delight, my best beloved, my wondrous mistress whose eyes are better than the sun, my Jenny! I am to appear at Ipswich! Ipswich is the town that's to have the honour and glory of seeing me first! Mr Coventry has agreed! I am to be a musician in Othello and have five speeches all in one scene. I know the play quite by heart as I've been prompting the company. Apart from that, I have made fine progress in candle-snuffing and must be counted as one of the best in the country. Oh Jenny, heart's delight! If only you could be in Ipswich to see me! Ipswich – Ipswich! It has a ringing sound. I am quite perfect in my lines and have *almost* got over my coachman's walk. Mrs J. says she wouldn't have known me now from what I was. But I hope you will always know me as my heart is absolutely unchanged. I have not spent above two pounds of my money and that on necessaries. Cleanliness being next to

Godliness, I salute you with a kiss. Your ever-loving, ever-faithful, ever ardent, Sam.

Every trade has its own particular malady, rising in severity from the left forefinger corns of the coachman to the indigestion of the merchant and bad dreams of the king. The gravedigger has his perpetual snivelling cold, and the brandy-merchant his madness. But of all diseases of occupation, the most mysterious and terrible is the actor's. Trafficking as he does in dreams, he is subject to a freezing of the air, an encasement in ice that strikes him down in the fulness of his pride. There is no early intimation, no headache, no sense of fever. At most, there is a slight dryness of the throat and a passing weakness in the bladder and legs; but these occur so immediately before the disaster itself that they are like warnings shouted when the ship has already foundered. This truly horrible thing is known as stage-fright and it struck down Sam Chichester at the very moment he stepped from the shadows onto the full glare of the stage in the Ipswich playhouse.

One moment he was painted, costumed and dancing impatiently in the wings ('Wings!' he thought to himself. 'No wonder they're called wings! I could fly –'); and the next –

'You're on!' said someone – and gave him a push.

Light, from six dim candles, blazed blindingly upward, and over it he saw the audience, as numerous as the stars, united in hostility and contempt. The force of the push was spent; he came to a halt. Had he been an oak, an elm, a mighty beech with roots grasping the bowels of the earth, he might have moved like gossamer; but movement had suddenly become impossible. Legs, feet, hands and tongue were imprisoned as if the air had turned to cold iron. The only sensation he felt was a powerful desire to go to the privy, but dimly sensed its impropriety.

In vain someone hissed his line at him; in vain someone tried to heave him from his rooted place. He had no thought in his head but instant death or worse ... and he blinked unhappily from side to side for some means to come by it.

He saw the prompter screaming silently at him – and beyond he saw Mr Coventry gravely shaking his head. Mrs Jamieson was making faces at him ... but it was no good; he was dead in every particular save a feeling that he ought to be more so. His face had been floured over and his lips and eyes expertly improved in red and black. Now he felt it all clotting and running down towards his chin in a thick, perspiring stew.

He stood thus for close on an hour ... yet he was assured afterwards that it had been for less than a minute. It was Mrs J. who told him, and he knew she lied out of kindness.

'You were fine, Sam,' she said. 'Nobody threw anything.'

'Was I, ma'am? Was I really all right?'

Dearest, loveliest Jenny! I have acted *twice* – and, without boasting, with terrific success! Everyone says I have a great talent and in no time at all will be playing longer parts. Even Mr Coventry was surprised and has suggested that, when this tour is over, he might get me taken – for a small premium – by one of the London Companies. He says they'd be mad to miss such a chance and leave me wasting my time in the Provinces! He really is a wonderful man, although not altogether easy in his ways. But I suppose one must make allowance for genius. Will you make allowances for me, Jenny, when I'm a genius? No; I should cross that out. I have a long way to go yet. Mr Coventry is still helping me and he's persuaded Mrs Jamieson to teach me to dance. I wish you could see him on the stage; he's quite another man. Even when he's been drinking! God bless you, Jenny; I love you and always will. Sam.

There was no doubt that Mr Coventry was a superlative performer when sober, and still very fine when drunk, though not to be trusted with above half a dozen lines without the prompter. Time and again Sam watched him from the wings and never ceased to marvel. Othello was his best part and the anguish of watching the noble figure of the Moor staggering under the malevolent skill of Iago was almost unbearable.

Unfortunately Mr Coventry off the stage was pretty unbearable, too. Already the company had lost two serviceable actors because they couldn't abide him. He seemed to take a malicious pleasure in wiping them off the stage as if they'd never been. When they were delivering their lines – necessary lines for the play – he'd stalk behind them with such eloquent gestures that they were left, mouthing stupidly, deprived of all notice or applause. Mr Minchin had lost a leg over a part; it was a marvel that Mr Coventry hadn't lost his life.

It was only his extraordinary charm that preserved him. There was something about his sudden smile, at once helpless and childlike, that softened the most affronted heart and gained him forgiveness. It was as if the Lord God Almighty having poured too much talent into a weak vessel, had sought to save it with an abundance of charm – to prevent its coming back with a knife stuck in it, so to speak, instead of a spoon.

He had only to smile, and spread his hands, and he charmed Mrs Jamieson into forgiving his philandering with a butcher's wife in Ipswich; he charmed Mrs Clarke into forgiving his philandering with Mrs Jamieson; he charmed even Mr Robinson (who ought to have been proof against it), into giving him, in addition to his own benefit performance, a shared one with Mr Minchin. However, he had not succeeded with Mr Minchin. The comedian's traditionally tragic heart remained obstinately suspicious and gloomy that Mr Coventry would do him down.

Sam had not yet found out all there was to this side of Mr Coventry's complicated nature. He was still totally unaware of how Mr Coventry had charmed him out of thirty pounds; consequently he continued to admire him and to perform every menial task and insolent demand the great actor made on him. He believed profoundly that one day he would learn all the secrets of Mr Coventry's art.

So far, Mr Coventry had been reasonably honourable in his

dealings and had not spent much of Sam's money; but now he felt sure that his harmless little swindle wouldn't come out so he opened his purse and embarked on a sea that was all port.

At first, this made him no more than intensely fond; he took to cuddling Mrs Clarke and Mrs Jamieson at one and the same time ... though he was very apt to fall asleep between them and have to be carried away to bed. But little by little he sank into more damaging ways and began to disfigure the stage.

His memory grew agonizingly short; and so did his temper. The prompter's task became fearful with anxiety as Mr Coventry would so swing and sway across the stage as to be frequently out of earshot. Once Mr Minchin, a good-natured man if ever there was one and liked by all, gave him his line; but a demon of fury had got into Mr Coventry. He swivelled round to the prompter's side where Sam was sitting unhappily over the text, and shouted:

'You, there! Damn you! What's the next line? Can't you read? Come out here and let the audience pelt you for a pig-ignorant sot!'

Attempts were made to remonstrate with him, even threats were used ... and finally he was persuaded or frightened into moderating his drinking. It was confidently believed that he'd remain dry until after his shared benefit with Mr Minchin in Bury St Edmunds.

Certainly there was a clear improvement, and all the scenes he played were scenes of the playwright's making; but Mr Minchin, who needed a success even more than he needed money, was not satisfied. He maintained there were still moments on stage when it was touch and go; a look of glazed malevolence would suddenly and unaccountably glide over Mr Coventry's face, as if he'd heard the voice of another prompter – with two horns and a tail. Then it would pass and he'd carry on; but the back of the scene would have been broken and there'd be limpness everywhere. Consequently Mr Minchin remained unconvinced by Mr Coventry's reformation and, as the time for the benefit drew near, worked himself up into a pitch of angry gloom. He declared solemnly before all the company that if Mr Coventry wrecked the benefit, he'd kill him.

'I've already lost a leg,' he said quietly, 'so it won't come too hard to lose my neck ... especially if it's in a good cause. So help me God, I'll do him in.'

Differences of opinion, such as the above, Sam omitted in his letters to Jenny. Experience had taught him that they quickly blew over, and that by the time she'd have got the news, sworn enemies would have become best friends, firmly united against someone else.

18

Freeze, freeze thou bitter sky,
Thou dost not bite so nigh
As benefits forgot ...

THIS was not entirely true; Mr Coventry had neither forgotten the shared benefit nor gone out of his way to injure it; but there could be no doubt that it had been his unsavoury reputation that had been responsible for the receipts being wretched.

The company were staying at *The Swan's Nest*, a small inn conducted by a widowed landlady who had once been on the stage herself and still liked the company of players. She was well thought of on the circuit as she sometimes allowed credit and was able to give useful advice concerning the great houses in the neighbourhood where an actor might most profitably apply for his benefit.

However, on this occasion her advice had not met with success; the local gentry who might otherwise have bespoken the entire house, declined to buy more than a couple of tickets apiece when they learned that 'that boozy old soak Coventry' was mixed up in it. It was common gossip that his appearances had become an embarrassment and an incitement to riot.

'As benefits forgot,' repeated Mr Minchin, whose share had amounted to a bare three pounds. He laughed – and his flour white face smashed like a dropped egg.

Mr Coventry shrugged his shoulders and remarked that he hadn't made a fortune, either; but he didn't press the point as he sensed a tide of anger rising against him.

The company were in the parlour, collapsed in gloom after their miserable hour and extending their sympathy to the comedian. Mr Minchin was never a great performer but, for a player, he was modest and consequently popular; it seemed monstrously unfair that he should be made to suffer not only for his lack of great talent but for Daniel Coventry's damaging reputation as well. Mrs Jamieson declared it was a damned shame, and the rest of the company stared at Mr Coventry with increasing hostility.

'Ah well,' said Mr Minchin, not altogether displeased at the way things were going. 'Little as it is maybe, this'll have to go a long way.' He patted his pocket. 'Three young shavers of pounds all the way to Plymouth on their own.'

It was well known that Mr Minchin had a wife and three children he was supporting in that town and it was generally understood that their circumstances were pretty wretched; consequently his little joke fell as flat as a coffin lid.

'You're a bastard, Daniel Coventry,' said Mrs Clarke, moving to take up a position beside her rival so that the two ladies, unusually united, formed a threatening pair. Mr Robinson, the manager and keeper of the peace, wondered if he ought to intervene, and, if so, how? The landlady hurriedly removed a knife that had been left on the table and hid it behind her back; but she made no attempt to leave the room. She, like everyone else, with the exception of Mr Coventry himself, was helplessly fascinated by the prospect of a storm. Even Sam was totally absorbed and watched breathlessly as the great actor retreated to the end of the room and endeavoured to keep the table between himself and his colleagues. He was looking alternately defiant and pleading.

Suddenly Mr Minchin shrugged his shoulders. He'd had enough.

'Forget it,' he said. 'I'm not one for playing tragedy. I get enough of it at home. Laughter's my meat and drink, so don't you all go robbing me of that, too.'

With that, he held up his hand for attention and executed a favourite trick of his that could always be relied on to bring the house down. He tucked up his good leg and spun round on the other like a top.

No one laughed. Indeed, the effect was the very reverse of what it might have been supposed the comedian had counted on. He looked quite dismayed, and Mrs Clarke dabbed at her eyes with the corner of the tablecloth while Mrs Jamieson compressed her lips with anger. There are few things sadder in the world than a clown who's failed to raise a laugh.

And it was all Mr Coventry's fault. The tragedian, pressed now against the parlour wall, being in turn, Othello, Hamlet and even King Lear, was a universal figure, capable of gripping the mind and exciting awe; but the poor clown, smiling feebly, remained embarrassingly particular. He was merely hard up and that treacherous, posturing scoundrel was to blame.

Abruptly Mrs Clarke flounced round the table till she was no more than a foot from the apprehensive Mr Coventry. Then she spat in his face.

'That,' she said coldly, 'is my opinion of you.'

'My dear,' murmured Mr Minchin reproachfully, but not without a certain glint of pleasure in his eyes, 'there was no need for that.'

Slowly Mr Coventry wiped the fine spittle from his cheek. There were tears actually in his eyes; but these he made no attempt to remove; he was not ashamed of them.

'You were wrong, sir,' he said quietly. 'There *was* a need. There was a need to bring me to my senses. Believe me, my friends – if you can still bear to *be* my friends – I've never meant to injure another living soul. Drinking myself to death – as I have been doing – has been no more than escape from – from myself. I never thought that what I left behind could have brought about such desperate misery. Mr Minchin, sir ... I cannot undo the harm I've done you. No one could do that. But for pity's sake, sir, accept this! My – my heart goes with it!'

With a sudden gesture he emptied onto the table the contents of his purse, which consisted of some twenty pounds remaining from the money he'd swindled Sam out of; he had already spent the rest.

'Take it, sir, take it! After all, "who steals my purse steals trash"!'

There followed a most absolute silence. Then Mrs Clarke stammered an apology; Mr Robinson breathed a sigh of relief and the landlady quietly put the knife back on the table; Mrs Jamieson said she was proud to claim Mr Coventry's friendship and declared him 'the noblest Roman of them all'; and Sam felt a lump the size of an orange rising in his throat.

Mr Minchin, somewhat red in the face, picked up the money; he knew there was no point in not doing so; besides, he needed it. He attempted to mumble some sort of thanks, but he felt it to be unneccessary. The sheer nobility of Mr Coventry's gesture had utterly defeated him. The bleeding tragedians always win in the end, he thought, with all his clown's pathos. He sat down feeling an absolute brute, while Mr Coventry emerged quietly from behind the table, a poorer but richer man.

Shortly afterwards he made his excuses and went outside. Sam would have joined him, but Mr Coventry, with a curiously melancholy smile, begged to be left alone: he had much to think about ...

Sam stared after him, his heart full of confused sensations of gratitude, pride and regret that all the world hadn't seen what he'd just seen; but over and above everything else there was a shining happiness that he could claim such a man as his companion and friend.

Mrs Jamieson touched him lightly on the arm; he started. She smiled amiably and asked him if he'd be so good as to hear her in her part? She knew he liked doing this as it gave him the chance of reading better lines that any that were likely to be entrusted to him; but to her surprise and mild pique, he begged to be excused, pleading that he had to write a letter. The truth of the matter was that the exhilaration he was feeling was almost choking him. He longed to confide his joy to *someone* ...

He had no clear notion of who he was going to write to ... Jenny, most likely; but equally to Parson Talbot ... or to nobody at all. The only thing that mattered was to unburden a teeming mind and a very full heart.

He went upstairs, light as air. His room, which he shared with the fiddle player, was at the top, crouching with a bent back directly under the roof. He reached the door, was about to enter – when he heard an obscure and hasty scuffling, like rats at supper. He thought it was the fiddle player, rosining his bow, when he remembered having seen him in the parlour below. He paused, pressing his ear to the door. The sounds continued and presently were joined by an urgent and peevish mumbling. Helplessly Sam listened; and as he did so his heart began to falter and to sink ...

'Where, o where ... does he keep it? Must be somewhere ... God damn it! These country louts ... everything done up so tight! I know it's here; that stupid bitch of his – Jenny – swore he had more than fifty pounds! Gave me thirty ... leaves twenty. And where the hell is it, I'd like to know. Can't have spent it. His sort hoards. The rainy day, and all that! Mealy-mouthed clods ... He'll never miss a few pounds ... more than likely he can't count ... it's for certain-sure he can't do much else, either! Ye gods! what a hempen homespun he is ... But still, as he'd say himself, mustn't look a gift horse in the mouth! Jesus! I'll turn ostler before I'm rid of him!'

A horrible coldness crept along Sam's limbs, freezing his skin so that he began shaking everywhere ...

'Ah! What have we here?' The voice had changed its tone; a note of breathless inquiry had entered into it; then came a low, rushing whistle.

'Jesus Christ! Or should I say, "angels and ministers of grace defend us"? I do believe it's the same and – and – where in God's name did he get it?'

Sam opened the door. Mr Coventry whirled round. His face was amazed, but by no means guilty. He was sitting on the floor, surrounded by Sam's possessions which he'd scattered in his search for money. He was holding up the pistol.

'Where did you steal this?' he asked almost threateningly.

'It's mine!' muttered Sam; there was a look on his face that should have warned Mr Coventry. But the actor was too absorbed in his own sensations, which, at that time, were incredulous and deeply disturbed.

'Is it, indeed? Is it? *Is it?* Wait here!'

Before Sam could halt him, the actor had rushed from the room, brandishing the pistol. Sam shouted out – then saw something shining on the floor. It was one of his razors that Mr Coventry had investigated and unwisely left exposed.

Sam snatched it up and followed after the actor with murder in his heart and hand. He heard Mr Coventry clatter to his room on the floor below. Sam half ran, half fell down the stairs; he was trembling so violently at the thought of what he was about to do that he could scarcely keep upright.

Mr Coventry's door was wide open; Sam went in.

'Now will you –' began the actor; then he saw the razor and the look on Sam's face. 'No!' he cried. 'Don't! Don't kill me! Only look – look on this! Please!'

He held out a case – a pistol case. There was a single weapon in it, lying beside the velvet grave of its twin.

'D'you see?' gabbled Mr Coventry wildly. 'D'you see?'

He laid the other pistol – Sam's – in the empty place. The two weapons were a perfect pair.

'Now will you tell me how you came by it? I gave it to – to someone ... a long time ago ... to a girl ... in – in Arundel, I think ... and there was a – a ring ...'

19

'ARUNDEL? You said – Arundel?'

'Yes – yes! For God's sake, put that razor down!'

'*Arundel?*'

'I told you. A girl I knew ... long ago. Before you were born. Why are you – you glaring at me like that?'

'A girl?'

'Stop repeating everything I say. You – you're not on the stage, you know ...'

'The – the girl. What was she like?'

'What business is that of yours? I told you, it was a long time ago. All right, all right! She was a – a pretty little thing. Dark-haired, as I remember ... no! I tell a lie! She was fair with blue eyes and –'

'Her name?'

'Good God! D'you expect me to remember the name of every silly, stage-struck slut I've met? What are you doing? Sam! No! Oh! Ah! You bloody madman! What's got into you?'

Mr Coventry was suddenly lying on the floor. He was clutching the side of his face where Sam had struck him. The actor felt as if all his teeth had been shaken from his head. He honestly believed that the young man had gone out of his mind and was severely frightened that further injury of a more serious nature was on its way.

'Tell me about her, Mr Daniel Coventry. Tell me more.'

'Why should I? Oh, all right ... only – only put that damned razor down! I was young at the time ... and she was young. I was appearing with a company in Chichester. Ha-ha! There's a coincidence for you! Sam Chichester! Well, she came to see me every day ... quite besotted with me, the poor dear. No! I tell a lie. We were in love. Yes, love. The springtime of the year, etcetera. I left her a keepsake: this pistol, and there was a ring ... I know there was a ring. I used them in the play she'd seen me in. Terrific sentimental value. Then we parted. That's all. I never saw her again. Of course, I'd told her she could always find me at *The Shakespeare's Head* in Covent Garden. I expect she cried and swore she'd come. But she never did. I suppose she's wed and fat and merry, now ... and the great Dan Coventry's a golden dream in her heart of hearts. Ah, well – we all plant our seeds in common soil and let them grow how they will! Perhaps at this very moment she's thinking of me tenderly ...'

'You dirty, heartless pig! I hate you – I hate you – I –' Sam's face, desperately white, vanished into his trembling hands. He sank onto the bed, and Mr Coventry, feeling the immediate danger past, rose cautiously to his feet.

'Well, now, my boy ... you haven't answered *my* question. How did you come by the pistol?'

'And you don't even remember her name.'

'Whose name?'

'My mother's.'

'Your *what*?'

'That stage-struck slut. She was my mother.'

'My God.'

Dazedly Mr Coventry stared down at the pair of pistols; he leaned against the wall for support; he whistled.

'I see it now! I understand. Of course, of course! How stupid of me. How – how is she, my boy? Tell me how she is. A lovely lady, that one. Why, I remember –'

'Dead.'

'What?'

'She's dead.'

'Oh! Oh dear! I'm sorry, my boy. I'm truly sorry to hear it. The loss of a mother is a tragic thing – perhaps the most tragic a man ever faces. We are not men of stone ... Tell me, was it long ago? And – and your poor father?'

'She never married ...'

'Oh! Ah! Hm! Well, no matter! Some of our greatest men are ... Remember Edmund? Stand up for bastards! Oh, I'm sorry about that! When did she – er – pass away?'

'On the day that I was born.'

Sam's answers were low and grinding. They reminded Mr Coventry of a play he'd been in; but he couldn't off-hand recall which one. It wasn't so much the words as the feeling of being led on and on to –

'A real tragedy, that! And yet – and yet merciful in its way. You've been spared the sharp grief of losing her. But – the pistol ... you haven't explained ... the pistol. How – when ... ? The – the pistol ...'

Mr Coventry's face suddenly went into an evening sky. Livid colours ran all over the mottled flesh, inflaming portions of it and bleaching others. He began to subside towards the floor, repeating over and over again, 'The pistol – the pistol –'

'It was my inheritance, Mr Coventry. Just before she died she said: "It was his father's." She was going to look for him – in Covent Garden. She was on her way to find my father ... my poor, poor father.'

Mr Coventry had reached the floor; he sat with his feet stretched out straight before him so that Sam could see his patched soles. Aimlessly he fiddled with the case of pistols; he raised his eyes timidly. Sam returned his gaze with a world of hopeless anger.

'Well? What now? What next – *father*?'

The words were as heavy as lead; and so was the silence that followed them. There was the sense of an hourglass having run out, with no one to set it going again. The actor had never known so long a pause; he looked instinctively to the left, as if for the prompter.

'There's a play, you know ... *The Child Hath Found his Father* ... but that's about Merlin, as I remember. *With all my heart I thank thee for my father* ...?'

He shook his head as fiery fragments of drama flickered through his brain, but left no light behind. He was moved as deeply as it was possible for him to be. There was no denying the force of the emotions that contended in his heart: now incredulity, now dismay, now joy ... He struggled to give them utterance, to form some sort of unity or harmony with the apparition sitting on his bed – for apparition it was, as white and still as any ghost. Desperately he clutched at memories of feelings as might a naked man clutch at clothing in a market place to cover his nakedness ...

'*Many a poor man's soul would have lien still* ...? *Come, come my son, I'll bring thee on thy way* ...?'

Sam watched him silently, and was put in mind of a heap of dead leaves and rubbish in a corner of a stableyard being animated by a little whirlwind ... now up, now down with an empty rustle.

'*My son then came into my mind, and yet my mind was scarce friends with him* ... *I'll tell thee, friend, I am almost mad myself – I had a son* ...?'

Tears had come seeping into the actor's eyes as if some bone-locked sea had been breached and was leaking away. He touched his wet cheeks and looked at his fingers as if amazed.

'*All the blessings of a glad father compass thee about! Arise and say how thou cam'st here* ...?'

He struggled to his feet and actually held out his arms.

'*But O how oddly will it sound that I must ask my child forgiveness* ...? *The – noble image of my youth* ...?'

'You make me sick.'

Unconsciously the actor jerked his head, as if to dodge a missile.

'My son – my son!'

'Your son – your son.'

'So I really have a son? God be thanked – I'm a father! *Our father which art* ... No, no! Not that. My dear, dear Sam! How long – how very long it's been! But now, after everything, we're together at last!'

'Together ... at last.'

Sam stared at the man who was his father. Everything inside him seemed to be congealed in a sea of mud. He was unable to move, to breathe, even. The slightest sensation was only achieved by the greatest effort; he no longer seemed to know how to feel or think. To his own surprise he found himself to be grinning. Had he gone mad?

Mr Coventry, encouraged by this, made as if to embrace him. Still grinning, Sam thrust him away ... and broke into laughter. He went on laughing, wildly, ferociously, helplessly. He could just make out his father's face through a fog of tears; he looked puzzled and a little frightened. But still Sam was unable to stop laughing. Dimly he knew there was a huge joke somewhere, but he needed solitude to find it. And he needed to stop laughing; the noise and strain were tearing his head apart.

'I'll go – go to my room – for awhile – let me go ...'

Jenny – Jenny – Jenny – Jenny! I am done for! That man, that devil, that lying, hateful bloated pimple of an actor (how I hate the word!) is my *father*! Yes – my natural father ... though how he could be natural only the devil knows! It was the pistol that gave him or, rather, both of us away. I feel so horrible – so sick and desperate. I've only just left him downstairs. I knocked him down. I wish I'd killed him! He doesn't even remember my mother's name. She was nothing to him – nothing! I can't tell you how I felt when he asked about her as if she was still alive and well!

God knows how many other Sams there are, littered about the world, scraping their livings and dreaming their crazy dreams of their 'other pa'! The pistol was a wretched trick ... but at least the ring has come to stand for something worthwhile. Oh Jenny! When I think of all my dreams about that pistol –

all the things I fancied I might become, because I believed it *meant* something. And now I find it was nothing more than a stage property! A piece of make-believe. And so was he. I used to dream of my other pa ... and it was a great comfort at the time. Now he turns out to be no more real than the pistol.

I always used to think there was something deep inside me ... something I'd got from *him*, mysterious *him*, for he was always a great sardonic mystery. But he's *nothing* – and so am I. I am empty, Jenny, empty, empty. When I was little, I used to imagine, because of certain things that had been said, that he'd been hanged. I actually had nightmares of him swinging from a gibbet, all black and shiny with tar. Now I wish those nightmares would come true! Yes – I hate him that much.

I'm frightened to face anybody now. I'm frightened even to go to sleep, because God knows what dreams I'll have. I might dream about Ma and Pa Chichester – and that would be horrible because I know there were times when I despised them and thought that my other pa, my true father (what a mockery the word 'true' can be!), was something immeasurably better than they. How can I face my good, my beloved Pa Chichester, even in my dreams? I might dream about the future – of years and years dragging by with that abominable man until one of us dies. I might dream about the lies he told me about my talent ... and that would be horrible, too.

What am I to do, Jenny? What am I to believe in now? I feel so lost and lonely. Can there be a God, Jenny, who watches this sort of thing and never lifts a finger to help?

Oh! if only the world was really all a stage – as the trash I live with keep saying. I could shut my eyes and be great again. Why not? Then open my eyes and everything would be make-believe ... beggars as kings disguised ... and even a Daniel Coventry as the prince he always used to be behind my eyes.

Why should the worse world be the real one? Why should the lies and treachery that even now is strutting downstairs – for I can hear him walking to and fro – be real and not a nightmare? Perhaps the real world itself is, after all, only a nightmare and one day we'll wake up from it and discover that make-believe was true all the time?

Oh Jenny, my love, forgive this misery. I expect it will pass; everything does in the end … everything, that is, except my love for you. And in the end, that will be all that matters. I love you – and that makes the world bearable … sometimes, even, it makes it marvellous.

So in which world does love have its home? Both, I suppose … a sooty town house and a fairyland country estate!

How shall I sign myself? 'Sam' seems nothing anymore. Which Sam? Chichester Sam? Coventry Sam? Then let it be Jenny Sam … Sam … Sam … Sam …

And so on over the page, line after line of 'Sam', till the letters no longer meant the word and were only an incomprehensible pattern on the paper, defying the dazed mind to make any sense of them.

He put the letter away, knowing as he did so that he would never send it. It was written to the Jenny in his heart rather than the Jenny of his heart – that Jenny who was part of himself, a turbulent limb of fantasies that wore Jenny's name like a mask.

He undressed and climbed into bed, leaving the candle burning as the fiddle player was not yet back. Presently there came a knock on the door.

'Who's there?'

'Your father.'

The door opened and Mr Coventry came in. He shut the door behind him and seated himself carefully on the fiddle player's bed, crossing his knees and clasping his hands before them. He regarded Sam cautiously.

'Whatever you're feeling and thinking now, Sam – and I can understand it must be something pretty tremendous – you must know that blood is thicker than water.'

'I do. It stinks more and attracts the flies.'

Mr Coventry looked patient. 'I swear to you, Sam, that if I'd known your mother was – was in that condition, I'd have come runnning to be beside her. I – I'm not all bad, you know …'

'Is there a good part, then? Is there a little bit still left?'

'Don't be childish, Sam. Listen to me as the grown young man you are. I – that is to say, your father is an artist, and an exceptionally good one, too. In my way, I've brought many people happiness and relief from the aching dullness of their daily lives –'

'Like my mother?'

'She loved me!' said Mr Coventry, with a spontaneous burst of anger. 'She really did. And that made her happy –'

'And killed her, too! She could have done without such happiness.'

'And you? Would you sooner not have been born, then?'

'Yes, yes! A thousand times YES!'

'Just think what you're saying, my boy. The good folk who looked after you – did they give you no happiness? That girl of yours – Jenny – hasn't she made life worthwhile? Friends, smiles, good times and fine weather ... would you have them all put in a wallet for oblivion? All these are the gifts of life, Sam. Can you really want never to have been? To be so surgeried out of memory that the very scar would never show? I gave you life, Sam ... and I see by your face you've enjoyed some of it. I'm not asking for gratitude; all I'm asking for is for you to acknowledge the gift with a little courtesy.'

Mr Coventry paused as if for a reply; none was forthcoming. He compressed his lips; he felt it was time he asserted himself; he disliked playing a secondary role.

'And another thing, Sam; your mother, God rest her soul, died when you were born. *You* never saw her ... never knew her dear smile ... her soft voice (it was low, as I remember; an admirable thing in women). Those memories are mine, my boy. Your anger on her behalf is a little far-fetched. Come – admit it! Isn't there something of the *performance* about it? Well, well! It's hardly to be wondered at. When all's said and done – you are my son!'

He couldn't help smiling as the rhyme fell into place; long

habit impelled him to rise from his seat on the bed as if for an exit, even though nothing was further from his thoughts.

Sam stared at him in profound hatred; the accusation had struck home. Guiltily he knew that there had always been something of the performance about even his deepest feelings. In Jenny's arms, he reddened to remember, he'd wondered how he looked; and in that very letter he'd just written in the flaming heat of passion and exposing himself utterly, he'd been as careful about spelling, stops and commas as if he'd been writing for a play. The actor had judged his son by himself – and he'd judged right.

'Not,' went on Mr Coventry carefully, 'that there's anything to be ashamed of in giving a performance. We are the mirror of the times, as the poet says. But we must always know what play we are in.'

He hesitated as if the thought had just struck him forcibly, and was causing him to ponder about the part he was called upon to play. He was trying, and was really trying very hard to persuade himself into loving the sullen lout who glowered at him. He was aware that some emotion was called for in which he had little or no experience. Vainly (in every sense of the word) he tried to trace some distinction in the boy's features, some fire of genius, some likeness to himself.

'You – er – resemble your mother, you know. You – you have something of her innocence and freshness ...'

'And you are a stranger,' said Sam harshly. 'You look like nothing I've ever known or wanted to know.'

He, too, had been studying his companion's features for some hint of familiarity – even the familiarity of a dream. Suddenly Jenny's word came back to him: 'I know that face as well as I know yours ...' He shifted uncomfortably.

'I am your father –'

'You were my mother's lover. That's all.'

'Didn't you know, Sam? That's what nature calls a father ...'

'To hell with nature, then!'

'You're making it very difficult for me, Sam, to –'

'Difficult for *you*? What about me? Do you know what you've done to me?'

The actor moved towards Sam's bed. He looked down inquiringly.

'What, Sam? Tell me what – and perhaps I can make amends? So far as I know, all I've done is to have given you life – even as I was given it. When I'm gone, you'll remember that. Remember, too, that your father lost a father, that father lost, lost his, and – and –'

He stopped, inwardly cursing himself for slipping into yet another part that was proving wrong. Words, words, words! He was the slave of them. Time and again they drew him further and further away from – *himself*. If only he could hit on the right mood, he'd strike the needful spark. Warmth, affection, respect … all these were waiting in the wings for their cue to come on. And love, too, was there …

But even as these sensations were passing through his brain, his face was still expressing the false consolation implicit in the lines he'd happened on. He had no control of it …

In consequence his father's look seemed to Sam to be gently mocking, as if the actor knew full well what damage he'd done to the boy.

'If only I'd lost you before I found you.'

'They say it's a wise child who knows his own father.'

'And a bitter one, too.'

'My dear boy –'

He stopped. There had been a sound on the stair. A moment later the fiddle player came in, red-faced and much the better for wine. He hummed, laid his bow and fiddle on his bed and sat down beside them to take off his shoes and stockings. Father and son watched him in silence; presently he became aware of it and began on a disjointed account of the merriment downstairs as if to excuse his intrusion; though he could see no reason why this should be necessary. After all, it was his room as much as it was the boy's; and whatever had been blowing up between Sam and Coventry could very well take itself off and explode elsewhere. Their rapid, awkward looks at one another annoyed and embarrassed him. He finished undressing, climbed into bed and stretched his hand out to snuff the candle.

'*Good night, sweet prince*', murmured Mr Coventry, '*and flights of angels*, etcetera ...'

In the darkness that followed, Sam clenched his fists so that his nails dug painfully into his palms. In spite of everything he'd said and truly felt, he couldn't help being bitterly humiliated that Mr Coventry had not confessed their relationship.

Outside the room, the actor stood quite still, as if waiting for a cue. Uncontrollable tears were running down his cheeks. If only the boy had said something – had called him 'father', a great warmth might have been kindled. His tears were for himself and expressed a sudden, desperate longing for some sort of anchor, a home for his emotions and his rootless soul.

At length he went back to his own room, even though he knew he'd have been better off walking the streets. Sleep was a consummation devoutly to be wished, but hopelessly unlikely to come. If he escaped from the present, it was only to fall into the past; and it took all his strength of mind to avoid a certain portion of it.

Presently, however, he succeeded and various visions of Sam's mother began drifting through his memory: Juliet ... Desdemona ... Rosalind ... He tried to fix her for certain, but it had been so long ago ... when he'd been young and near the top of his profession. Not that she'd vanished altogether; he felt quite sure that he remembered the smell of her hair and the sound of her voice. Her son brought that much back to him. Stood to reason that the lad would be bitter with him ... After all, it was human nature; and really, he must do something for the boy. He owed it to himself; a man may easily be judged on, as well as by, his son. But one must be quite clear about this. There was no question of guilt, or debts or obligations. The pour soul in Arundel was dead and gone. Doubtless the good Lord above had already made reparations in that quarter, and given her a decent part. If one worried oneself sick about every walk-on, a performance would never get off the ground. The play's the thing! Must tell Sam that. The play's the thing wherein I'll catch the conscience of – of –

He paused and shuddered. His gaze had fallen on the case of pistols. The boy had forgotten his own. Mr Coventry bent down. His hand hovered over first one, and then the other. Would Sam know the difference? *He* knew. He touched one; he shivered and shook his head. He picked up the other and crept back upstairs. He waited outside the room to hear the sounds of sleep; then he slipped into the room and silently laid Sam's pistol beside his bed.

This was an honourable thing for him to have done . . . even though he wished wearily that he'd been able to do otherwise.

20

EVERYONE travelled outside, excepting Mr Minchin, the fiddle player and Mrs Robinson, the manager's wife. The huge ungainly vehicle jolted and trundled out of Bury St Edmunds on its way to Colchester to the accompaniment of shouts and shrieks and sights unholy as Mrs Jamieson and Mrs Clarke tossed their tattered skirts, Mr Coventry bowed to the world and an Irish acrobat, taken on in Stowmarket, attempted to stand on his head.

Only the ancient horses seemed grave and properly serious as they dragged the dream-world out of the town and into the landscape under a wintry sun. Perhaps they were brooding that when they died and were boiled down into glue or some other such useful substance, the dream-world would perish with them as if they'd never been – 'and leave not a rack behind?'

Mr Robinson's horses had lived too long among players not to have picked up the occasional line. Or perhaps they felt an extra weight to their burden ... for surely the tumultuous thoughts and feelings of the newly discovered father and son must have weighed *something*? The immense weight of knowing taken on by Sam must have been measurable in *some* scales?

Supposing a man takes London into his head, brooded Sam – the whole brick, clay, wood and granite town with its teeming people, fat as Dr Bratsby, thin as paper, their clothes and boots, their dogs, cats and horses and buckets of stinking swill – would he weigh a grain more than before he thought of it all?

If a whole town was nothing, what then were love, longing, hatred and dismay? No more than weightless illusions that did business with one another like bankrupts who couldn't have bought an ounce of oil between them.

One man goes about with the affairs of the world on his mind; another thinks only of his mistress's breasts. Regardless of thinking, both weigh the same; but cut off a finger, or even a lock of hair from one – and there's the difference! Yet no man kills himself for the loss of his hair ... and every day men die for love and hate.

How stupid it is to live and die for things that have no weight. Why not pretend they never were? Who's to know? Those two ageing ladies dozing jerkily on top of the coach? The red-haired acrobat rubbing his neck to make it more flexible? Or that smallish, ugly man, sitting opposite, frowning at the passing fields and plainly not seeing them?

What a big, veinous nose he had ... and what baggy cheeks!

Only yesterday there'd been a youth called Sam Chichester, with strong ties in Dorking and another pa, once hanged but since then improved into a ghost of some sardonic splendour. Now that stretch of life that took in *The Red Lion*, *The Flying Cradle* with all inmates and daily passengers, seemed like an abandoned road, quite cut off; all that remained was a short grim stretch from a stone named 'Arundel' to the mottle-faced frowner over the way.

Towards dusk, the great waggon tottered into Sudbury and nosed about till it found a suitable inn. An ostler came out, peered at the horses by lantern light, then went away declaring that if they were unharnessed, there'd be nothing left to hold them upright; so Sam did the honours while the company unloaded themselves for the night.

Throughout the entire journey Mr Coventry had uttered scarcely a word. Ordinarily he was a talkative man, and this abnormal silence was commented on by Mrs Jamieson at supper. Receiving no response, she conjectured that Mr Coventry was still grieving over the money he'd given away. Mr Minchin, the sheepish beneficiary, took the hint and ordered a bottle of port wine to be put before the melancholy gent at the end of the table. Courteously Mr Coventry acknowledged the gesture, filled his glass and passed the bottle on. When it reached him for a second time, he begged to be excused. He had had enough. As he did so, he contrived to catch Sam's eye with a look that implied: 'Did you notice what I've just done?'

While the company were exclaiming in good-natured astonishment, Sam wondered if the meaningful look preluded another night visit. He was fully persuaded that such a visit would be repellent; yet when no visit took place, he experienced a distinct feeling of disappointment. However, next morning when the company were bustling about the inn, preparing for departure, Mr Coventry plucked Sam aside and, with a serious expression, said:

'I've noticed, my boy, you're inclined to move your head and eyes together.' He tapped the side of his nose confidentially. 'Never do that. Eyes first – then head. Make each motion register. One of the things, my boy – one of the things you should know.'

Before Sam could get over his surprise, he'd melted away, and the next seen of him was on top of the coach, sitting patiently with folded arms and a dignified expression. He formed a striking contrast to the rest of the company who milled and fluttered about him like torn-up paper, till the sudden resurrection of the horses scattered them into their seats.

After about twenty minutes of travel, Mr Coventry leaned over, touched Sam on the knee and said:

'You bend the elbow too much. Move the arm from the shoulder. The gesture must be seen from the gallery, you know. Remember that, my boy.'

This was followed by a further silence on his part and a further astonishment on Sam's. Mr Coventry stared impassively at the road ahead; then he nodded at Sam.

'Never learn the lines till you've learned the man, laddie. A bad habit, that. I've noticed it beginning in you. A part ain't an overcoat with you inside it. A part must be taken *within*. Remember that ...'

Remember this, remember that; I've seen you do this, I've heard you do that; dear boy, laddie, Sam, dear ... Every half hour, it seemed, some fresh hint, sly secret, trick of the trade occurred to Mr Coventry and he'd pass it on. But always confidentially, as if anxious to display no special interest that might be commented on. When the coach halted between high hedgerows for the passengers' easement, and Mrs Clarke and Mrs Jamieson flounced off in search of bushes to bloom behind – like rare flowers – Mr Coventry hastily told Sam the Seven Modes of Utterance, and had begun on the stages of a passion, when everyone came back, buttoning and smoothing themselves; at once he grew aloof again.

This curious and, to be truthful, faintly ridiculous behaviour of his survived the journey and carried on during the season in Colchester, where, in some respects, it grew even more eccentric. Although there were many occasions – between rehearsals or in the early mornings – when they might have been together without interruption, the actor never took advantage of them. He seemed to be frightened of being private with Sam for any length of time. Instead, he picked on moments when interruption was almost inevitable to confide some small particular of performance, some comment on the way he'd secure a striking effect; then someone would come and all feeling of intimacy would disappear and be replaced by the most casual of exchanges.

He's still ashamed to own me! thought Sam angrily, and responded with coolness and apparent indifference; nevertheless he took careful note of all the instructions he thus furtively received. Some day, he swore to himself, he would force this man into recognition and admiration and make him see that what he'd begotten was capable of eclipsing him.

In the meantime, however, it was impossible not to notice a steady improvement in Mr Coventry and be affected by it. He'd given up drinking – or, at least, he'd given up getting offensively drunk. Nightly, at *The Black Swan*, where the company lived, he would take no more than two glasses of wine and then retire with immaculate steadiness and courtesy.

Othello, *Julius Caesar* and *King Richard the Third*, suitably altered to accommodate a thin cast, were the chief plays given; and Mr Coventry was outstanding in all three. Mrs Jamieson, in a rare moment of generosity, declared she'd never seen him better – even in his younger days when he'd filled Drury Lane. There was such solidity in his playing, such marvellous timing and such humanity that she could never recall having seen in him before. She was not ashamed to admit that his performance of Othello's death scene made her weep real tears – which the true and natural death of her true and natural husband under the wheels of a waggon, she recollected moistly, had failed to bring about.

'And why not?' she asked defensively, feeling that she was creating a wrong impression on Sam. 'Othello, after all, was a great and glorious hero, dying in a wash of poetry fit to drown the sun. Mr J., I'm sorry to say, was a small, skinny fellow wanting his right eye; and he died with a grunt in a pool of mud. But perhaps,' she went on, observing a shocked look in Sam's eyes and not wanting to be thought heartless, 'the tears I never shed for Mr J. are all mixed in with those for the Moor? I surely feel a great ocean of grief rising up inside of me; and I know Mr J. is swimming about there somewhere ... and all the other sad things that come to mind. It's just that when I see one, I think of the other and I feel all warm and tender. But there's no help for it: the ocean's name is Othello. It ain't my fault, Sam, if I'm sensitive to poetry! And I'll tell you another thing: after I've had a good cry, I'm a new woman!'

She looked at Sam half appealingly; and he, unable to resist an actress, beamed affectionately back.

'Why, you've caught Daniel's smile!' she laughed. 'Take care you don't pick up his bad habits along with his genius. You're beginning to be very like him, you know!' Sam shuddered at the actress's unknowing penetration.

That night he dreamed of the day when Pa Chichester had been shot. There he was again, lying on the kitchen table in *The Red Lion*; only this time the coachman was dead.

' "He loved not wisely but too well," ' whispered Sam easily. But Ma Chichester stared at him with horror and dread. Sam recoiled in dismay from himself. What was becoming of him?

21

AFTER Colchester Mr Robinson's company toiled into the wilds, bringing a touch of poetry to such unlikely spots as Dereham, Swaffham, Hingham and Holt. The theatrical horses moved along the dull, flat roads with the mournful air of extinct creatures looking for a grave – 'a little, little grave; an obscure grave'. Like Mrs Jamieson, they too sailed their private griefs on a general ocean.

Sometimes as they passed along the featureless landscape, the company sang, and sometimes, when the weather was too bitter for the fiddle player to risk his fingers, they rehearsed on the tottering stage of the waggon's top.

Little by little Sam Chichester had advanced in the profession. His lilting coachman's walk had been replaced by the player's easy swagger, which was always most evident among 'the heathen' – as, with affable contempt, the inhabitants of the small towns were known.

Although not strikingly handsome, he had learned to appear so, and had acquired a real air and a flashing eye that brought him much agreeable admiration from the daughters of the heathen. He was inclined to stalk down high streets and strut into the smaller taverns where he'd fling himself into a chair and take up an attitude of poetic melancholy calculated to stir all but the most ignorant hearts.

Shameful to relate, there were times when he felt so full of himself that he forgot even Jenny; but always, when the company moved on, he remembered and was consumed with guilt, calling himself a beast, a brute and a worthless scoundrel not fit to fasten her shoe.

As of old, the notion of a vehicle and the moving of the road restored motion in time ... and time wore a train of memories seventeen years long. Then would the look of melancholy on his face grow fathoms deep; Mr Coventry would watch him curiously, even a little sadly – and enviously, too.

'Quite the little Hamlet, ain't he?' remarked Mrs Clarke, contemptuously on one such occasion. She disliked Sam for a number of reasons, but chiefly because he preferred the company of Mrs Jamieson to her own.

Sam reddened and forced a laugh; but Mr Coventry unexpectedly came to his assistance and declared that it wouldn't be long before Sam was playing the prince entire. He said this quite seriously – perhaps with the intention of provoking Mrs Clarke further. Certainly, he succeeded.

'Don't be a fool, Dan Coventry!' she snapped. 'The boy's no more than a bundle of tricks. *Your* tricks, I grant, but empty tricks nonetheless.'

Mr Coventry scowled. 'Tricks, you say? As far as I'm concerned he's got more native talent in his little finger than some performers I could mention have in their whole persons. He's something quite out of the ordinary – and if you can't see that, you must be blind! Believe me, there's an inborn quality there! He's got the seeds of genius all right!'

The actor's voice had gone shrill with anger; Mrs Clarke retired offended – and Sam struggled to hold back a grin of ironical amusement at Mr Coventry's sudden display of parental pride.

Nevertheless, absurd as it all was, he couldn't help being affected by it and wondering, over and over again, how much his father's defence of him had been prompted by personal vanity and how much by genuine regard? At length he came to the altogether happy conclusion that Mr Coventry would never have spoken out so forcefully for vanity alone. He really must have seen something in Sam.

From this unshakable belief it was but a small step to feeling himself thrown away on the almost invisible parts he was still allotted; and he took to wishing various disasters on other players so that he might be given the chance to shine in their parts instead of twinkling intermittently in his own.

Once, in Yarmouth, he got a laugh that still sounded in his memory like a coronation anthem. He'd given a new turn to his line and accompanied it with a little skip and a movement of his arm . . . and the laugh had risen at his bidding like the Red Sea. A wild, fierce joy had filled him; he loved all the world and he felt as light as air. Henceforth the smell of candles and lamp-black, the sweetish taste of vermilion and the unbearable excitement of waiting nightly to be born on the stage made every hardship seem but an insignificant interruption in his progress to the stars.

Towards the end of March a heavy fall of snow obliterated the roads, sealed up the towns and transformed the landscape into a white memory. The weather turned furiously cold; the snow froze and a deep silence settled over the countryside. None but the most desperate journeys were undertaken; all other travel came to an end. Four-day visitors found themselves extended into timeless guests in households that became hotbeds of whispers and resentful looks. Travelling salesmen and merchants were sealed in with what should have been overnight adventures; day after night they grew stale and threadbare, murdering their own memories before they'd had a chance to live.

From Yorkshire to the Thames, companies of players wore out their stock on the bored heathen, and only the coach horses benefited. Peering about them and seeing everywhere a white, fluffy world, they conceived the notion that they'd passed painlessly away and were now rewarded with a heaven where no coaches ran.

Then, after six weeks of time frozen still, the weather relented and remembered it should be spring. Guiltily, the snows shrank back and a delicate dusting of green transfigured the bushes and trees. Like Noah's doves, travellers sped from their imprisonments, affections revived, partings became cordial and only the coach horses lamented as various tousled demons in the shape of ostlers invaded heaven and made it once more hell.

Mr Robinson's company yawned topplingly out of Aylesham – and Aylesham yawned a little as they went. Some three or four young girls waved the great vehicle good-bye, and maybe a tradesman's wife or so dabbed her eyes in a private corner of her bedroom window as Brutus or King Richard went out of her life. A butcher's daughter sighed, and remarked how grandly that young Mr Chichester had blossomed and graced the big parts in the weeks gone by; but her mother sniffed and declared that he was all very well for a child, but he was nothing, simply nothing! beside the man ... ah! Daniel Coventry!

'And was it snowing when you were in Arundel?' asked Sam Chichester, squinting in the April sun and nodding coolly at Mr Coventry with all the careless philosophy that a seventeen-year-old player was capable of. He was seasoned now; but to whose taste it was early to say.

'No,' said his father, making strong efforts to remember one thing while forgetting another. 'It was one of those afternoons when all the world looks good.'

'An afternoon, was it? Only an afternoon?' His voice hardened; his air of assurance seemed to crack, like a bad glaze. Mr Coventry glanced uneasily at their companions on the coach's roof.

'Some hours,' he muttered. 'It – it's hard to remember now. Time stood still, as they say.'

'Some hours? That was generous of you. You might have got away in, shall we say, twenty minutes?'

'I – I thought we'd done with all that! Must you keep on?'

'Oh yes, yes. I'm sorry. I was only curious. You can't really blame me. It's only human nature. I'm glad it was a fine afternoon, though. At least I was planted in sunshine. I hope it rained soon after? Tell me, did it rain soon after?'

'Be quiet – be quiet!'

Sam smiled; but without pleasure. He knew quite well that such conversations embarrassed the actor and put him at an acute disadvantage. A wretched sense of propriety overcame the man and he was reduced to stammering awkwardly. Nor did these conversations give Sam any satisfaction; indeed, they were unpleasantly painful to him; but they were the only means he had of asserting himself and paying the actor back for certain cruel and humiliating tricks he'd taken to playing.

Whenever they were on the stage together, and he was doing well, his words securing silence, his movements being applauded, Mr Coventry would suddenly obliterate him. He'd produce some tricky piece of brilliance, some extraordinary, unexpected gesture that would so captivate the audience that he, once-admired Sam Chichester, would be left open-mouthed with none but the prompter's eye on him. Time and again he did it – and always with a quick, triumphant look at his son as if to say: 'Did you think that anyone watches you when *I* am on stage?'

Even when Sam had the lines, he'd listen in such a way that his very silence drowned Sam's words.

Once Sam came out with it and asked him furiously why he did it? But the actor had smiled innocently and patted him on the shoulder. 'You did very well,' he said; and gave no other answer. It was as if he himself had been unaware of what he'd done. So Sam struck back whenever he could.

'I suppose,' murmured Sam vindictively, 'that you left her the ring and the pistol as payment for services rendered?'

'For pity's sake!' hissed the actor, blushing patchily. 'Must you degrade *everything*?'

Further conversation was halted by Mrs Jamieson's beginning to sing. Overcome by the bright splendour of the morning, she stood up and let fly with:

'It was a lover and his lass . . .'

Almost directly she was joined by others, and Mr Coventry

186

looked pleadingly at Sam for him to bury his resentment and swell the song. But the boy's face had grown sombre; a sharp melancholy was pricking at his eyes, making him blink and rub them.

The movement of the coach had once more brought on his time-sickness. As he jolted from side to side, he was back in *The Flying Cradle*, between two great caped figures who screened him from the world. What if Pa Chichester was dead, as he'd once dreamed? He groaned inwardly and cursed himself for never having been to Mrs Nelson's, never having written ... Guilt had stopped him, then more guilt for his guilty neglect ... He glanced at his other pa with confused hatred.

'*In springtime, the only pretty ring-time,*' trumpeted Mrs Jamieson, clutching her yellow hat with its green ribbons and looking like a daffodil from the spring before last.

'*Sweet lovers love the spring.*'

The last line had been Mr Coventry's. His voice was warm; his eyes appealed to Sam. 'It *was* a pretty ring-time,' he murmured. 'I loved truly –'

'*Between the acres and the rye ...*' came the shriller tones of Mrs Clarke from the vehicle's interior. She had begun at a different place from her rival and defiantly led her own choir.

What if Pa Chichester was still alive and watching for him to come home along the London road? What if his ma was still tramping Covent Garden in search of him? How terrible not to know whether they were alive or dead but just to be playing games with their memory?

'*How that a life was but a flower,*

In springtime ...' soared the Irish acrobat, skilfully underpinning Mrs Jamieson's reedy soprano.

'You can't measure time by the clock,' breathed Mr Coventry into his son's unwilling ear. 'That afternoon in Arundel was a lifetime long ...'

'Mine!'

'*And therefore take the present time,*' carolled Mrs Clarke and Mrs Robinson, happily finding themselves in thirds.

'*With a hey and a ho and a hey nonino!*
For love is crowned with the prime
In springtime, the only pretty ring-time,'
warbled Mrs Jamieson briskly, finding herself quite by chance in sequence with the choir downstairs.

'*When birds do sing hey ding a ding, ding,*
Sweet lovers love the spring.'

They passed by a smallish wood of oak, hornbeam and holly where bright buds spotted the layered air like embroidery on a veil. The sun drenched down, exposing the grey and brown architecture of trunks and branches among which small, precise birds proclaimed their neighbourhoods like tiny Mrs Clarkes and Mrs Jamiesons ...

'*It was a lover and his lass ...*'

All together now the company rollicked out the song as music and springtime caught them unawares. They toppled through a village, pelted it with stolen flowers – and left it singing behind them.

'*And therefore take the present time ...*' sang Sam at last, to the evident pleasure of his loudly tenoring father.

'*With a hey and a ho and hey nonino ...*
For Love is crowned in the prime
In springtime, Sam – the only pretty ring-time!'

They came to a crossroads where, of all things, stood a gibbet; but even this grim thing had been made seasonable. Long fallen into disuse, its cage had been replaced by a basket loaded with blossom. Sam, inexpressibly moved by the strange sight, sang out with all his heart. He gazed at his other pa whose dream self had sometime swung from such a landmark ... and he rejoiced that flowers now bloomed in his dream tomb.

The coach turned south; Mr Robinson hauled valiantly at the reins – for all the world as if two mettlesome chargers were at the ends of them. A conveyance was approaching. An open-topped waggon bearing a coloured mountain of clothing on which were perched two women and a quantity of children. It moved cautiously drawn by a solitary horse that might have been ancestor to Mr Robinson's pair, making them seem almost frisky. Walking beside this venerable creature, ready to assist it when necessary, were some half dozen crowned heads, carrying various swords, spears and items of scenery.

'Well met by sunlight!' shouted a tattered duke who was bearing on his back the nether parts of a dragon, like a St George with the evidence.

A mirror had been held up to nature – or, rather, to un-nature. It was another company of players, travelling north. A tremendous warmth was suddenly kindled, and amazement and delight as like souls met in the wilderness. Even the horses inspected one another with rueful fellowship as they were dragged to a halt and the roadside overflowed with ragged royalty talking kingdoms, triumphs, spoils, nineteen to the dozen. Comedian met comedian; tragedian stepped apart with tragedian; actresses skirmished and managers shook hands and wondered where the money went. Even little children were princes, and two of them had been murdered so often in the Tower that they cried bitterly if they missed their good-night smother from their wicked uncle.

They fastened themselves onto Sam and eagerly told him how they'd been snowed up south of Colchester and how, between that town and Chelmsford, they'd lost their dragon's head in a snowdrift. The Lord alone knew what consternation there'd be when the snow melted and the executed monster glared forth!

They shrieked with laughter, then, more seriously, begged that if Sam's company was travelling that way and heard of part of a dragon found in the snow, he'd transmit it to Richmond in Yorkshire – Templeton's Company. By the by, what company had they the honour of meeting with? They liked to know, as they collected names ...

'Mr Robinson's.'

'Did you say Mr Robinson's?'

One of the women had overheard him and now approached. 'Yes, ma'am.'

'The one with Daniel Coventry?'

Proudly Sam indicated his father who was half listening to a colleague.

'Then you must have a Sam Chichester with you?'

Even more proudly Sam acknowledged himself. He beamed with pleasure and wondered which of his performances had made him most famous?

'I've a letter for you,' said the woman, staring at him curiously. 'It was forced on me in *The Shakespeare's Head* in Covent Garden. I took it on the off-chance as the poor soul seemed beside herself. I understand there's five more such letters travelling the roads in search of you. What a thing it is to be pursued by love! Better than the bailiffs, eh?'

She fumbled in a cloth bag and produced a stained and folded paper that already looked time-battered enough to be an heirloom.

Sam grew pale and trembled so that he could scarcely take it from her. Of a sudden, the April world, full of gold and song that had engulfed him, vanished and he was alone in a bleak place with winds whirling through him and accusing faces staring at him from the trees, the coach-wheels, and the dusty road itself . . .

'Thank you – thank you –'

He retreated to a quiet place behind one of the vehicles. For a moment he thought of tearing up the letter unread; he was sure it contained horrible news . . . and if he never read it, then it never happened. Then he reflected there was no use in that. Five other letters were hunting him down and sooner or later they'd find their mark. His hands shook violently as he opened the paper and began to read:

Written at the dictation of Miss Jenny of *The Bunch of Grapes* who orders me to say that she has sprained her wrist and cannot hold a pen.

Sam smiled with enormous, but guilty relief, and read on:

Mr Sam Chichester, I wish to know if you are alive or dead as I've not heard from you these four months past. I keep dreaming you are done in under a waggon or a fever and I must know for sure. Excuse me. There's other gentlemen waiting and I ought to tell them if I am bespoken or not. None of us is getting any younger, you know. I been to Covent Garden regular, just like you said, but since four months not so much as a fly's arse. And take that smirk off your face or I'll wipe this rag round it, so help me I will. But I am not writing all on my own account as you must know I wouldn't demean myself in that way. Pardon me, but I took the liberty of calling at Aldersgate Street to see if you had written to your Mrs Nelson. I'm sorry to say the news in that quarter ain't good.

Here Sam stopped reading. A sickness, a dreadful apprehension overcame him. He waited for it to pass before he could see the words that followed.

There was a Parson Talbot present who spoke very serious about your ma and pa in Dorking. He thanked God he'd met with me and said it was destiny brought him to London on that day which was not his usual. I told him you'd gone for an actor and Mrs Nelson went through the roof. He said to tell you Pa Chichester is in a bad way of mind and he fears the snail has perished inside its shell. He said you would know what he meant. He begs you to come *home*. He undertakes to break it to your pa about being an actor as the old gent is so mad on the truth that a lie out of you would kill him as he would be sure to find out. Perhaps the truth will do him in as well, but leastways it would be a cleaner end. I did my best for you and told them that you was considered a *genius* in the trade; and the parson said he hoped so as it would need genius to undo what's been done.

Your ma still goes to the Garden. I seen her two or three

times but didn't like to talk. She looks real poorly, but I expect it's in the course of nature – her being so old, I mean. Then Mrs Nelson told me something that made me cry when I got home and thought about it. Your pa has made you a birthday present. Carved it out with his own hands. Took him months, she said. Oh Lord, Sam! What must be going on inside him all this time!

I must close now as the gent what's writing this down says it's more than he contracted for, especially as it's to be done six times over. I got a birthday present for you, too. Made special by the good Lord Himself; and it took Him sixteen years! It's your ever-loving Jenny.

'What is it, son?' murmured Mr Coventry, coming up beside him and attempting to read over his shoulder.

'Sad news?'

Savagely Sam pushed him away.

'I must go back – I must go back!'

22

MR Robinson's horses continued trudging south, printing their weary hooves in the same earth that had received them months before, wondering, maybe, at the folly of voyaging so long to be in the same place. On and on they staggered, with the same towns looming up before them, the same meagre stables waiting to take them in ... and the same rowdy load of madness that was their life's burden, dancing and singing in their wake as if God had two legs instead of four.

Swaffham – Norwich – Diss – Bury St Edmunds ... One by one they came and went, but where was the hoped-for paradise that kept them going? The paradise where old horses would surely warm their bones before the everlasting bonfire of coaches and players roasting for their crimes.

Instead, their crimes increased; the great coach, already as heavy as a world, was made heavier yet. Mr Robinson had purchased a magician's cell, a shipwreck and several parts of an island from a bankrupt manager in Diss, piled them on the waggon, and put *The Tempest* into rehearsal.

Luckily for the horses, all the complicated agonies of Sam weighed nothing beside all the hopeless lumber of make-believe.

Perhaps a better youth than he, a nobler heart and a nature less given to impossible dreams, would have sped like an arrow to Dorking, flung himself at Pa Chichester's feet and washed them with his tears? Certainly a young man less in love with the stage and not so easily tempted by a good part would have caught the next coach and gone home. There was such a youth, somewhere, in Sam; for such thoughts as these did trouble him horribly, kept awake of nights and ringed his eyes with black. A dozen times he'd been on the point of rushing off, even on foot, to kneel before the crippled coachman. But somehow, he hadn't gone and was still with Mr Robinson's; and worst of all, each time this horrible determination surged up in his heart, it had been just that little bit more open to reason, argument and, ultimately, persuasion.

If he went in his present state, with nothing accomplished, his money spent, the grim old man would surely scorn him and declare that he'd returned because he'd failed and needed help. This would be intolerable, and Sam burned with shame at the very thought of it.

Scoundrel! Coward! Ingrate! You know in your heart of hearts you're afraid to go back! Yes; afraid of an old cripple ... afraid because you've half forgotten him.

That's not so! I remember him in every particular! Do you suppose me to be so cruel and hateful as that?

Then why have you never written to Mrs Nelson to find out if he's alive or dead?'

Because ...

Because each neglected week has made it harder; and in that murky heart of hearts there lurks a hope that all will solve itself in time. The grave answers everything, doesn't it?

That's an abominable accusation! I truly long to go back to him; but only when I'm to be seen. That's the only way he'll know it's love and respect that brings me back – not need.

And when will that be?

'*Very soon, now, my darling, I will be back,*' he wrote to Jenny from Bury St Edmunds in a fit of passionate sincerity; and followed it up with an outpouring of love, well mixed with jealousy concerning the waiting gentlemen, very proper to a seventeen-year-old lover suffering the pangs of every variety of guilt. '*And tell Mrs Nelson, if you should see her again, to thank Parson Talbot for his good offices and tell him he's wrong about the snail being dead in its shell. Believe me, I know ...*'

This almost boastful confidence stemmed partly from an obstinate refusal to accept even the possibility of so crushing a disaster, and partly from a sudden and wholly unexpected improvement in his dramatic skill.

The extremes of his feelings during the days following the receipt of Jenny's letter had lent his performances an abstracted nervousness that prompted Mrs Jamieson to declare, quite spontaneously, that she'd been unable to keep her eyes off him – even when Daniel Coventry had been on stage. Missed cues and botched entries went for nothing; the feeling was all ... and he had it.

He played Duke Clarence in *Richard the Third*, so that in addition to his present concerns, a host of memories of that play gave his reading of the lines a deep poignancy. Once again he was in the fairground at Dorking with Milly and Joe; once again he was in Joe's cellar, brooding over the fateful butt of malmsey ...

Mr Coventry played King Richard, and, as always, was marvellously good in the part; but somehow *his* Richard was a long way from the demon king who'd stalked the stage in Dorking, long ago. Most likely Mr Coventry was a hundred times better than that forgotten player, but the first Richard still held the stage of Sam's memory, and was quite gigantic. There was simply no competing with him.

Weirdly Sam felt himself to be acting out his own dreams; for the ancient, shadowy monarch had often been dissolved into the ghost of his 'other pa'. Now, when the other pa himself was dissolved into King Richard, he seemed woefully shrunk. *You* are not *he*, thought Sam contemptuously. *He* was more devilish, more fascinating ... *He* was a king! He found himself looking down on Mr Coventry; and he acted like it.

It was because of this striking success that he was offered the part of Ariel in Mr Robinson's new production of *The Tempest*. It was more than Sam's flesh and blood could withstand to deny himself.

'*My dearest, ownliest love, my sweetest Jenny, I am on my way back,*' he wrote from Stowmarket. '*I am coming back in triumph!*' Here caution modified enthusiasm; he temporized. '*Very, very soon now. Just a little longer, Jenny. If I was to leave directly, all would be lost. I am at the very edge of great success.*' Then conscience overcame him; his writing changed its slope and the words had a pinched look. '*Believe me, my darling, I go through agonies every night wondering if I'm doing the right thing. To abandon all would be so easy!*' Once more the writing changed and rushed like a river in flood, submerging all unpleasant obstacles, '*But I know I must not. For the sake of both of us and my art I must suffer the pangs of conscience and come out the better for it. It's the only way! So be patient, sweetest Jenny ... you are bespoken!*'

At the end of May, Mr Robinson's company gave *The Tempest* in Colchester. Sam played Ariel and Mr Coventry was Prospero. Still smarting under his defeat in *Richard the Third*, the actor put out all his powers – and acted Sam right off the stage. Never had his authority been more intolerably great; and when, at the end of the play, he relinquished his magic, it was the magic that seemed deprived. Ariel was dismissed, rather than freed, like a dull child out of school.

Smashed and humiliated, Sam burned with fury against the actor; he could have murdered him, he could have done, in short, all the extreme and violent things that had so amazed and appalled him when first he'd fallen among players.

He cursed himself for having been seduced into staying with the company when he knew he should have gone at once to Dorking. Had he obeyed his simplest duty, all would have been over by now: recriminations, anger, scorn, jibes, the shame of failure ... Forgiveness alone would have been left – hard-won, but durable. Instead of which, the worst was still before him, inexorably nearer and immeasurably worse.

Time no longer halted when motion ceased; time was itself

a coach that dragged him unwillingly on. A second of Jenny's letters found him at an inn to the south of Colchester; it was like an arrow in an open wound.

He stood in the yard with the letter in his hand, staring down at it in fixed dismay. It had reached him via Oxford, and had a battered, fateful appearance. For a horrible moment he feared it contained something new and desperate; he lifted a corner of it – like a terrified gambler peering at a dealt card. It was the same letter; there was no need to read on. He began to crumple it up – but could not. He unfolded it and forced himself through the painful words. They came at him bitterly and reproachfully, as if aware they'd been pushed aside before. The thought crossed his mind of destroying the other letter and swearing this was the first news he'd got, so that his subsequent weakness, vanity and cowardice would be cancelled out. After all, who would know? But he'd already written to Jenny! At once he fell into an unreasonable rage against her for standing in the way of a possible escape. Next he raged against Parson Talbot and his destiny-mad interference. How dared he drive such knives into someone else's heart? And worst of all he raged against the grim crippled coachman for haunting him and seeking to die in his shell.

The whole world had risen against him, turned itself into a web in which he was helplessly enmeshed ... Yet it was not a web; it was a huge, implacable coach, driven by a madman towards a precipice. There was no escape; wherever he went, whichever road he travelled, the direction always turned out to be the same. The way ended; the precipice yawned.

Mr Coventry crossed the yard and saw him standing stock-still with the letter in his hand. He began to approach, but was halted in his tracks by the look Sam gave him. It was neither welcoming nor the reverse; it was as remote as the stars. He went away bitterly lamenting that his son – his own flesh and blood – should have such secrets from him. He went into the parlour and moistened his sorrows in port, as a direct consequence of which he slackened his grip on the night's performance and unwittingly permitted his son to shine.

After Colchester came Bishop's Stortford and then Hertford – and all the way the unseen battled raged: the battle of a Prospero unwilling or unable to free his Ariel, a Prospero who must needs crush his Ariel, or truly peg him in the entrails of an oak before he himself left the haunted isle; in short, a Prospero as jealous as Othello ...

At times, the battle's issue was in doubt; the boy, in ferocious mood, almost overcame the powerful enchanter. But never for long. Talented as Sam was, he was no match for his father. Mr Coventry's genius was shaped, seasoned and concentrated; there could be no absolute victory against it. Whatever Sam had inherited from this immensely talented man had been diluted by the gifts of his dead mother. Haplessly mixed in with his father's genius were the fatal ingredients of gentleness, faith and a deep innocence. They damped down the fires; they caused him to watch where he stepped; he shrank from riding rough-shod over tender ground.

In black moods, Sam cursed these laming qualities – and found himself raging against the girl who'd shackled him with them. In a curious way the anger helped him; he discovered that the more furious his inner state, the more powerful was his presence on the stage.

He received the third of Jenny's letters in St Albans; it had gone in a huge half circle as far as Bristol before turning and winging its way back. That night he was cheered to the roof and, for the first time, began to feel that the precipice ahead might be spanned. The old sensation of flying had returned. What need had he of roads when he'd grown wings?

He wrote no further letters to Jenny; he reasoned that he would be with her almost as quickly as any such letter could arrive. He had fully persuaded himself that this was the only reason; but the truth of the matter was that he was deeply and superstitiously frightened of losing the sensation of inner success. Committing himself even to faraway Jenny seemed to sap his essence and leave him enfeebled and purposeless. More and more he turned inward as if to seal up any crack or weakness that might let his fermenting genius leak away.

The company stayed three nights in Barnet, giving *King Richard the Third* and *The Tempest* in the courtyard of the principal inn. Sam triumphed in the gory history – but in the other, deeper play, he drowned ignominiously.

Mr Coventry, with the smell of London in his nostrils, dwarfed everything, turning the whole play into Prospero's dream. Everyone, everything seemed a figment of his imagination; Ariel, Caliban, Miranda, even the tempest itself existed only in his mind's eye; and when he turned his back, they ceased to exist. And he turned his back pretty often.

Sam came off the stage in tears and not all Mrs Jamieson's comforting, 'It looked quite different out front, dear,' could restore him.

'You'd be surprised,' she said, striving to keep the angry bitterness out of her voice, 'how little them cheap tricks of his make their mark. And as for that bloody orange he kept fiddling with – I'll ram it down his throat, so help me!'

The orange in question had been another of the actor's unexpected inspirations. He'd produced it from his robe and it had become, in turn, each of the characters; he talked to it instead of to them, tossed it in the air, stared at it deeply when it became 'the great globe itself'; and, at the play's conclusion when the great enchanter gave up his magic, he flung it into the audience where it was fought over like gold.

'What chance did I have against an orange?' wept Sam furiously. 'And a rotten one, too!'

Mrs Jamieson nodded. 'But did you see the fellow who got it? A great burly lump of a bumpkin, with his shirt all torn, a button off his coat and a scratch down his face like a church door! You should have seen him looking at it – frowning, rubbing his dirty head, wondering where the magic had gone!

He all but burst out crying when he saw how he'd been took in!'

Sam sniffed; Mrs Jamieson offered him a filthy handkerchief and impulsively bestowed a highly flavoured kiss on his cheek.

'I'd change you for him any day of the week, including Sundays!' she declared. 'That – that over-ripe Romeo!'

Partly mollified by this generous tribute to his personal charms, Sam returned the handkerchief and the kiss, and went back on to join in with the last bows.

Mr Coventry, flushed with pleasure, stretched out his hand to Sam.

'Aren't you proud of me, son?' he muttered, as he acknowledged the tumultuous applause. 'One day it will be all yours. I promise you!'

One day ... one day! One day, he Daniel Coventry would give his last performance and then reveal to the world that Sam Chichester was – to the best of his belief – his only begotten son. 'No matter!' the heartbroken crowds would cry. 'You stay with us, Dan Coventry! Stay with us a little longer! There's no one who can take your place!' 'But I *am* staying!' he'd laugh. 'Behold! Dan Coventry the Second!' (Damn it! The lad would have to change his name. Who ever heard of an actor called Sam?) In this way the farewell would be turned into another beginning. It would all be the same, the glorious same all over again! Once more he'd be back among them in his youth, in his vigour, in his pride ...

These intoxicating thoughts occupied the actor increasingly; he savoured them, relished them – but studiously avoided doing anything more definite than that. After all, the boy was not at all ready yet ... and he himself was a great way from retirement and had perhaps his finest triumphs to come; the lad had by no means seen all that his father could accomplish ... oh yes, there were still peaks to be scaled. And it didn't end there. Other things, other obstacles remained to be overcome. The ties with the foster home were not yet severed; the letters Sam had received had plainly unsettled and disturbed him. Mr Coventry felt his father's heart aching that his only son should be distressed by strangers.

All in all, he considered, there was little point in yielding up his place to a child whose heart still lay elsewhere – to a child who, though his own flesh and blood, was someone else's in spirit. And the spirit was everything.

As was usual with him, he began to transmute his circumstances into the play, lifting it bodily and shaping it to fit. It really was very like ... In the play he had a much-loved daughter, whom, like everything else, he must needs set free; but before he did so, he loaded her intrusive lover with chains. Before he relinquished a jot of his power, it had to be *seen*; he *had* to bring the world to its knees ...

It was by no means enough to compel his son's admiration; he must also break the keepers of Sam's soul. The old coachman and his dull wife! The rivalry leaped out at him and he was glad of it because he was sure of his course. Once and for all he would show these earthbound gaolers of Sam's heart that they'd reared a lad with wings. They must be brought to understand that their task was done; the mighty eagle had swooped down to claim his fledgling and bear him up to the mountain heights!

'Hey, mountain, hey!'
'Silver! there it goes, Silver!'
'Fury, Fury! There, Tyrant, there! Hark, hark!'

The actor felt a thrill of ecstasy as the play's lines sang in his head and he dreamed of himself soaring above the world with quicksilver Sam in the shadow of his wing, sharing his divine laughter and contempt for the crawling hedgehogs far below.

Before the company left Barnet, Mr Coventry wrestled with

himself and then with Mr Robinson whom he urged and nagged into putting off the proposed Kentish circuit in favour of visiting Arundel and Chichester, taking in Dorking on the way. He'd been given to understand, on the best authority, that *The Red Lion* in Dorking had a good courtyard – and dear Sam would surely take pleasure in appearing before his old friends.

Although Mr Robinson had put up a pretty good fight before he agreed to abandon the Kentish circuit, it was nothing to the battle Mr Coventry had waged with himself before he suggested the change. He shrank from the very idea of Dorking; but there was no help for it. He thrust an unwelcome memory back into the darkness where it belonged and resolved that he, Prospero-Coventry, would once and for all dissolve his son's lingering love for the coachman and let him see it for what it was: 'the baseless fabric of a vision'.

23

JULY came in like a dirty great kitchen-maid, slamming clouds and spilling water everywhere. The Town teemed with it; the roofs shone and the steeper streets, under rushing films of rain, seemed forever hastening away to better-class neighbourhoods. The *Two Gentlemen of Verona* – as Mr Robinson's mettlesome horses had come to be known – plodded hopelessly down sleek Monmouth Street, as if trying to catch it up. Behind them, the preposterous vehicle, piled high with soaked scenery, prominent among which was the bargain shipwreck from Diss, rumbled on emitting its customary melodious uproar. Swarms of naturally washed urchins followed, pelting it with horse dung; and, every now and then, a window would be slipped and a gnawed apple or a lump of old pie would be hurled out to the accompaniment of dramatic shrieks and abuse.

Presently the conveyance came to a halt; the puddled assailants declared a truce and formed a diminutive guard of honour as the company disembarked and went into the costume warehouse. Seized with a sudden good humour, Mrs Jamieson curtsied – and straightway won a dozen hearts. The doors swung wide to admit her, and she vanished to a long, loud whistle of awe.

'Cor!' said an infant with a face as old as the hills.

Sam gave him a penny, and, for a moment, felt like a king. A cheap crowning; he smiled ruefully ... then, as he stared up the drowned street towards the very spot where Jenny had lost her shoe when she'd run after the outgoing coach more than a year before, his spirits sank under a leaden weight of gloom.

'Monday at Southwark,' called out Mr Robinson.

'We leave at nine.'

Sam nodded, and began to drift away. Mr Coventry emerged briefly, gazed after him, but made no decided effort to hold him back. Two or three of the undersized human beings – one hesitated to call them children without proof of age – followed royal Sam in the hopes of further largesse; but by the corner of the street it was plain he was a defunct soul, a dead duck and good for neither child nor beast. He didn't even know his way about, and such ignorance, to the urchins, was hilarious and contemptible. He asked the way to Aldersgate Street, and was justly misdirected. After about ten minutes he found himself at Charing Cross and was forced to ask again.

To his dismay he found he'd have to walk the length of the Strand and so pass the neighbourhood of *The Bunch of Grapes*. He cursed the urchins for having exposed him to such danger, and hurried on with shoulders hunched and face averted. He was terrified of meeting with Jenny and was filled with guilt and shame for avoiding her and going directly to Aldersgate Street instead.

The news of the company's proposed visit to Dorking – to *The Red Lion* itself – had thrown him into confusion. A host of wretched thoughts and fears plagued him; he was obsessed with sensations of impending calamity from which he attempted to take refuge in various fantastic superstitions he'd not had since he'd been a child. For instance, he must touch all the posts that marked off the pavement from the streetway; if he missed one it would mean disaster. He found himself pushing passers-by aside, and not daring to apologize ... for that, too, was part of it. Now he must walk with closed eyes for twenty-seven paces; if he opened his eyes too soon, it would mean disaster. He knocked against an elderly lady who poked at him savagely with an umbrella. He must ask the next man he passed what time it was; if it turned out to be more than fifteen minutes after the hour, then it would mean disaster.

'Ten minutes after four o'clock.'

Thank God – thank God!

His journey to Aldersgate Street was itself a part of this web of superstition. He'd got it into his head that if he met Jenny before he'd fetched Pa Chichester's present to him, then it would mean disaster.

What was the disaster that so terrified him? It was the coachman's discovery that Mr Coventry was his natural father. The very idea filled him with misery and dread; he couldn't bear the thought of the crippled old wreck being exposed to the baleful arrogance of the actor.

He crossed Newgate Street and found himself at last in Aldersgate Street. He sighed with a relief that he knew to be ridiculous; he'd obeyed every whim of destiny, not a post had gone untouched. He broke into a run ... and then, twenty yards down, on the left hand side, he saw Jenny!

'Christ!' she said. 'What a face to meet with! Come to me arms, Sam darling, and let me kiss a little colour into it!'

All was lost! For a moment he actually hated her, and he stood frozenly as she embraced him and poured out her full heart in excitement and affection.

It turned out that she had forestalled him. She was just on her way back from Mrs Nelson's, having collected Sam's present which she had under her cloak. She'd left messages at *The Bunch of Grapes* and in Covent Garden that she'd gone to Aldersgate Street. Expecting Sam hourly, over a period of some days, she'd been leaving messages everywhere, so that her movements were tolerably well known to a surprising number of people. In fact, in her own modest way, Jenny had become quite famous ...

'Which one of 'em told you I was here?' she asked, cuddling into Sam's arm and drawing him back along the way he'd just come.

'No-one,' he muttered. 'I – I –'

Her grip on his arm loosened as she understood that he'd been going directly to *The Bull and Mouth* without bothering about her. She bit her lip, then reasoned that maybe he'd been put off near Aldersgate Street and had only been meaning to pop in before rushing to her arms. Now she came to think of it calmly, it was the likeliest explanation.

They reached *The Bunch of Grapes* and Jenny importantly informed the other barmaid to forget the message that had been left as the gentleman had very naturally found his own way and was here before her very eyes. If anyone wanted her, she was just going upstairs now to show him his room.

'But it's not five o'clock –'

'He's me betrothed.'

'Lor!'

Jenny frowned coldly, then hastened after Sam.

'She couldn't keep her eyes off you,' she said, shutting the door of the little room and leaning back, the better to admire her lover. 'You've turned out quite handsome. I'm glad I waited.'

Sam struggled awkwardly – and returned the compliment as best he could.

Jenny smiled wryly. 'I expect you'll be wanting your present? I got it here, Sam. I must say, the old gent's very clever with his hands ...'

Pa Chichester's gift turned out to be, once more, a whip; but this time it was not a coachman's. It was a short, gentleman's whip with the handle carved in the shape of a winged horse. The beast had been skilfully and indeed beautifully fashioned; it had been taken in a high trot. It was only in the depiction of the wings that the artist had failed a little; the old man must have been watching one of Mrs Roggs's chickens ...

Sam took it silently and went over to the window. Jenny watched him, noting with rueful admiration how he'd filled out and held himself more upright. He'd acquired quite an air, an assurance ... but in her heart of hearts she wasn't entirely sure that it suited him. She knew that he and she were a year older now; but somehow his year seemed to have gone a different way. Maybe something had been gained – but something had been lost, too.

Sam continued to examine Pa Chichester's gift, frowning and turning it over and fingering the carving as if by so doing he was touching the old fellow's hands that had laboriously worked it. Imperceptibly Jenny shrugged her shoulders. There was no doubt that this meeting she'd looked forward to for so long was turning out as sour as last night's wine. She sighed and shook her head; then an expression of some determination came over her face. She'd invested a year of her heart in the young gentleman; she wasn't going to cut her losses till she was sure they were losses; she believed in putting up a fight. She went over to the bed, gazed reminiscently at the pillow, then sat down. She frowned as if she'd suddenly been accused of something unladylike; she folded her hands in her lap with an air of broachable propriety. Although she wasn't making herself cheap for anybody, there was no sense in pricing herself out of the market altogether.

'Sam, sweet,' she began, then chuckled. 'Sounds like flowers, don't it? Sweet Sam – penny a bunch! Who'll buy? Dirty Molly downstairs, I shouldn't wonder. Did you fancy her, Sam? But not after all your grand actresses! Have you been true to me, love? Best not answer that! Just you tell me I was worth waiting for! That'll be enough ...'

She craned her neck to catch a glimpse of her face in the mirror to satisfy herself that she *was* worth waiting for. She wished she hadn't. She swore inwardly; the bloody rain had done for her hair; she looked like the backyard mop ...

'I got a nice nature, though,' she mused. 'Very loving, and all that ...'

She went on with her affectionate chatter, but the conversation remained obstinately one-sided. She began to grow irritated and longed to get up and shake her inattentive lover. Why didn't he come over to her? Couldn't he see that she was all but demeaning herself? What was wrong with him? Had he, perhaps, got too grand for her and was he being bloody miserable because he felt himself obliged to her? There wasn't any need for that sort of thing! Hundreds was ready to step in if she stepped out. Respectable business gentlemen with their own carriages ... young fellows with prospects ... God help us, she wasn't so hard up that she'd break her heart over a twopenny ha'penny actor!

She asked him, quite casually, what his intentions were, now he was so famous? He *was* famous, wasn't he? Certainly he looked it. Was he, by any chance, going to see the old gentleman in Dorking? Or was that sort of thing beneath him nowadays?

'For God's sake, Jenny!' he cried out at last and turning to her a face that was a mess of tears. 'I'm going on Monday ... with *all* of them! It's –'

He broke off, being unable to tell her what it was that was steadily eating him away. If only he'd sent her that mad letter he'd scrawled when he'd found out about the pistol! Then at least she'd know ... But as it was, every word, every thought and every event added to his unhappiness and fear. The coachman's gift, with its mixture of slow love and clumsy imagining, had all but broken his heart ...

Quietly Jenny slipped off the bed and put her arms round him. She said she'd been a selfish cow; if she'd been half a woman she should have guessed he wasn't himself. (Though Christ knew how, she thought to herself.)

'To have to act in front of *him*,' muttered Sam; 'he'll despise me for it ... he'll hate me! And even if – but what chance have I got against – Daniel Coventry? You don't know what he's really like! He's a – he's –'

Once again he broke off. He felt himself to be suffocated by secrecy.

'Never mind,' said Jenny, crying with relief that Sam's distress wasn't on account of any shortcomings of hers.

'I'll be there! Promise! I'll be watching and shouting my

heart out for you! Here,' she sniffed, fishing a handkerchief from her bodice and offering it to him. 'Mop up, love. It's got to come out one end or the other; and, as they say downstairs, the more you cry the less you piss, darling ...'

With triumphant delicacy Jenny refrained from disturbing her betrothed after that. She reasoned that he was in the throes of some spiritual battle and that she, physically she – of the earth, earthy – would only get herself bruised by coming between him and himself. So she stayed below and gave in her warning to her employer, saying that circumstances had arose that made it necessary for her to shog off on Monday. She flounced about a good deal, loftily referring to her 'intended', her 'bespoken', her 'betrothed' and her 'gentleman' who was the first actor of the age and the natural son of a wealthy landowner in Sussex to boot.

To some extent this promotion of Sam helped Jenny to subdue a creeping uneasiness that was at the bottom of her heart; but in unguarded moments it rose up and terrified her with the bleak possibility that she was demeaning herself by clinging to someone who had no further use for her.

'And when will you be wed, miss?' inquired dirty Molly, half derisively, half enviously.

'Toosdy,' said Jenny, dropping a glass and abstractedly pushing the pieces behind a barrel with her foot. 'If the parson's sober.'

Early next morning, which was Sunday, Sam went to Panton Street to pay his respect to Dr Bratsby, his benefactor. His reasons for this visit were as complicated and muddled as his feelings. Certainly there was pride in his new profession and a natural desire to show off to the fat, sentimental doctor; but there was also a longing to hear again those tales of his beginnings. Although at first those tales had exasperated and disheartened him, now they seemed oddly necessary to his well-being. He felt them to be an insurance against oblivion.

He'd spent a disagreeable night waiting in vain for Jenny, and at last falling into a fitful sleep full of dreams of falling huge distances from slowly crashing coaches. Shrill shouts had echoed continually in his ears, faces came and went, and the hedgerows rushed by in a dappled green confusion. When he awoke, he felt bruised from head to foot ... and had suddenly remembered Mr Roggs of *The Red Lion*, poking his head round the door to see how 'the tiddler' was getting on ...

From this the longing had sprung up within him to have his memories revived by someone else. He craved to hear again about Joe and Mr Roggs and *The Flying Cradle* spanking along the winter's road, with the coachman and his guard, muffled to the eyeballs, swaying like a pair of tattered owls ...

Dr Bratsby's footman recognized him at once and ushered him within. Was the doctor at home, or had he gone to church? He could always call again ...

The footman looked momentarily surprised. Didn't Mr Chichester know ... hadn't he heard? Sam's heart misgave him; he grew cold. Had – had the doctor passed away? No. The footman shook his head. Not yet. But there wasn't much to choose.

He'd been struck down, even at his dinner, by a most violent apoplexy. It was quite the most violent the footman had ever seen. His eyes had seemed to come right out of his head and he'd fallen into the mutton ...

At first, his life had been despaired of, but prompt bleeding had saved him. Yes, he lived, but despair was his life, you might say. Now the old gentleman could just lie in his bed ... had to have *everything* done for him, if you know what I mean. Tragic for a doctor who'd seen it happen to others; so many bedsides he'd stood over, shaking his head at relatives ... Now a younger doctor came and did the same for him. One supposed it was life, though.

But come and see him by all means. He can't hardly talk, but the sight of Mr Sam Chichester is sure to warm the cockles, if you'll pardon the expression. And he ain't had a visitor in a month . . .

The stricken doctor was accommodated in the dining room. The table had been moved and an enormous bed brought in on which Dr Bratsby, or a careful image of him, lay in a landscape of pillows. He looked remarkably clean and untroubled, with his large, fat hands resting tenderly on the upper slopes of his stomach.

'It's Mr Sam Chichester come to see you,' said the footman; then repeated the information more slowly and loudly. 'You can never tell if he's asleep or awake,' he added in an undertone to Sam.

The doctor was evidently awake. His eyes glimmered open and his hands quivered like murdered butterflies.

'He wants you to go over to him,' explained the footman. 'You can tell that by the way he rolls his eyes. Wonderful, really, what he can do; considering.'

Hesitantly Sam approached the bedside, not knowing what to say. He felt ashamed of his own good health – and because he could offer the luckless man no real comfort.

Dr Bratsby's lips were moving – not with any marked vitality, but rather like a pair of sleepy worms round a hole in the ground.

'He's saying something,' said the footman encouragingly. 'He does, sometimes, you know. But of course, it's not much. You couldn't expect it, really.'

Overcoming a strong repugnance – for the doctor, despite his childish scrubbed aspect, smelled unpleasantly – Sam bent low to catch his words.

'. . . 'member . . . 'member . . .'

'That's "remember"', interpreted the footman.

'Wunnerful 'ime . . .'

'Wonderful time,' said the footman, with a distinct air of pride in his master's accomplishment. 'He's quite chatty now you're here.'

'Nigh ... Oxon ... Sippy ... 'member ... wunnerful 'ime ... enver 'orget ... you ... me ... res' ... dinn-dinns ... 'member .. 'member?'

'He's going on about your visit last year,' explained the footman, quite excitedly 'He really remembers it! There's no telling what goes on in his head, you know! You've really set him going this time, and no mistake!'

'Wunnerful, wunnerful ... wunnerful see you ... 'member dinns ...'

His flabby flesh seemed to prickle with enthusiasm.

'I'm on my way to *The Red Lion*!' cried Sam urgently. 'Remember *The Red Lion*? That night – long ago? *The Flying Cradle – the baby*?'

' 'member,' said Dr Bratsby, his eyes glimmering anciently. 'Always 'member ... here ... in woom ... dinns ... wunnerful, wunnerful 'ime ... nice oo see ... so nice ...'

'Remember *The Red Lion*?' pleaded Sam pathetically; but it was no use. As decently as he could, he fled from the mumbling old gentleman and the terrible house in Panton Street. His birth itself had been wiped away; the custodian of it – his benefactor – had let it go.

At half past five on the following morning, Sam left *The Bunch of Grapes* to make his way to Southwark. He departed like a ghost, wakening no one – not even Jenny. On his bed, propped against the pillow, he left the barber's box. Inside was the pistol and all the money he possessed. He intended the gesture to be taken as a confirmation, strong as holy writ, of his love. The appalling similarity to his father's action of long ago did not strike him till he was well on his way south.

24

A T about half past four on the Monday afternoon, a respect-
ably dressed melancholy-looking person, giving his name as
'Robinson', arrived at *The Red Lion* in Dorking. In spite of
himself, Mr Roggs, the proprietor, was impressed by the
stranger's voice and bearing. He knew a gentleman when he
saw one – which he regretted to say, wasn't very often nowadays; all brass and bluster, as they say up north.

The stranger was welcomed, offered refreshment – and
then picture Mr Roggs's confusion and shock when he learned
that the person giving his name as 'Robinson' was no better
than the manager of a company of players! Feeling himself
to have been taken in, he grew red in the face; he called his
lady, he called his cellarman – and Mr Robinson began to feel
quite uneasy. He had never come upon such hostility to the
profession before. He judged that it proceeded from some unhappy experience in the past; he hastened to assure Mr Roggs
that his company – fresh from triumphs in London and the
north – were considered by many to be the aristocracy of the
stage. Indeed there was, among their number, in addition of
course to world-famous Daniel Coventry, a brilliant young
actor who, Mr Robinson always understood, would be peculiarly welcome at *The Red Lion*: a Mr Sam Chichester ...

'Oh my God!' said Mrs Roggs.

'Not the tiddler?' said Joe.

'Amen,' said Mr Roggs, for no other reason than feeling it
gave him the last word.

Mr Robinson's uneasiness mounted. It was clear that young
Sam's welcome was going to be a somewhat mixed affair, to
say the least of it. But the great lout of a cellarman – of whom
Mr Robinson had been most frightened – turned out to be

well-disposed. By the time Sam's health and prospects had been inquired after and generously answered, the atmosphere turned quite cordial and Mr Robinson's request to be allowed to give a play in *The Red Lion*'s spacious courtyard on the following day was refused quite courteously.

Mr Robinson sighed; then it would have to be *The White Horse*.

Mr Roggs shrugged his shoulders. He hoped no offence would be taken but *The White Horse* was the more suitable establishment for fairground larks, being less of a family house and not so particular ...

Far from taking offence, Mr Robinson quite understood and entirely respected Mr Roggs for his openness. All the same, he hoped that all those who wished him well would attend at *The White Horse* to applaud Sam Chichester ...

'It's really him, then?' asked Joe incredulously. 'And he's an actor now?'

'One of the best,' said Mr Robinson casually.

'It seems a shame,' mused Mrs Roggs. 'And on his first visit ...'

'Never at *The White Horse*,' said Mr Roggs, with all the instant decision of the born leader, no matter which way he was facing. 'Say what you like, ma'am. Fret and fume to your heart's content. I know you women; but I won't have our Sam exposed to ruffians what don't know a play from a pigsty. You send out your bills, Mr R. Tomorrow at *The Red Lion*!'

Something was going on; the old coachman was sure of it. It was something to do with the yard. They were swilling it down and dragging benches across it. He could smell the sweat of excitement in the air ... and voices were agitated.

'Careful – careful, or you'll split it!'

'A bit more room – more room, there!'

Then again, they wanted him out of the way; and when he asked them why, they fobbed him off with some rubbish or other. So he'd dragged himself off to his little room with its convenient hoist and everything to hand and sat on his bed like a punished child. Suddenly the whole building had seemed full of strange noises; he tried to make them out, straining his ears for snatches of conversation; then Milly came in with a mug of ale for him. He refrained from questioning her; it wasn't her place to tell him. Nevertheless she gave him such a look that he was sure the excitement was some concern of his. Thereupon a deep sense of injury settled on him and he refused to talk to Milly or anyone else.

He just sat and stared out of the window onto Mrs Roggs's kitchen garden whose every root and leaf he knew by heart. Though folk said – and sometimes he heard them, for people often imagine the crippled are either simple or hard of hearing – that it would be a mercy when his last hour came, he didn't particularly think so himself. He lived each day for itself alone; when the sun shone, he was pleased; when the weather soured and no horses ran, he was gloomy. Sometimes he attempted to read the books Sam had left behind; but they were hard for him. However, he enjoyed the maps and engravings of curious animals, often marvelling that they could stand upright and get their nourishment. Of an evening, Parson Talbot would come and play him at backgammon, in exchange for his agreeing to learn chess, which the parson preferred; but chess, with all its devious movings and plannings, fretted and troubled his essentially simple mind.

Best of all he liked Joe, and had made one of his rare excursions into the town when Joe had got married to Milly; and lately he'd gone again for the christening of their first-born. Joe had insisted on calling the infant 'Balcombe', and Chichester had been honoured by the cellarman's remembrance of his own old wish.

Oh, yes, *he* remembered ... His memory, considering his age, was very good. He still remembered every twist and turn of the road; he remembered the pretty, treacherous look of it under frost, when a man had to go careful; he remembered putting out his elbow to keep Sam from falling sideways ...

Indeed, every moment of that tiddler's life was engraved on his mind with scrupulous care and exactitude. What was it: sixteen year? And what was it now? A year and two months without him. That left fourteen year and ten months to get through before the boomy ache he felt would be smoothed away. Sixteen years for sixteen years; such was the old coachman's arithmetic ... though he'd admit to no one what the notches were for on his crutch.

He wondered if Sam had got his present – and what he'd made of it? He'd enjoyed the carving of it, but the wings had worried him. He'd only put them in because they were the sort of fancy the lad had always liked ... Mr Roggs had grinned at them and, when he'd thought the old fellow wasn't looking, he tapped his head expressively. But the coachman took this sort of thing in his stride; he knew that Mr Roggs was a man who had to have his opinion of everything ... and he was a man who was entitled to his causes and resentments.

Chichester had always been aware of his obligations to *The Red Lion*; in the bad weather he'd got Joe to make him a harness and handcart so that he could at least bring in wood for the parlour fire. Unluckily the effort had brought on such cramps and stitches that he'd been laid up for a week after and had been a great deal more trouble to everyone than he had been before.

During that week he wouldn't have been sorry to have passed away. When the pain had kept coming over him in waves so that he'd moaned and cried like a baby, he'd found himself remembering a certain face, wild with desperation – a certain face all mottled with temper – a hand holding a weapon that glittered in the sun. Once more he heard the explosion and felt something kicking him in the back ... But when afterwards Mrs C. had gone on and on about that face – with vengeance and murder plainly written in her eyes – he'd held his tongue. A man must have some secrets.

Presently he heard the coach come in; but instead of dragging himself out to meet Mrs C., he stayed where he was. He wasn't going to expose himself to any further shovings out of the way. He wondered if they'd tell *her*? He supposed so, and pictured the whisperings and glancings towards his room. Would she come and share with him?

He shrugged his shoulders and stared at the scratched and cracked door panel of *The Flying Cradle* that Joe had fixed above his bed. He reached up and polished it with his sleeve. As he did so, the mottled, desperate face came back into his mind – and the pistol. The pistol! Of all things, he hated it most in the world. It had enslaved the boy; it had murdered the family. From the day it had come into Sam's life it had been the magic monster, the enchanter. The pistol, the damned, damned pistol!

He gripped one of his crutches and began banging it on the floor, which action had become a mark of blind fury with him. Mrs C. came hurrying in; she stared at him. Her face was dead white and pleading. He stopped his banging; he examined the look in her eyes. Yes; he'd been right in his deepest feelings.

'It's him, ain't it!' he muttered. 'That's what it's all about out there. He's coming back, ain't he?'

Helplessly, Mrs C. nodded. 'Tomorrow ...'

'*Full fathom five my father lies* ... No, no, *thy* father ... *thy* – *thy* ...' muttered Sam with almost humorous aggravation. He knew he'd get it wrong; it touched too closely on his own situation. Nonetheless he must make every effort; if nothing else he would be *word* perfect in his part.

He and the company were staying the night in a small establishment on the edge of the town. He was thankful for this as it enabled him to concentrate his mind on what was to come. The play; everything else had to be banished from his thoughts. Somehow or other he would rise to great heights, and the old coachman would be proud of him. Much as Pa Chichester might have despised players, he was a man who respected craftsmanship above all else; he would know if something was well done; and if he, Sam, did well, the old man would know, in his heart of hearts, where he'd learned true craftsmanship: on *The Flying Cradle* ...

Of his bones are coral made;
Those are pearls that were his eyes;
There is nothing of him doth fade ...

True, true. Unfading, Pa Chichester stared into his mind's eye; and unfading, too, was the memory of the crutch that had been hurled through the window ...

He shivered, and returned to whispering his lines. All his ambitions were now fixed upon this single occasion; he *must* succeed.

And yet, at the same time, he knew this to be impossible. His other pa would never let him. He was still a child beside that particular enchanter. He wished now that he'd warned the actor that the coachman was little more than a crippled wreck of a man. Then, at least, Mr Coventry might have had some pity and allowed Sam the chance to shine. Or would he have done even that? Sam shook his head; the actor's pride armoured him in iron; nothing could ever get through to him. That very evening Sam had seen him sweeping up and down the dingy corridor, gesturing as if to pluck 'the cloud cap't towers and gorgeous palaces' out of the air. Sam had caught his breath at the sheer magnificence of the gestures; Mr Coventry saw him and smiled.

'Tomorrow,' he said meaningfully. 'You'll be *really* proud of me ... son.'

Sam's heart had fallen; he'd stood, feeling quite sick with dismay. From the best of motives, the actor was preparing to annihilate him in front of those he loved best. And Sam knew too well how completely he would do it.

25

THE playbills had promised for seven o'clock; but by the time the theatrically inclined portion of Dorking had arrayed itself and gathered murmurously in the yard of *The Red Lion*, it was all but eight. The sun had fled, shadows formed in dense ranks, and the half dozen stage candles flickered in the warm air, turning the patched curtain that had been strung across the yard into a strange green wall that billowed, bulged and shivered with the birth pangs of mystery.

Parson Talbot, a keen playgoer in his youth and himself an amateur of the art, sat between the coachman and his stern lady, explaining the action of the play; but the Chichesters had no ears for him. Instead they sat, quite rigidly, with eyes fixed on the curtain that seemed to writhe away from their steadfast gaze. They were both dressed in their best coaching livery (Oh! the awkwardness of getting tight breeches onto dead legs!) and presented a curiously ornamental aspect, like a chimney-piece pair in glazed earthenware.

Parson Talbot passed the coachman a playbill – which was studied with scholarly care; even though another such bill, eyeworn and carefully folded, was at that moment inside the coachman's pocket. He ran his great gnarled finger along the names until he came to: 'Mr Sam Chichester as Ariel.'

'What's Ariel?'

'A spirit, in the power of Prospero. I told you.'

'A spirit, eh?'

The coachman subsided into contemptuous grunts and handed the playbill back. The curtain billowed again; a brief sight of robed figures scampering provoked a murmur of excitement. Then all was calm again. Parson Talbot glanced at the coachman – and was mildly surprised to observe an intentness in the old man's aspect ... as if sudden vision had quite transfixed him. Chichester's eyes were glittering; his mouth was drawn in a fierce, tight line.

He had, in that unlucky instant, glimpsed a figure, seen a certain face ... then it had vanished and he'd been left with it in his mind. His hands fumbled for his crutches; he found and grasped them as if to crush the wood itself. Mrs C. leaned across.

'Was it *him* you saw?'

'Who? Who do you mean? Who's *him*?'

'Sam.'

'No – no! It weren't Sam.'

Mrs C. settled back; her expression was troubled.

Parson Talbot, between them, felt the threads of destiny tightening across him like cobwebs.

The curtain moved and Mr Robinson, in an old black cloak, appeared and begged for silence: the play was about to begin. A grand expectancy gripped the audience. Somewhere, Joe found Milly's disengaged hand and squeezed it. ('Oh Joe!') Balcombe, in her other arm began to whimper.

Faces, ordinarily sour, casual, world-weary, spirituous, seemed suddenly painted with wonder. Once more Parson Talbot glanced at the coachman; he hoped with all his heart for a miracle. The old man's eyes were screwed up like needle-points; he was trembling.

Abruptly, the curtain jerked and galloped back, sending the candle flames flying. The bargain shipwreck from Diss stood revealed, and *The Tempest* began in all its opening fury. The boatswain raged, the courtiers snarled and the mariners prayed as their little world came tumbling about their ears.

Backstage, in confined space, Mr Coventry strode to and fro, billowing out his gaudy gown like a pagan sky ... and Mrs Jamieson made her hair sweetly wild and lost twenty years of a rich, full life under a quarter inch of vermilion and flour. Sam, in tinsel and feathers, with streaked face to represent lightnings, flexed his muscles, danced up and down – and peered from the wings for a glimpse of faces he longed to see.

He thought he saw 'Spare Joe', standing on tiptoe at the back, his mouth set ajar to catch flies and impale them on ragged teeth. Eagerly he searched for others he knew, but the curtain cut him off; the bargain shipwreck jolted away and was replaced by Prospero's cell and a palm tree like a gibbet. Mrs Jamieson arrayed herself on the ground – Prospero drew breath, seemed to swell, and stood poised in the wings. The curtain opened ...

'That's him!' breathed Parson Talbot. 'Daniel Coventry!'

The parson had seen him before; in Arundel, once ... There was no forgetting Daniel Coventry and the extraordinary effect of his presence. It was as if a wind had swept through the audience, rustling them and brushing them forward like autumn leaves.

But the crippled coachman remained as stone. Only his eyes had changed; they had grown enormous. The glimpse he'd had through the curtain had been confirmed. He, too, had seen Daniel Coventry before ...

The coachman's heart seemed to blaze up inside of him; the pain was unbearable. He brought his crutch down on the ground with a crack like a pistol shot.

The actor was momentarily distracted; he glanced haughtily, angrily across the audience. The sound had come from in front. Slowly he ranged the row of faces. He came to the crippled old man with the burning eyes. He paused; he staggered slightly, as if struck. He faltered in his part, and was aware of liquid dripping from his hand. For an instant, he thought it was blood – that substance being on his mind; then he realized he'd squeezed the orange he'd been holding to a pulp.

'Oh the heavens!' said Miranda in the uneasy person of

Mrs Jamieson. The actress had sensed the distraction and was frightened the play would collapse.

'*Mark his condition and th' event; then ...*'

Prospero's lines continued to emerge from Mr Coventry's lips, but they were like dead men's worms wriggling out of his brain. He no longer had control of them; they came and went as they pleased.

'*Come away, servant, come! I am ready now,*' he mumbled, feeling a spark of hope coming back. He longed for the presence of Sam by his side; his loneliness was frightful.

'*Approach, my Ariel: come!*'

'It's Sam!' burst out his ma.

'Sam!' cried Joe and Milly together; and Balcombe began to cry.

'Our Sam!' declared Mr Roggs, claiming *The Red Lion*'s own.

'Sam!' called 'Spare Joe' from the back.

'Sam!' whispered Pa Chichester. 'Sam ... Sam ...'

Of a sudden, the old fellow's spirit began to move and alter the fixed and deathly landscape into which it had recently been cast. He dragged his thoughts from the one and watched the other, the lively boy, so urgent and rapid to please. With mounting satisfaction he observed the skill, the craft in every movement; and presently his lips began to move as if to follow the swift, intricate speech and unravel it for his own, slower mind. He tried to catch Sam's eye – did so – and was rewarded a hundred-fold.

'Look, look!' he cried out, unable to hold his tongue. 'D'you see what he's holding? My present! I made it for him! I carved it out ... that there nag with wings! See how he holds it? Lord, Lord, he's good!'

The feathered Ariel seemed to dance on air; and in his outstretched hand he carried the old man's gift. It was his brilliant

answer to Prospero's orange; he turned the whip into a wand
of the most distracting magic.

I boarded the King's ship; now on the beak,
Now in the waist, the deck, in every cabin,
I flamed amazement ...

With bewildering movements the whip drew masts and
bowsprits in the smoky air as the spirit related his uncanny
mischief to his master. And that master stood, dazed and
stupid, wooden as a gallows' post, so that one might have supposed that this Prospero was the servant of Ariel ...

Once off the stage, Mr Coventry staggered into a corner.
He doubted if he could continue. His mind was full of the
most terrible occasion in his life. The memory he'd struggled
so long to push and drink into oblivion had suddenly risen and
confronted him!

'Stop – stop!' he moaned to himself as a certain sunny day
near Dorking flooded into his head. Seven years ago, and still
as sharp and hatefully clear as ever.

He had been in a state of desperation. That was his excuse.
He had been frantic to escape certain pressing debts; his chief
hope had been to reach Dorking before the fair departed. He
knew he'd have been able to join the players. They'd have
been glad of him; after all, he *was* Daniel Coventry. (He
wished to God he was anyone else!)

He'd walked for miles ... then, like the answer to a prayer
at a spot where three roads met, he'd seen the coach coming.
He could remember every scrap of sunlight glinting on it.

'Stop – stop!'

But the coachman never slowed.

'Stop – stop!'

He'd pulled out his pistol. Why? He'd only meant to
frighten ... he couldn't help it; he was an actor ... all the
world was a stage – everything was really make-believe ...

'Stop – stop! Or –'

Why had the coachman glared at his weapon like that? Why had he . . .

Oh God! He rubbed his wrist where the whip had snaked round it, and he tried to shut his ears against the sickly grunt the coachman had given as the bullet had struck him in the back.

'Dan Coventry! Dan Coventry! You're on!'

Mr Robinson was gesticulating. Wretchedly the actor rose. He craved for something to drink, to steady him before he took the stage again and faced the man he had shot seven years before on Oakwood Hill. The old man with crutches in the front row who had glared up at him in burning accusation; the old man whom he knew, instinctively, to be Chichester.

The play ran its course; the courtyard of *The Red Lion* seemed to swell and swell till the tumbledown old world was engulfed in the new. The Irish acrobat worked wonders as Caliban; Mr Minchin brought the house down as the clown and Mrs Jamieson bewitched all but the keenest sighted with her antique youth and charm. But over and above them all soared Ariel – that strange, wayward spirit, peevish to be free.

Sam could scarcely believe in his own success; it seemed as supernatural as the play itself. Everything he'd feared from Mr Coventry had inexplicably come to nought. He wondered if he could have misjudged the man? Between the acts he approached him hesitantly, expecting to be rebuffed.

'You were . . . very good, Sam,' the pale, exhausted actor forced himself to say; and it was a great effort to him. Every instant he expected a hand on his shoulder and the fatal accusation to be made; it was as much as he could do to stand upright. He'd always believed he'd killed the man; but now, although relieved of the guilt of murder, he faced the terror of being caught. 'You – your people should be proud of you. I was . . .'

Tears of gratitude filled Sam's eyes. This man, this great

actor who could have wiped him off the stage, this strange 'other pa' of his, had deliberately, yes, *deliberately* underplayed his part so that he, Sam, might have a triumph. When he'd said, 'Tomorrow you'll be really proud of me,' he'd meant just that. Sam was proud of him. The sheer nobility of the actor's renunciation overwhelmed him and he was ashamed that he'd never credited his own father with such generosity. It moved him inexpressibly to discover how wrong he'd been, and he hoped to God that he, too, if the situation arose, would be able to rise to the occasion. He liked to think that he might have inherited something of his father's quality. Daniel Coventry was a man in a million.

The performance came to a rousing end at five minutes after eleven; the audience, happy, bemused and partly uplifted, shuffled achingly to get what it could of Mr Roggs's refreshments before weaving its ways home to dream on the haunted isle with its fierce and beautiful spirits.

When the magician had reliquished his art, there had been a tempest of cheering as Ariel and Caliban had danced, hand in hand, to celebrate their freedom. Then each had danced alone, and then together again, and no one had seen anything to equal it before.

At last the yard was emptied; the candles were snuffed and the curtain taken down. Parson Talbot rose and gently touched Mrs C.'s arm. She, as conscious of destiny as he himself, smiled and nodded. Together they moved away and left the old coachman alone in his place. His stern face was rich with tears as he stared and stared at the dull stretch of courtyard where Caliban had dragged wood and been wracked with cramps, and Ariel had sung and danced.

But he was not altogether alone, and perhaps he knew it. Sam was in the shadows. He had been watching and waiting for the coachman to be by himself. Now the moment had come; the old man sat surrounded by a silence that seemed to be increased rather than broken by the cheerful sounds from *The Red Lion*'s parlour where Mr Roggs was entertaining the company and lording it over kings.

As lightly as the spirit he'd so lately been, Sam crept up to the quiet figure. At first, the coachman seemed unaware of the intrusion. His thoughts were elsewhere, and his eyes were fixed on what had been the stage. Sam knelt at his feet.

'Sing me that song again, Sam,' mumbled Pa Chichester. 'The one about your pa being all corals and pearls and suchlike. I liked that ...'

So Sam rose and went back onto the stage and sang and danced as he'd never done before; while his pa cried with pleasure and thumped the ground with his crutches to accompany his beloved, never-begotten son.

26

O h the world was good! Till three and four o'clock in the morning Sam was in the parlour – the hero of all the hours there were! Joe said he'd always known Sam had it in him; he'd thought so when he'd watched him in the tent at the fair. Mr Roggs couldn't get over it, didn't even make an effort. Kept remembering the night Sam had been born and wondering how he'd come to this. The Lord surely worked in mysterious ways – but they were nothing to *The Red Lion*'s! Now would it have turned out the same if they'd called the tiddler (begging the young gentleman's pardon!) 'Hassocks'? He doubted it. He remembered when he'd been 'Poggs' he'd been a different man altogether. Most likely there never would have been a *Red Lion*, and never a Sam to do it credit!

'Have some more of your *eek wine*, Mr Chichester,' he said affably. 'It's a very particular occasion, sir.'

This was an extraordinary secretive piece of Mr Roggs's wit – and the only one he'd ever actually come out with. He'd been driven to it by the years of sacrifice of his private office to the coachman who never ought to have survived anyway. He'd found out that 'equine' meant horse-like, and had played with that and the notion of Chichester's personal appearance for several weeks before venturing on: 'A special little something for you, Mr C. Up north they call it *eek wine*. I fancy it'll suit you.' Then he'd gone away, killing himself with secret glee.

Solemnly the old man took his tankard and returned to a steadfast contemplation of his boy.

The players had all gone back to their lodgings; nothing of them remained beyond a litter in the courtyard and the lingering smell of the stage. The meeting that Sam had dreaded had failed to come to pass – and the last fear had been removed from his heart. Uncertainly Sam had asked the actor to meet Pa Chichester; but Mr Coventry had shrunk back and vigorously declined. Sam concluded it was from delicacy and his gratitude to his other pa was consequently increased. Mr Coventry had hopped into the ancient coach with terrific rapidity and had vanished like a ghost.

He was mortally terrified that the old fellow would suddenly appear and accuse him; in fact, he couldn't fathom at all why he'd been spared. He wondered if it could have been out of contempt? Certainly he'd given an abominable performance.

At the very word 'performance', his terror diminished. Anxiously he seized on the word and, by means of it, beat the hastiest of retreats from that dour world where underwear perished and men went into holes.

He recalled his very real disaster in the play and shuddered almost humorously; he felt quite ashamed to receive Sam's gratitude for his 'generosity'. Such an idea quite shocked him; but, before the night was out, he came to accept it with pride. Mr Coventry was nothing if not adaptable; all was in the mind ... Perhaps by worldly standards this was not an honest thing; but otherwise it was not so unworthy. Many a man is made good by being thought so ...

'I can't see why this Daniel Coventry's name should be higher up than yours, Sam,' said Mrs C., studying her copy of the playbill. 'To my mind you was a thousand times better.'

Laughingly Sam disclaimed, and set about praising the great actor to the skies.

'It was because he wanted me to do well, you know. He knew you'd be out there, in front. So he gave me the stage – handed me the play on a dish. That was a wonderful thing he did, ma. I was truly proud of him for it ...'

'I'll to bed, now,' said the coachman abruptly. 'I've had too much of that there eek wine, Mr Roggs.'

He scraped to his feet and swayed off out of the parlour.

Sam watched him affectionately and then returned happily to his boasting till 'Spare Joe's' efforts to catch his attention at last succeeded. Would there, by any chance, be an opening on the stage for a young 'un like himself? He was on the look-out, you know, for other employment ...

Awkwardly Sam realized that the world had been going on in Dorking, too; so, with as good a grace as he could muster, he sat and listened to the tale of Joe's wedding and Milly's move from *The White Horse* and the new cottage they'd got and how the hoist Joe had made in the privy had fallen down when Mr Roggs had taken it into his head to try it out after a heavy night. And he never interrupted above a dozen times.

The old coachman sat on the side of his bed; his head was dazed with wine and thinking. He'd had no choice but to spare the man who'd shot him. He had known, with absolute certainty, that the man was Sam's natural pa. Ever since the day on Oakwood Hill when he'd seen the pistol in the man's hand (for he'd flourished it like a lunatic!) and had recognized it as the spitting twin of Sam's, he'd suspected. More damaging than the ball that had broken his spine, this same suspicion had been eating away at him, driving him further and further into a dark shell. Then, coming upon that man again, studying him with foreknowledge and fanatical care, resemblances, like-nesses leaped out as plain as day. Much as he hated the man, he could not bring himself to make a child's nightmare come true: to have a father hanged.

He dared not even destroy the boy's pride in the man, and that unearned gratitude for a false generosity. Instead, he must put up with it all and let the lie go unchallenged.

He laid down his crutches for he thought he heard Sam coming, and, childishly, he did not want to be caught out of bed. He heaved himself to comfort by means of Joe's hoist, lay back and closed his eyes. The play returned to him, but with differences. It wasn't Ariel he saw, or even Prospero; it was himself as Caliban, wracked with hatred and cramps. Alas, the magician had not let him go. He and Ariel would never dance together. Nonetheless he must leave the lie be – as if it was the truth.

He hoped, when Sam should come in, he'd bring no light. He didn't want it to be seen that he was still in his clothes. Mrs C. would be angry with him for spoiling them ...

And what was so special, so holy about the truth? He opened his eyes. It was as if an entirely separate voice inside his head had put the outrageous question.

'It's that there damned eek wine,' he mumbled. 'It's no more than gut-rot!'

He sighed, relaxed a little, and unconsciously recalled the last words spoken from the stage by that man with the mottled face.

As you from your crimes would pardoned be,
Let your indulgence set me free.

Well, he'd obliged. The fellow was free; and it seemed that being free was all that mattered ... in the play, that was ...

Freedom, high-day! High-day, freedom!
'Ban, 'ban, Ca-Caliban!

That was a good tune, too. Must get Sam to sing it some time ... Sleep came nudging in among the old man's thoughts, pushing away teasing problems and leaving calmer matters to spread in peace ...

Dimly, as in a dream, he heard the door creak open, and, through flickering lids, he saw a well-remembered figure creep in and go towards the window and the other bed.

The boy knew, of course; he must have known who his natural pa was. But that was all he knew. He could not know, nor ever would, if the old man could help it, what he, Chichester, knew. The old coachman smiled as he sensed the dark figure kneeling for his nightly prayers. Everything was as it ought to be. The lad had respect – respect enough to hold his tongue and say nothing to him or anybody else of who this Coventry really was ...

'God bless Ma and Pa Chichester and ...'

So ... he and Mrs C. still came first. That was good. The lad was grown enough to divide his heart and lose none of it. Truth, lies – what did they matter in the end? They were all horse-dung left behind under the wheels.

Yes indeed, there's better things than truth, Chichester; and if we *are* such stuff as dreams are made on, then for Christ's sake let's dream our best ...

Only a tiny fraction of him now remained outside the dark embrace of sleep. Feebly he raised his hand and touched the wooden panel of *The Flying Cradle* above his bed ... which action he performed nightly with certain silent requests; then he climbed aboard. A moment later he'd cracked his whip and the horses were away.

The young woman in the coach sat in her corner and frowned with great hostility at all attempts to bring her into conversation; even the mildest glance drew from her a look of outraged modesty. Plainly, she was not to be trifled with; indeed, the shrewdest among her fellow-passengers surmised that she *had* been trifled with at one time and that the world was now paying the penalty.

She was not a remarkably pretty young woman, but she was undeniably attractive; hers was not a face easily forgotten – and, by the determined scowl on it, it was not a face that was going to be forgotten. She had got on at Aldersgate Street with a battered trunk that had been put outside, and an old mahogany barber's box with brass corners that nothing would part her from. She sat clutching it as if her very soul was kept inside.

Thus, on the Wednesday, travelled Jenny. After prolonged and stormy thought she had decided that she would not be demeaning herself by going to Dorking. Her sole purpose was to return Mr Bloody Chichester's property.

When she'd gone to his room on that dreadful Monday

morning, all bright and loving and full of good thoughts, and then found him not there, she'd not been able to believe it. He was playing some trick – hiding under the bed or in the privy; but then, when she'd seen the box, opened it (as was her right), and found the pistol and the money, she'd come out with words that shamed even her own reflection. She'd been paid off. Money and goods for services rendered. He – he'd took her for a – a bleeding whore.

She'd burst into tears and sobbed her guts out; but they'd been tears of outrage. She'd gone down to the parlour where her trunk was packed and ready. She'd looked at it, kicked it, and burst into tears again. She'd been ill-used by all creation; and worst of all she couldn't abide the thought of dirty Molly's jeers when she heard of Jenny's gent absconding. Well, the cow *wouldn't* hear. Jenny had given in her warning and she was an honourable female of her word. She opened her trunk, popped in a pair of pewter tankards she'd always fancied, and, as haughtily as she could, had humped her belongings out into the street.

A bad patch of road outside of Tooting caused the coach to jolt and sway. The gentleman sitting next to Jenny found himself tossed against her.

'Shog off!' said Jenny with quiet dignity. 'Don't you dare paw me.'

They were all the same. Give yourself, fresh as a rose, to one, and they all come snuffling after, like mice into cheese. She should have listened to her ma; she knew it. Never mind; whatever else she'd lost, she still had her pride.

For instance, she'd not gone hot-foot after him that black Monday; nor had she gone on the grey Tuesday, either. No; she'd stayed in a stinking lodging-house near St Paul's, brooding on mankind in the most unflattering terms. She was glad to say, however, that she'd never seriously thought of making away with herself. She wasn't going to give him *that* satisfaction. True, she'd gone down to the river to have a look; but it had gone slithering and slopping by so bleeding wet and cold that she'd gone straight into an establishment for a port and brandy to get the taste of it out of her thoughts. So here she was, Jenny from *The Bunch of Grapes*, coming like thunder out of a clear Wednesday sky, to douse her lost lover in mortification and shame. What she'd given him was beyond price; like rubies. So she was intending to give herself the final pleasure of casting his payment back in his baby-smooth face; like pearls before swine.

The coach made good time and came in to *The Red Lion* at Dorking at half after three o'clock. The young woman, pushing everyone aside, alighted and went straight into the parlour, still clutching the barber's box. 'God save us!' said Mr Roggs. 'It's happened again!' All the world was there, sitting round a table and staring at her like she was a corpse with two heads. But no Sam.

'I – I –' she began, and held out the box, which was her only credential. She felt a terrible desire to burst into tears again. 'I – I –'

She peered into corners, hoping for Sam. Her face, pale and stained from travel, reflected everything she was feeling. She looked lost, forlorn ... Her eyes, brimming over now, regardless of her inward indignation with herself (she always cried easily and despised herself for it), caught his ma's. Lord! that fierce old dame was certainly glaring at her!

'It's Jenny, ain't it?' she said abruptly.

To Jenny's amazement, she saw a pair of tears, like mint-new bullets, hop out of her eyes and roll down her shockingly weathered cheeks.

'From *The Bunch of Grapes*,' mumbled Jenny, who knew it to be ladylike to give an address.

Then the old girl got up, came towards her – and before Jenny could tidy or even sidestep, she found herself seized by Sam's ma and hugged and hugged till she heard a hook go somewhere.

Naturally Jenny sobbed her guts out again; it seemed only polite as Sam's ma was doing the same ... and through the bubbling of tears, she heard other voices – all of them – calling out her name.

'Jenny – Jenny – it's Jenny!'

So they really all knew about her? He must have mentioned her, then. He – he'd not forgotten! A wonderfully agreeable sensation of warmth and satisfaction with the world intruded on her former annoyance. It turned out that she certainly hadn't demeaned herself by coming. She – she –

'Oh ma'am!' she wept into Mrs C.'s shoulder or thereabouts. 'I thought he – he'd gone an' left me! And – and I love him like anything ...'

Mrs C. stroked her hair and reflected dazedly how like in colour it was to that other one's hair. It seemed to the one-time guard of *The Flying Cradle* that she'd been given a second chance. The nameless outcast of seventeen years before, who'd died in her arms, had returned. This time she would not let her go.

Jenny felt herself being disengaged. A moment of panic seized her. Whose hook was it that had gone? Was she about to be shamed by something coming adrift in front of everybody? But before such a disaster could strike, she was enveloped again – this time in an embrace she knew every inch of.

'Why, why, my darling, didn't you come on Monday? I left everything I had in the world for you – just so's you'd know you *had* to come! I've been sick with longing and worry –'

Christ! thought Jenny. 'I – I had a bit of a cold,' she lied effortlessly. 'Didn't want you to catch it, love.'

He stood back. She beamed damply at him. 'Honest.'

'Have you met my pa?'

Fresh alarm overcame her. His pa – the grim, frightening old coachman! And she looked such a wreck! She plucked at her hair, straightened her gown; she peered uncertainly at the bulky figure with the crutches. The coachman regarded her impassively. Jenny went up to him and curtsied. She dabbed at her eyes with a corner of her sleeve. She *must* make a good impression.

'Pray excuse me complexion,' she said; then sniffed genteelly. 'But as they say, the more you cry the less you piss, sir.'

Little Balcombe was crying; curiously Jenny watched as Milly fed and comforted her son.

'Don't he ever bite?' she asked uneasily; she herself was portly with life to come.

'No great teeth yet,' said Milly. 'It's not more'n a tickle, really.'

Presently she put Balcombe down and asked Jenny to watch over him while she went down to the cellar with Joe's lunch. Almost directly Balcombe started crying again. Jenny picked him up and gave him her finger. He bit it. She swore and carried him upstairs to find another plaything; then she came down again and laid him in his cot. He kept quiet. Milly came back.

'What did you give him that for?'

Little Balcombe, his piggy eyes alight, was struggling to play with Sam's glittering pistol.

'He's a boy, ain't he?' said Jenny defensively. 'Boy's like things like that.'

'I don't hold with giving him murdering ideas in his cradle.'

'My Sam played with it.'

'And what'll he say when he comes home and finds you've been lending his precious birthright to my Balcombe? That thing was with him always. I remember, even when he was a tiddler and sweet on me, he wouldn't let it go.'

'He don't care about it any more,' said Jenny shortly. 'He's got me instead.'

'All the same,' said Milly, 'I don't choose to see a son of mine playing with something made for killing. It's not natural.'

'My Sam don't think like that. He says it's no more than a stage property ...'

'It's all very well for your Sam, acting his head off in Kent or somewhere. He's an actor, after all ...'

'My Sam says we're all actors, really ...'

Milly shrugged her shoulders; but nevertheless removed the pistol from Balcombe's grasp. He howled as if the sun had been wrenched from his sky; so Milly gave him her breast again. It seemed to satisfy ...

Jenny looked out of the window; the December sky was darkening with threatened rain. She sighed, and picked up a half finished shirt that was meant for Sam's birthday. Then the rain came down. It poured and poured, drenching the fields and town; and among many other things, it washed away some writing on a card.

This was in the churchyard. Lately there had appeared, in the far corner, propped against a falling stone marked 'Arundel', a bouquet of wintersweet. No one knew how it had come there; there was no more indication of the sad admirer's identity than there had been of that mysterious, nameless young woman herself. There was only the card on which had been written:

Then to the elements
Be free, and fare thou well!

Then the rain came down and washed it away.

END

Also by Leon Garfield

THE GHOST DOWNSTAIRS

Mr Fast, the mean-spirited clerk, signed away seven years off the end of his life in return for the riches of the world, but never imagined the little lost spectre that would come to haunt him.

ADVENTURES OF THE BOY AND THE MONKEY

Tim and his monkey Pistol lived by their criminal wits in long-ago London, but Newgate gaol and a convict ship put a stop to that.

BLACK JACK

Tolly Dorking's fate is enmeshed with those of two other people: Black Jack, the murderous escapee from the gallows, and Belle, a mad girl who awakens his love.

DEVIL-IN-THE-FOG

An eighteenth-century story about fourteen-year-old George Treet who lives with a family of strolling players and is torn between pride in his profession as an actor and pride in the noble birth he is told is rightfully his.

JACK HOLBORN

A pirate adventure story in the best Stevenson tradition, bursting with fascinating characters and dominated by the figure of the mysterious captain.

SMITH

A twelve-year-old pickpocket is hounded through eighteenth-century London for a document he stole by accident.

THE STRANGE AFFAIR OF
ADELAIDE HARRIS

Harris and friend lose his baby sister, Adelaide, in an experiment. They search desperately to find her, but it looks as if she's gone for good, and in her place appears an unknown gipsy waif ...

MISTER CORBETT'S GHOST
AND OTHER STORIES

A chilling supernatural tale of an apprentice who wished his master dead – and got what he wanted. Also two other stories about a painter's assistant and a battle at sea, and a mutiny of convicts.

If you have enjoyed reading this book and would like to know about others which we publish, why not join the Puffin Club? You will be sent the club magazine, *Puffin Post,* four times a year and a smart badge and membership book. You will also be able to enter all the competitions. For details of cost and an application form, send a stamped addressed envelope to:

The Puffin Club Dept A
Penguin Books Limited
Bath Road
Harmondsworth
Middlesex